# Non-Prophet Murders

# Non-Prophet Murders

*A Grit and Grace Mystery*

BECKY WOOLEY

GRIT AND GRACE Publications · Chattanooga, Tennessee

NON-PROPHET MURDERS
A Grit and Grace Mystery

ISBN 10:0615850480

Manufactured in the U.S.A.

*Dedicated to my husband, Bruce, and daughter, Amanda,*
*and to my loving brothers and sisters*
*at Brainerd church of Christ in Chattanooga, TN, who have been*
*unfailingly and uniformly supportive.*
*Also, to the countless, Christian church staff members*
*who remain dedicated, devoted and discreet.*
*Thank you.*

Acknowledgement to Dr. William David Spencer, author of *Mysterium and Mystery: the Clerical Crime Novel.* Thank you for your unselfish encouragement and for clueing me in on what sort of mystery I have written.

O wad some Power the giftie gie us
To see coursels as ithers see us!
It wad frae monie a blunder free us
An foolish notion:
What airs in dress an gait wad lea'es us,
An ev'n devotion!

ROBERT BURNS,
TO A LOUSE
ON SEEING ONE ON A LADY'S BONNET AT CHURCH


*Son of man, describe the temple to the people of Israel, that they may be ashamed of their sins. Let them consider the plan, and if they are ashamed of all they have done, make known to them the design of the temple—its arrangement, its exits and entrances—its whole design and all its regulations and laws. Write these down before them so that they may be faithful to its design and follow all its regulations.*

EZEKIEL 43:10–12 (NIV)

# Contents

# 1

# The Primrose Path

TRUMAN "GRIT" GRIFFIN bent his six-foot-two inches against a sudden, cold rain and ran across the New Jerusalem College campus toward Bennettville Holy City Zionist Church and the office of college founder and pastor, Newell Post Lawson. As he slopped through several of NJC's countless January puddles, he exercised the first of several civil rights he was on his way to reclaim—freedom of speech. *A simple and satisfying pleasure,* he concluded.

*And freedom of religion,* he thought. *No more required attendance at Holy City. No more of Lawson's jingoistic, Zionist sermons.* He stepped in another puddle up to his socks and remembered the question he intended to ask when he got to Lawson's office: What exactly do you plan to do with the few million, pesky Muslims who might take exception to the rebuilding of Solomon's temple?

He slogged the last few yards to the church and hurried through the vast foyer. His heavy steps echoed from hard, unadorned walls like a barrage of water balloons and left foot-shaped puddles on the marble floor. He arrived at the door to Lawson's suite, still dripping.

Lawson's secretary, Virginia looked up from her desk disapprovingly. "Speak of the devil," she said. "I was about to post a letter to you, Mr. Griffin." She emphasized the "Mister" and waved an ominous looking envelope.

Grit followed Virginia's glare to his muddy feet and Lawson's expensive carpet. He lost some of his bravado, but forged ahead. "I need to see Pastor Lawson."

"Pastor Lawson isn't in, Grit. You need to make an appointment."

"I can't make an appointment. I won't be here."

She opened the appointment screen on her computer. "When do you expect to return?"

Grit took a deep breath, leaned across the wide mahogany desk and explained.

When he finished, Virginia handed Grit the official looking envelope. "In that case," she said, "you need to see this now. Provost Chessman sent it over yesterday, and Pastor Lawson signed it this morning just before he left." She waved Grit to a nearby chair.

He sat, dampening the upholstery. The three-page missive listed Grit's many violations—including smuggling alcohol into the dorm (the one job skill he had learned in two-and-a half years as a Bible major)—and, in careful legalese, served Grit with a formal dismissal.

"Fine," Grit said on his way out—his one word, farewell address.

* * * * *

After her graduation from Bennettville Christian High School, Amy Grace Willis began working as a receptionist at the local Dodge dealership. She planned to work for a year, save up some money, and then take advantage of her partial scholarship at the local branch of the state university. Her modest dress and thoughtful speech, though apropos to her long, dark curls and frank, innocent smile, set her apart from the world-weary car salesmen and life-hardened mechanics. Her first week at the reception desk gave new meaning to "on-the-job training."

"Hey sweetie, let me talk to Bobby John." A woman's voice twined like kudzu through the phone.

Grace dutifully paged the married salesman who, after answering, left hastily, calling over his shoulder, "Grace, honey, if my wife calls, I'm in a sales meeting."

Fast cars and faster women; chauvinism was alive and well in the car business.

Julie, the finance manager, gave Grace daily instructions. Tuesday it was, "I'm not takin' calls from my baby's daddy, and if Alejandro calls, tell him he can kiss my—"

Grace mentally modified Julie's message to fit her own scruples, then clarified which baby's daddy. By week two, she had seen all but one of the guys in the cleanup area smoking pot and had met the owner's mistress and her brand new Viper.

Maggie Harris, was a notable exception to the general tone of Grace's work place: first, she did not swear, and second, her cute, coltish body parts did not bulge from or wallow under skimpy clothing. Grace learned that, in spite of very little upbringing and no financial resources, Maggie's persistence and ambition had won her a hardship scholarship to New Jerusalem.

Much later, Grace learned that Maggie had met Grit Griffin there, and that he, upon learning that Maggie was not a Christian, had dutifully assaulted her with the New Jerusalem version of the Gospel—Christ will reign in a literal kingdom in a literal Promised Land for a literal thousand years. Maggie had not been impressed. She wanted to know about Jesus now—not at some distant Apocalypse. Now—when she had to put her alcoholic mother into bed. Now—when she battled demons of loneliness, fear, and anger—not a conquering Jesus reigning on an earthly throne but a loving Jesus reigning in the hearts of men. Grit plumbed his shallow, legalistic faith and hit bottom. That next semester, Grit dropped out of school.

Now, Grace wondered why she and Maggie, as straight-laced and unglamorous as they were, had been hired in the first place. She was amazed and horrified by the self-destructive behavior around her, but her overwhelming reaction was love and pity. She tried to understand. What if this small city car dealership was the best she could hope for? What if she didn't have college waiting for her? Would she too seek comfort in sex or drugs? And she wondered why Maggie, though not a Christian, seemed to feel the same.

Grace cared about her coworkers and knew intuitively that judging, blaming or condemning would not help. She also knew that God's love could set them free. Her innate awareness and acceptance of grace was leading her further and further from the legalism her father preached at the Bennettville One True Church.

\* \* \* \* \*

Grit did not want to face his parents after being tossed out of New Jerusalem, so he had stayed in Bennettville. Within a month, Haley Philben crawled into his life in a low-cut sweater and a high-cut skirt.

To Grit she represented freedom from religious concerns and life choices in general. For six months, the couple "lived on love" and credit—insulated from faith or reason. But Grit was still a "good ol' boy" with a smattering of Christianity; he believed in love, and marriage. In August, reality, which had circled impatiently, sank its teeth into Grit and shook; he was ashamed. Part of his shame grew from a true concern for Haley. Physical passion had morphed and moved from his nether regions to his heart. He loved her.

He pawned his drums—a true sacrifice, but not particularly lucrative—bought a cheap ring and a cheesy "I love Haley" tattoo. But what he intended as a loving proposal, Haley turned into a hateful confrontation. She was happy as long as the money and good times lasted, but she had no use for love. It frightened her. She packed her things, and most of his, and left.

Grit slipped into depression and alcohol, barely holding on to his minimum-wage job and living in a low-rent studio apartment. What happened to Haley, he did not know and tried not to care. He imagined her sailing into the sunset. Actually, she rode west on the back of her new lover's Harley.

* * * * *

Every Tuesday morning, Grace's mom, "Miz Dinah" to church members, taught a Bible class for infants and toddlers at the Bennettville One True Church. This Tuesday, as always, she sat a bit lopsided but triumphantly cross-legged on a small cushion in the floor of the church nursery. Her lush but graying locks poked from a hand towel fastened to her head with a tattered strip of cloth. She wore an orange striped bathrobe. A dozen or so equally accurate Biblical costumes hung in a closet at home.

She had been lowering herself into the lotus position at least once a week in a church nursery somewhere in the Bible belt for the last twenty-three years. For the last four, she had found it worthwhile to pray to her fifty-year-old knees for forgiveness on the way down and to ask the good Lord for comfort and salvation when she attempted to rise. Between prayers, she found redemption in the drooling faces of the squirming, gurgling infants safety-belted into jumper seats and arranged in a semi-circle at the extreme limit of her bifocals.

This Tuesday morning, she squinted at four insouciant faces happily crossing and uncrossing their own unfocused eyes toward plastic versions of baby Moses and his sister Miriam that she held just within reach of their flailing arms. Prophet and prophetess swam giddily in and out of focus.

"Mo-o-o-ses," Miz Dinah intoned, "Mo-o-o-ses," her smile in spasms, attempting to form itself around her wonderfully long O-o-o-s.

"Mo-o-o-ses was a baby just like you."

She broke into song,

"Just like you, Just like you,

"Mo-o-o-ses was a baby just like you,

"So very long ago-o-o."

"Miriam was his sister, yes indeed,

"Yes, indeed, yes, indeed.

"Miriam was his sister,

"Yes indeed

"So very long ago-o-o."

At heart, Miz Dinah was more actress than teacher, a holdover from her "wicked" days as a drama major. But she did not analyze. She picked up a small covered basket and held it toward the wayward limbs of her charges.

"Pat the basket, Mackenzie, honey."

Mackenzie's errant extremities made contact; for an instant, both eyes were on target.

"Good girl! Mo-o-o-ses' basket." Miz Dinah enticed another customer. "Benjamin, pat the basket." She guided a hopelessly disobedient hand to its owner's objective. "Very Good! Good, Benjamin. Very G-o-o-o-d."

Benjamin, finally able to grasp the illusive basket, could not let go. By pure instinct, he drew the inedible toy toward his all-purpose mouth.

"No, no, Benjamin, just pat the basket, Benjamin." Miz Dinah gave a gentle tug. "Benjamin, let Hannah," tug, "Let Hannah have the"—tug, "BASKET!"

Hannah began to yowl as the five-minute buzzer signaled the eminent return of doting mothers and the moment of truth for Miz Dinah's knees. She carefully unhinged her visual aid from Benjamin's involuntary but tenacious grip then gave Hannah and Matthew access. Each in turn willed a recalcitrant hand toward the target and reacted in holy surprise upon contact—a baby miracle, followed by a fully mature one; Miz Dinah stood up. Up being the position she achieved once all of her joints, especially her knees, had indeed forgiven her.

She issued a vanilla wafer to each sweet communicant, cleaned four faces, eight hands and matched diaper bag to child just in time for the last bell—another Baby Bible class down, and another crop of angels beginning a study of the Mosaic Dispensation.

Last week had been the last of several lessons on the Patriarchal Dispensation. These four students, as the hundreds before them, had petted the rubber snake, tapped Noah's wooden ark, groomed his animals, snatched at Esau's hairy arms (a woolly sheep skin), felt Jacob's rocky pillow, and stroked Joseph's embroidered coat.

But the Mosaic Dispensation was Miz Dinah's favorite. She had G-rated props to simulate each of the ten plagues. (It had taken several years to come up with a proper carbuncle.) She had a red dishpan rigged to divide the waters, stone tablets inscribed in Hebrew, and every year she built the walls of Jericho out of Rice Krispy treats.

She had even, after much trial and error, come up with tangible props for six of the Ten Commandments. She had nothing suitable for idolatry or blasphemy. Adultery and murder were out of the question.

In the end she simplified the concepts into pat phrases that the babies might understand, in a year or two.

"Thou shalt not covet thy neighbor's wife," and "Thou shalt not commit adultery," became "Don't grab another child's toy." "Thou shalt not murder" came out "Don't hit anybody."

Over the years Miz Dinah developed her own primitive theology; every action was right or wrong, good or evil. Every person was saved because of their good deeds or damned because of their sin. The Patriarchs and Prophets were exempt, she reasoned; after all, Abraham and Jacob lied; Moses committed murder; Aaron worshiped idols and Isaiah ran around naked.

Some Old Testament stories could only be taught to adults, and some would never be mentioned in Sunday school, at any age.

* * * * *

Thomas Willis was always pressed for time on Wednesdays. Today was no different; he had two visits to make before evening Bible class, and he had struggled with his office printer for the last twenty minutes.

"Blasted, confounded, piece of junk," he mumbled under his breath. The doorbell rang. He prayed it was not what it turned out to be, someone in need.

Sylvia answered the outside intercom, "Hello? Could I help you?"

A tentative female voice replied, "Is the Pastor in?"

This question revealed two things: First, the questioner was not, nor had she ever been, a member of any One True Church. If she had, she would know that OTC preachers were not called Pastor. Officially, ministers had no titles at all. In practice, they had to be called something. The choices included, Brother, preacher, minister, pulpit minister or even simply Mr.—never pastor, reverend, or, heaven forbid, priest or Father!

Secondly, the lady was in need of Brother Willis' precious time. Sylvia buzzed Brother Willis' office. He had heard the exchange and asked Sylvia to set up an appointment for another day, but the woman persisted.

"I have to see him today. I need to talk to him now!"

Thomas checked his clock and mentally gave the woman ten minutes. "I'll see her," he told Sylvia, "but call me in ten minutes, and leave your office door open." This last precaution was standard for ministers meeting alone with females; it prevented unfounded rumors and costly lawsuits.

The woman at the door, Loretta Harris, had been wandering up and down Miller Street for the last three hours—her only companion a cheap bottle of wine in a paper bag. She had stopped to pee at the gas station, to pass out in the grass behind the grocery and to stare at the various churches lining the street. The One True Church seemed the least formidable. She rang the bell, ready to admit to her helpless condition and to beg for the crumbs from Christ's table. She needed to hear the promise of forgiveness and to gain the hope of repentance.

Sylvia ushered Loretta into Willis' painfully small office. The obviously inebriated woman wobbled unsteadily until guided to an equally wobbly, under-stuffed chair where she settled in—all too comfortably Willis noticed. He had no time for this. He got right to the point.

"You are drunk," he said.

As if she did not know.

"You have no business being here in your condition, and you are wasting my time. Come back when you are sober. You are on the road to Hell, and no one can help you but yourself!"

Loretta had chosen the wrong church.

When Maggie got home from classes at New Jerusalem, she found her mother in worse shape than she had been in years, babbling about damnation and crying uncontrollably. It would be days before Maggie heard the entire story, and even then she wasn't sure her mother had the facts straight. But she knew this much, Brother Thomas Alexander Willis had damned her mother in ways that he would never understand.

# 2

# Deep Water

TROY MICHAELSON returned to campus late that summer with his master's degree and a bride, Amber. Pastor Lawson had hired both to teach communication classes beginning in the fall. A week after his and Amber's arrival in Bennettville, Troy caught sight of Grit standing in a coffee shop. He and Amber hurried in.

Troy slapped Grit on the back and made introductions, "Amber, this is Grit, I mean Truman, Griffin."

Grit managed a smile and an automatic, "Grit's OK, uh . . . Hi." He extended his hand while admiring Amber's green eyes and sassy, auburn bob. "No wonder I haven't heard from Troy for a while," he said. "Looks like he had better things to do than call me."

"Yeah, man, sorry about that." Troy apologized. "I didn't mean to blow you off. We sent you an invitation."

Awkward silence.

Grit fumbled for something to say. *I was homeless and drunk?* "It's just that I . . . uh."

"Do you have a minute?" Amber asked.

Grit wasn't sure if he did. He was not ready to debate religion, and he certainly did not want to alienate a friend.

Troy pointed to an empty table. "Here, have a seat. I'll get us some coffee. What would you like?"

Grit took his black, Amber ordered latte. Left alone with Amber, Grit couldn't find words to start a conversation. She smiled, and asked about school. He was explaining why he had left New Jerusalem in January just as Troy returned with the coffee.

"I've given up on legalism, too," Troy said. "I'm 'determined to know nothing but Jesus Christ and him crucified,'" he quoted the apostle Paul.

"How did that happen?" Grit asked.

"It's mostly Amber's doing."

Amber chuckled. "But I wasn't even a Christian when we met. And when I found out he was a fundamentalist, I just thought, 'like that's going to happen!'"

"Amber's parents are professors at a state university," Troy added. "They teach that human beings are just a higher life form. And they think all religions are just myths made up to explain anything people don't understand."

"When I left home, I jumped in and out of religions as often as I changed college majors," Amber said. "Nothing held my interest. I was just a stew of questions like: Where did I come from? What am I here for? I went down some pretty lonely, dangerous roads."

Grit opened his mouth to empathize.

Amber put down her empty cup. "Do either of you want a refill?"

Both men said, "Sure," and Amber took their cups to the counter.

Grit watched her effortless stride. She was tall and confident— more confident than any female of Grit's acquaintance. Everything about her suggested she was not the type who would find Troy irresistible.

Troy read Grit's thoughts and laughed. "She was definitely not overwhelmed by my charm."

Grit took a deep breath and said what he was really thinking, "I have a lot of questions about my faith," he confessed. "If I have any."

Amber returned with three steaming cups and three long, oval pastries on a small tray. Grit picked up a pastry and inspected.

"Biscotti," Amber said. "It's Italian."

Grit took a bite. "Sort of a cross between a cookie and toast," he said. "I like it."

Troy took a piece. "I know where you are coming from, Grit," he said. He gestured toward his wife. "This woman challenged me with her questions more than I satisfied her with my answers."

Amber handed Grit his coffee and took her seat. "I didn't need new answers," she said. "Troy needed new questions—questions neither of us had ever asked, like: How do we know God exists? How can we know that He cares?"

"I had never even thought about such," Troy agreed, "stuff like: What does God have to do with morality? What difference does it make? Why should any religion be better than another?"

"But the one that really stumped us both was, 'Why is there such a disparity between the teachings of Christ and the practices of institutional Christianity?'"

"Once we got the questions right, the answers came. They weren't simple or easy, but they were clear and true," Troy said.

Amber smiled and took Troy's hand. "We both confessed Christ as Lord, and I was baptized."

Troy kissed his bride. "Four months later we were married."

Grit changed the subject. "How did you ever get hired to teach at New Jerusalem with all your 'heretical' beliefs? And why would you want to?"

Amber laughed, "I think we slipped in under the radar."

Troy agreed. "We're the 'stealth' communications teachers. I've never told Pastor Lawson or anyone at the school about my new understanding of things, and before I left, I talked to him about coming back to teach. At the time, he was my hero. He's an amazing speaker."

"You're right about that." Grit grimaced.

Amber continued, "We stayed in the Zionist Christian fold all along; we didn't really know where else to go."

"Believe me, we looked." Troy added. "We just don't fit into any mold."

"But, why come back?" Grit asked.

"I didn't want to," Troy said. "I knew we could be walking into trouble, and I didn't want to drag Amber into a religious war."

"God has something for us to do here," Amber added, "regardless of our own welfare."

"I believe New Jerusalem is going to have to understand and adapt to our post-modern culture or die," Troy launched into a sermon. "Christians have to stop fighting each other and start fighting Satan. We need to stop hating sinners and start saving them. How can any non-religious person see past American Christianity to Christ? Christians need to be one as Christ and the Father are one—one in love, one in purpose, one in the Spirit."

Grit listened through two more rounds of biscotti. Troy and Amber's answers rang true—the most resonant: the Gospel is spread by living and dying for Christ, not, as Lawson had taught, by killing for the Kingdom. He was ready to enlist. "So where do I sign?" he said.

\* \* \* \* \*

After that first meeting, Grit, Troy, and Amber met regularly to ask God for guidance. He obliged, and Deep Water was conceived— conceived by the Holy Spirit. The gestation was, of necessity, clandestine (New Jerusalem students were not supposed to worship away from Holy City), and the birth took place in a somewhat disreputable accommodation (the unused under-story of Grit's employer).

But the comparison to Christ's nativity went no further; no angels announced the arrival; no magi worshiped. Instead, the first few Sunday night meetings consisted solely of Grit, the Michaelsons, and about ten Christian friends.

The name, "Deep Water," occurred to Grit after much prayer and a few beers. What else could you call an outreach that met under a bar called "The Dive"? Troy liked the implications; water is the first requirement to begin and sustain both physical and spiritual life. And the meaning of life? Deep Water indeed. Grit drew upon the knowledge he had gained, in spite of himself, at New Jerusalem to lead Bible based discussions at the monthly worship services.

The building, in a slightly seedy section of downtown Bennettville, had two stories, each with an entrance at street level. The bar, on the ground floor, fronted Main Street. Stairs near the front led to a downstairs hallway. At the end of the hall, a door opened into the stark basement space soon to become Deep Water. At the back of that space, was an exit to the parking lot.

With much work and love, Deep Water became a comfortable, conveniently located place to hang or chill as needed—a place to talk, a place to worship. Amber painted a brief paraphrase of the story of Nicodemus, on the stair wall:

*A religious official came secretly one night to check out what a very dangerous but amazing man had to say about the meaning of life. The man told him, "Everyone needs to be born again." The official had never heard of such nonsense, and, in a tone that probably meant "Are you nuts?" asked, "Can a fully grown man go back into his mother's womb?" Jesus answered, "You must be born of water and the spirit."*

At worship services, unusual, even bizarre, artistic expressions of faith rested in hallways, hung from ceilings, rang from the rafters, and drifted through the crowd—stimulating the senses, challenging the intellect, and fostering personal faith.

But forthright, non-denominational Bible teaching and unapologetic Christian orthodoxy put some of the simply curious off, and the fellowship shrank to the faithful and committed: Grit, Troy and Amber; Troy and Amber's fellow teacher, Ricky Cruz, and communications student, Kale Edgar. Gradually, a number of new seekers—either invited or otherwise enticed—joined the tangle, and a few more unfettered-but-fervent Christians found their fellows.

One of the first people Grit thought to invite was his agnostic friend, Maggie. Maggie, in turn, invited her coworker, Grace Willis.

# 3

# Love and Grit

"GOOD MORNING, NEW JERUSALEM!" Ricky Cruz's imitation of a Vietnam-era deejay was full of irony; most of his listeners did not find this Monday morning, the first day of classes after Easter break, good in any way. He had taken the early shift himself to let some poor student sleep a little longer and doubted if anyone other than Pastor Lawson was listening. Lawson kept a strangle hold on the entire department. No one with an ounce of imagination lasted long—except Ricky.

"This is 'Crazy' Ricky signing on from mighty WNJC, eighty-eight point one, FM, the voice of New Jerusalem College, broadcasting from the basement of the Barrett Baxter Bible Building."

The New Jerusalem radio and television department owed its existence to Lawson and his "Holy City  Zionist Christian Hour." But diminished enrollment and lack of funds meant that Lawson's baby was a bit undernourished. "Mighty" WNJC barely broadcast beyond the New Jerusalem campus. Ricky and his students, poor but proud, kept the radio station running in spite of ancient equipment and an outdated music library. Regular listeners had to have a large antenna and a taste for easy-listening.

"We begin our usual programming with those consistent hit makers, the U.S. Air Force Orchestra and Chorus. Here's their latest chart-buster, 'The Star Spangled Banner'. You know the words, people. Wake up! Sing along!"

Ricky clicked the first track on the CD, flipped off his mike, and took a second sip of his still-scalding coffee. He waited for the last measure, flipped his mike back on, raised the volume, and warbled, "AND THE HOME OF THE BRAVE!"

His ad-lib patter was a constant irritant to Lawson. All WNJC deejays, student or faculty, were required to stick to pre-approved, censored scripts. But Ricky, as the only "minority" faculty member (unless you counted the one female who had taught Home-Economics and English literature for the last thirty-five years) was not intimidated by threats of discipline or dismissal; he was absolutely necessary and virtually irreplaceable.

In the late '70s, New Jerusalem had "integrated"; in other words, the school recruited a number of black basketball players and a couple of ethnic students to retain its eligibility for federal grants and student loans.

That limited outreach garnered one Rick Alejandro Cruz, soon known by all as "Crazy" Ricky. Four generations back, Ricky's progenitors were Puerto Rican. His actual racial or ethnic mix was a matter of conjecture. To all appearances, he was Caucasian, but, at New Jerusalem, his dark Latin eyes, sumptuous hair, and Standard American accent set him apart as a "foreigner."

Only on the otherwise homogenous campus of New Jerusalem would Ricky's slightly off-kilter humor and unknown ethnicity garner a label of "Crazy," but he relished the title and fostered the image. He kept the administration worried while staying just within the limits of the student handbook. No sandals? Ricky painted his shoes to look like sandals and bare toes. No long hair? Ricky wore his just-short-enough-cut in a bushy tangle.

After graduation, Ricky spent a few years in the broadcasting business but returned to New Jerusalem to teach when Pastor Lawson moved his Holy City broadcast from radio to television. The pay was awful, the situation strained, the position powerless, but Ricky wanted to teach, and he wanted to bring a small measure of adventure to New Jerusalem. The NJC administration decided to overlook that flaw and hired him anyway. Experienced communication faculty was hard to come by—minority faculty was impossible, and anyone teaching at New Jerusalem had to have the added qualification of allegiance to the Holy City Zionist Christian Church. That demographic tended toward more prosaic occupations and bluer blood.

Ricky was a loose cannon on and off the air. He conducted his classes barely within school regulations. Since students were not allowed to patronize movie theaters, Ricky showed movies in his classes. Students could not attend other churches; Ricky invited guest preachers to speak. Pastor Lawson and the board stayed one step behind him, closing the barn door and chasing horses.

* * * * *

Deep in the Texas desert, in room twelve of the Giddy-Up Motel, "Sex and the City" reruns flickered on the television. Sarah Jessica Parker, in perfect makeup and runway fashions, looked as realistic as a space alien beside the dingy walls and broken furniture. The air-conditioner was frozen into uselessness, and the door stood open to the heat and dust from the gravel parking lot.

Haley Philben heard the Harley skid to a stop and a bawling string of oaths. Lover boy had apparently cheated the wrong cowboy.

She started throwing her things, and the motel's towels, into a plastic grocery bag.

More oaths, and a warning to, "move it!"

Haley grabbed her purse and her boots, ran out barefoot, and threw her leg across the saddle. The cycle roared away under a midday Texas sky set on broil. The outlaws were just ahead of the posse, but they had their bankroll; next stop, Vegas.

About fifty miles into Arizona Haley felt sick. The only signs of habitation on either side of the road were neglected huddles of travel trailers going nowhere. Sand blasted her face, grated between her teeth, and sat on the back of her tongue. She was nauseated and cramping. She squinted against the sun. Just ahead was a small general store.

"Babe," she said. "I need to stop."

He cussed under his breath, but braked hard and slid into the drive, nearly throwing her.

"Could you get me a cold soda?" she asked and headed for the outhouse behind the store.

"Buy your own damn soda." He lit a cigarette.

Dry heat and sunshine took care of most of the outhouse smell, but there wasn't anywhere to wash, and an old telephone book served as toilet paper. Haley sat over the hole in the rough plank and peed—still no period. She tore out a scratchy Yellow Page and did what she could, then rubbed her hands on her jeans and went in the back door of the dim, unair-conditioned store. It smelled worse than the outhouse, and her stomach roiled. She bought a Coke from the machine. A sharp-eyed clerk watched her wander around two short rows of groceries. Near the back, she was surprised to find health and beauty items. On a top shelf were individual rolls of toilet paper. *Damned miser.*

She was even more surprised to find what she was looking for: a bottle of hand-sanitizer and a pregnancy test. Outside, lover boy revved his engine and swore loudly. She stuck the items in her pocket, ran out the front door, dodging the clerk, and jumped on the bike.

In a filthy restroom outside a desolate gas station in New Mexico, Haley confirmed that she was pregnant. She told her lover. Two days later, in Nevada, she overheard him trying to sell her to another biker for a heavy leather jacket. She took off with the clothes on her back and the rings Grit had given her. She pawned the latter for a bus ticket to Bennettville.

Wind, cigarettes and fear had hardened her face and vocabulary. Nicotine stained her teeth and nails. Liquor and drugs dulled her mind. She was pregnant, hopeless, and broken.

* * * * *

On Maggie's first visit to Deep Water, Grace was in tow. Grace, whose teetotaling ancestors had contended for generations that Jesus turned water into grape juice, was aghast.

"Maggie, this is a bar!"

"Don't worry, it's not open, and we're going to be in the basement." Maggie reassured.

"What if somebody from my church sees me?"

"If they're in this part of town, they won't want you to see them either."

"But, I don't drink!"

"I know. It's OK. Grit told me that Deep Water doesn't serve alcohol."

Grace relaxed, but Maggie continued, "Except at communion and before and after church."

Grace was speechless and remained so until introduced to Grit Griffin at the bottom of the stair. He did an appraisal: thick curly hair, large brown eyes, and the sort of sweet, soft curves that caused his mind to consider love and commitment, at least briefly, before his body lusted for more immediate attention.

He gave Maggie a hug, but settled for shaking Grace's proffered hand. "Welcome to Deep Water," he said. He was supposed to remain at the bottom of the stair to meet and greet, but he was desperate. "Stay right there," he said to the girls and hurried up the stair to catch Kale on his way

down. "I need a favor, man," Grit whispered, and explained his dilemma. Kale was conscripted. Grit took Grace's arm. "Let me introduce you to some people." He spent the rest of the evening with the two women, but his need to be near Grace was evident.

* * * * *

Services that night were, as usual, preceded by refreshments, open to discussion, and centered on communion. The informal atmosphere encouraged unrestrained participation and unscripted questions. These passionate, expressive Christians immediately accepted Grace into their fellowship in spite of her conservatism, and their fertile Christianity fed and watered her withering spirit.

Grit and Grace found themselves working as a team answering many of Maggie's questions. By the end of the service, Grace and Grit had each other's numbers—and not just on their cell phones. Grit was the sort of unharnessed, likeable teddy bear that Grace, the daughter of a strict and distant father, found irresistible.

The next day, Grit returned to his tattoo artist, who managed to change "I love Haley" to a fairly readable "I love Jesus."

Grace attended monthly worship services and haunted Deep Water as often as she could excuse herself from her parents. Her first Sunday evening visit had caused a flood of recrimination from her father and tears from her mother. Grit and Grace agreed it was too early in their relationship to cause a family rift, so, as often as he could stand it, Grit attended morning service at Grace's church.

* * * * *

After a few months, regular Deep Water attendees began calling themselves "Divers," an allusion to three of Deep Water's unique characteristics: 1) the name of the bar above their heads, 2) the "divers"ity of their fellowship, and 3) every Christian's soggy, underwater initiation.

The first two honest-to-goodness converts were Maggie Harris and Buddy Crutcher, also a scholarship student at New Jerusalem. Each had attended a few meetings at Deep Water and had stayed after for discussion and Bible study with Grit, Grace and the Michaelsons. Buddy confessed Christ and was baptized in February while Maggie died to sin, was buried in baptism and resurrected in April. She and Buddy risked a lot; New Jerusalem students caught attending churches other than Holy City could be expelled.

But they were willing to take the risk. Someone was eating, studying, talking, praying, or all of the above nearly every evening, and Sunday worship meetings continued to grow. When The Dive was open, Joe Uptain, the owner, allowed access to Deep Water through the regular street entry and the stairs. For Sundays, Troy, Grit, Amber, and Ricky had keys to the door from the parking lot.

Rumors that a group of New Jerusalem students and teachers were holding church meetings away from Holy City reached the school administration two days before Easter.

# 4

# The Right Reverend

NO ONE, NATIVE OR VISITOR, could miss the many billboards throughout Bennettville advertising Greater Bennettville First Methodist/Baptist/Episcopal/Holiness Alpha and Omega International Tabernacle. Consequently, the youthful, smiling visage of The Reverend Bishop Reverend Bishop, in custom-tailored white suit, hot pink shirt, and clerical collar, became a staple of the area media diet. The billboards featured the handsome, single minister in massive proportions. Next to his portrait was a quote from the Gospel of John, "If I be lifted up, I will draw all men unto me."

Partly because of his name, Reverend Bishop had always considered himself exceptional. His mother, Calendula Bishop, had named him Reverend to honor the preacher who had taken her in during her pregnancy. When she died, three days after Reverend's birth, the preacher and his wife felt obligated to keep him.

Reverend knew. He knew that he was an accident and a cross to bear, a Christian duty bestowed on dutiful Christians. But he thrived, his will springing from a secret well dug by his mother's hope and fed by his forbearers' tears. That will lifted his head when he entered grade school during the early years of integration. It manifested itself in an appetite for power and it motivated him to personal achievement and political ambition.

At Bennettville High, Bishop led the debate team to a state championship and excelled in basketball. His name, shortened to "The Rev," became known well beyond Bennettville.

With fame and accomplishment, Bishop gained loyal friends. With fame and accomplishment, Bishop gained unforgiving enemies.

Bart Crutcher fit both categories.

When "The Rev" hit Bennettville High as a freshman, Bart was a starting forward on the basketball team. After, Bart was a benchwarmer.

He hated Bishop and wished him dead. Bishop returned the sentiment, disguised in the form of favors—favors that were best kept secret— favors that could be called in, any time. Bishop could wait.

After his graduation, Bishop made it known that he intended to major in Bible, but his secret ambitions remained political; the pulpit would be his access.

To test his own mettle and the local political climate, Bishop applied to New Jerusalem College. He was, predictably, rejected, but he left that fight for another day and accepted a scholarship to the Methodist/Baptist/ Episcopal/Holiness Alpha and Omega International Bible College located in Mississippi. Bishop studied Bible reluctantly. He studied people relentlessly. By his sophomore year he had gained renown throughout the South as a persuasive speaker.

With his degree in Bible came his ordination in the M/B/E/H Alpha and Omega International Tabernacle denomination. The now "Reverend" Reverend Bishop returned to Bennettville and began a series of revivals in the Bennettville High gym where the city had watched his previous triumphs. His sermons, a mixture of traditional Gospel and political rhetoric, instilled both spiritual fervor and worldly acumen in ever growing crowds.

The attendees reached critical mass at about two hundred. With that number, The Reverend Reverend Bishop founded Greater Bennettville First M/B/E/H Alpha and Omega International Tabernacle in a rented hall and started a building fund. That summer the congregation broke ground and began building the "permanent" tabernacle. That oxymoron was completed a year later. "The Rev" hired a tailor, appointed himself Bishop, and left his nickname behind.

The furnace of ambition grew white hot, and The Reverend Bishop Reverend Bishop began to forge alliances and hammer out political deals. He unashamedly wrapped his Gospel message around two causes: minority rights and legalized gambling—somehow managing to convince his hearers that either goal could answer the question, "What would Jesus do?" His congregation swelled to eight hundred plus.

Bishop culled the most zealous: a small squadron of self-important men and a larger regiment of lonely women. He appointed six of the squadron members to the office of elder and the remainder to the office of deacon. The regiment of ladies became Handmaidens of the Lord, anointed to serve Greater Bennettville First M/B/E/H Alpha and Omega International Tabernacle's most urgent spiritual needs, as determined by The Reverend Bishop Reverend Bishop.

With this army, Bishop organized the various minorities of Bennettville into The Rainbow Unity Party and convinced them that a gambling casino in Bennettville would end unemployment and save souls. Never mind that gambling was illegal in the state; laws could and should be changed.

By the early eighties, without holding public office, Reverend Bishop represented a constituency of thousands. He was revered by the entire Methodist/Baptist/ Episcopalian/ Holiness denomination; guarded by a squadron of elders and deacons; worshiped by a regiment of handmaidens and protected by an as-yet untarnished reputation. He was ready to call in favors—the first call went to Bart Crutcher.

* * * * *

The call to Crutcher Tow and Stow came in at 2 a.m. on a Saturday. Bart's business number was still in the yellow pages, but he had lost his driver's license to a DUI three months before and could no longer do business, legally. He woke, cursing the phone company for not changing his number. And he cursed the idiots who left their cars to be towed on a Saturday morning: kids parked in private lots, sports spectators in tow zones, drunks taken to the tank. He was about to disconnect the call when he felt the need to curse the caller directly. He picked up the receiver. A familiar voice sent a stinging fear up his spine.

"Bart, this is Reverend Bishop. Do you remember?"

Bart remembered. He remembered "The Rev"; he remembered the favors, and he remembered the reason he needed to return those favors without question. How could he forget? Those memories had the half life and toxicity of nuclear waste.

"Yeah, I remember. What d' ya want?"

"I heard you might need a little help."

As a matter of fact, Bart did. It had been less than a year since his wife Meta's death, but in that short time Bart had managed to drink away his business and most of his friends. Now he was in danger of losing his son; Children's Services had been sniffing around since Bart's day in court. He had fended them off by working at odd jobs and keeping a housekeeper/sitter, but money was running out. Meta's small life insurance policy had barely paid for her funeral. The housekeeper had already made allowances, but she needed her money. All Bart had left was his tow truck. If he sold that, he could never revive his business.

Bishop continued, not waiting for Bart's answer. "I have a job for you; just a small favor, and I'll see to it that you are well paid."

And so it had begun. At first, Bart went out in the wee hours and simply towed any vehicles left in the Tabernacle parking lot. He towed abandoned clunkers. He towed cars impounded by the police. He hauled off vehicles left by rendezvousing lovers, but it mattered not to Bart. He didn't want to know where they came from or where they went after he left them across the state line.

"Serves the idiot owners right for leaving them in the first place."

Bart was driving with a suspended license. He painted his tow truck black and traveled the back streets. He found other good spots for "picking peaches" and faster ways to make them disappear.

After a year, Bart renewed his driver's license and slowed his drinking, but by then he had stepped too far over the line to care what laws he might be breaking or who he might be hurting. He began teaching Buddy the business.

Buddy took to thieving like a pro. After several years in the business, he got greedy. It was Buddy who suggested they put a chop shop on the back of their remote property, and Buddy who built "the Varmint" to transport their loot. Bart agreed. Buddy never asked him where the money came from, but he knew it wasn't a bank.

Though The Reverend Bishop Reverend Bishop's investment became quite profitable, Bart saw only a small portion. That was the deal. After all, Bart was operating illegally. Bishop's involvement was peripheral and unverifiable. If Bart were to protest, Bishop had only to pull the plug, leaving Bart to suffer the consequences of crimes past and present. In sober moments Bart thought that getting out from under the machinations of The Reverend Bishop might be worth doing time, but sobriety brought a painful question: What about Buddy? Why had he involved his son? Sober thinking sent Bart back to the bottle.

Bishop gained recognition and power daily. Influential but anonymous friends financed trips to the state capital where he assured legislators that the profits from a casino in Bennettville would benefit education. He made those assurances on tony golf courses, in pricey restaurants, and during complimentary gambling sprees. Sometimes he assured them that underprivileged preschoolers would be the benefactors. Other times he made oblique references to the elderly, the unemployed, or to welfare mothers. But, he assured them, someone would learn something somewhere, if only the legislature would see the light.

His regular trips to Washington were even less subject to scrutiny. Who financed them and why were not public knowledge. The Reverend Bishop Reverend Bishop's power and influence spread like an illegal drug.

\* \* \* \* \*

Martha Elizabeth Lawson stopped at the light on the corner of Seventeenth and College and checked the visor mirror. Her fine, graying hair was steadfast and immovable in a sleek bun, her lipstick and earrings were likewise secure. A bright pink blouse, the only truly colorful item in her wardrobe, lent color to her face and accented her deep blue eyes. But Martha was not pleased. Her small face featured a large, non-complementary nose and a receding chin. "Well," she said, "you can't make a silk purse out of a sow's ear."

This was only the second time Martha had attended one of Reverend Bishop Reverend Bishop's Abigail meetings, and trepidation was giving her the "whamdoodles"; her hands were freezing; her face twitched, and she talked to herself as she guided her nearly silent, deep blue Lincoln toward the Greater Bennettville First Methodist/Baptist/Episcopal/Holiness Alpha and Omega International Tabernacle.

"I should have taken something."

She had not felt this crazy since menopause, but she drove on. Today, Reverend would know everything. She had revealed a portion of her feelings at the last meeting, and that partial revelation had nearly overwhelmed her.

Bennettville's sleepy Saturday morning streets were quiet and empty; Martha would be early. Newell Post Lawson, her husband and Pastor of Holy City Zionist Christian Church, had left the house before she dressed, presumably to make final edits on his sermon for tomorrow morning. He was not likely to call home, but prickles of guilt made her heart race.

"I should have taken something."

*Maybe a drink?* That would not do for the wife of Pastor Newell Post Lawson, and Martha could not buy liquor anywhere in the state without being recognized.

Her whamdoodles urged her to turn around. She summoned the part of herself that could do what had to be done and continued down College Street past Holy City and the affiliated New Jerusalem College.

Soft morning light blurred the harsh angles of the stark, utilitarian buildings. Holy City Church was a sprawling series of sterile, steel-gray boxes topped by a cultrate, chrome-covered cross. Pastor Lawson had supervised the design. The form-follows-function architecture and excessive footprint spoke not of grace and peace but of an obviously intimidated architect and of Pastor Lawson's penchant for power.

At Thirteenth Street, Martha involuntarily hit her brakes; there he was, the bearded figure Bennettvillians had come to call "Moses." He had stood on that corner, robed in white and carrying a placard, night and day for the last six years. Martha shivered. Did he live somewhere? No one seemed to know. Today his sign read, "REPENT! Thou shalt not commit adultery."

"Oh Lord! Why didn't I take something?"

But Greater Bennettville First Methodist/Baptist/Episcopal/ Holiness Alpha and Omega International Tabernacle loomed ahead. An early critic's characterization of the structure as a "neo-classic, Egyptian, tobacco barn" was as close as anyone had come to describing the steep-roofed, rough-hewn "Tabernacle" and its incongruous, colonial steeple.

Martha parked in the back. As arranged, the back door was open; no one would see her coming or going. She walked into the hallway behind the office and through a second door that opened to the main hall. Her whamdoodles did not care for the busy, green and purple carpet and told her so. The hall ended at a grandiose, wood-paneled door bearing a heavy brass plate, "The Reverend Bishop Reverend Bishop." The door was locked, the building silent.

*It's been cancelled,* Martha thought. She looked down the empty hallway. *I should not be here.* She did not consider that The Reverend Bishop might be somewhere else in the building, nor did she remember she was early.

Oh, why didn't I take something? She felt faint. Panic took her feet and carried her back to her car and home.

* * * * *

The Reverend Bishop had stopped briefly in the restroom. He emerged from his ablutions perfectly attired in alligator shoes, deep red, hand-tailored suit, orange silk shirt, and designer tie—his unruly hair tamed by a fifty-dollar haircut. He sauntered down the hall (it's elaborate décor equal to his own sartorial splendor) and reached his office five minutes after Martha bolted. Taped to the door was a clipping from the Bennettville Sentinel, which was stapled to a handwritten note.

Bishop read both, crumpled them in his hand and searched the building. He was alone. He picked a candle lighter out of the janitor's closet and walked out the back door to the parking lot. Three minutes later, he reentered, locked the door, replaced the lighter and returned to his office to work on his speech for the Rainbow Unity Picnic while he waited for the Abigails.

* * * * *

For a flag waving, chicken eating, ice cream melting good time, no one could beat the Rainbow Unity Picnic held every year on the Saturday before Memorial Day on the grounds of Greater Bennettville M/B/E/H Alpha and Omega International Tabernacle. State politicians who knew what was good for them, from county judges to the Governor, made an appearance annually; to them the good will of The Reverend Bishop Reverend Bishop was a necessary commodity.

This year the Handmaidens of the Lord had outdone themselves in the way of food. Proceeds from the fried chicken, fried apples, fried pies, fried tortillas, French fried potatoes, deep fried turkey legs, deep fried corn on the cob, deep fried corn dogs, deep fried dill pickles, deep fried funnel cakes, deep fried Twinkies, and refried beans were more than enough to finance the auxiliary's trip to the National Handmaidens of the Lord convention in Memphis, Tennessee.

Picnickers also brought their own dishes to share on a long table in the shade. The spread included offerings from take-out coleslaw to homemade coconut cake. Regulars knew to stake out their favorite dishes and head for them first.

The Rainbow Unity Picnic was the premier venue for free advertising in the county. Politicians, caterers, realtors, contractors, landscapers, service clubs, and churches rented booths and passed out samples, gadgets, or souvenirs.

Holy City Zionist Christian offered tiny bottles of water from the Jordan River, military recruitment brochures, and New Jerusalem College pamphlets.

One True Church members gave out King James New Testaments with additional pages of Holy writ entitled "The Plan of Salvation" and "The First Century Pattern for Worship."

Victoria Sellers Realty scored big time with free cardboard fans; the day was unusually warm for May, and Victoria's picture fluttered at eye level in nearly every hand. Complimentary paper fans were not new, but these had a twist; Victoria's picture was printed on an attached CD containing all of her real-estate listings, and anyone who downloaded it would be linked to her website. Before the day was over, every politician in attendance and two funeral directors had asked her where she had them printed.

Ricky Cruz, freelancing for WBTN talk radio, roamed the grounds chatting with anyone who fancied two minutes of local fame. He ran into a number of New Jerusalem students: Kale Edgar and

Maggie Harris were earning service credits by manning the Holy City booth; Tom Dixon, who interned at WBEN TV, was shooting tape for a segment on the six o'clock news. Buddy Crutcher was impossible to miss, passing out business cards from the cab of his father's bright orange "Crutcher Tow and Stow" truck. The crowds began to thin around two-thirty.

Two-year-old Honesty White lost her lunch in the car on the way home. Her parents attributed her illness to a hastily eaten corn dog and carsickness, but at six o'clock the toddler was still erupting and had become lethargic. Her parents rushed her to Bennettville Memorial where she was immediately admitted.

Mr. Trenton Townsend, Sr., who had never been sick a day in his long life, came home from the picnic complaining of stomach pain and nausea.

Later that night, the Reverend Bishop Reverend Bishop also fell ill.

\* \* \* \* \*

Before church service at Holy City the next morning, in the center of Pastor Newell Post Lawson's massive desk, in the center of Pastor Newell Post Lawson's massive office, in the center of Pastor Newell Post Lawson's massive church, a neatly typed note lay, conspicuously and inexplicably. No one had seen it delivered, nor had anyone been in the office since.

It read:

THE PROPHET SPEAKS

You shall not commit adultery.

You shall not make for yourself an idol formed like a woman nor like a viper that moves along the ground. You shall not covet thy neighbor's wife, nor set your desire on his maidservant.

I am a jealous Prophet.

YOU HAVE SEVEN DAYS TO REPENT.

I set before you today a blessing and curses—the blessing of forgiveness if you listen and obey, or this curse if you do not. Deut. 12

Just as sleeping with another man's wife brings you pleasure, so it will please the Prophet to watch you die in ecstasy.

Pastor Lawson entered his office as always just before the Sunday broadcast from Holy City to adjust his "Jesus Saves" necktie and check his comb-over. He saw the note, glanced at the title and scanned the page without his reading glasses, which were with his "preaching" Bible on the pulpit just beyond the door. No address, no signature, not much sense. He would take another look later, but it seemed to be a random sermon outline. Maybe Virginia, his secretary, had found it on the Internet and left it for him. She knew next week was "Commandment Sunday" and that he had chosen to speak on "Thou Shalt Not Commit Adultery." He smiled at the irony.

He replaced the note, checked his hair one last time and exited the office onto the auditorium dais. The hot TV lights sent a momentary draft through the door; the note fluttered unheeded off the desk and under the bookshelf behind, never to be seen again.

Next week's sermon would be Newell Post Lawson's last.

\* \* \* \* \*

The unimposing, squat Bennettville One True Church roosted on Miller Street, three blocks east and five blocks south of Holy City. Sometime before Wednesday evening service, a handwritten note was placed among several last minute announcements on the lectern of the church's preacher, Thomas Alexander Willis.

It read:

*The Prophet Speaks:*

*You shall not give false testimony against your neighbor.*

*I set before you today a blessing and a curse. Listen and receive forgiveness or ignore and be cursed. Deuteronomy 12*

*YOU HAVE FOUR DAYS TO REPENT*

*Just as it pleases you to reveal the indiscretions of others, so it will please the Prophet to bring you to a shocking end.*

Thomas barely got to his classroom before the bell rang, although he had spent the entire day at the church and skipped lunch to work on his lesson. The Lord's work was never done and did not include spending time with his wife, Dinah Lee, or their daughter, Grace.

Somehow, at five feet, five inches short, Thomas Alexander Willis was formidable—ramrod straight, slim, and imposing. Dinah had very little trouble appearing submissive though she was three inches taller. Willis had acquired showy, but self-conscious theatre major, Dinah Lee Mason, her freshman year at state university. For some unholy reason, Dinah was dangerously attracted to fellow actors and found this preening, vainglorious man irresistible. Their consequent courtship and marriage was not so much a romance as a natural phenomenon. He towed her in his wake like a leaf in a gutter, and she accepted his every pronouncement as Holy Writ. At twenty-four, Willis decided he needed a wife. He briefly surveyed the world outside his own ego, saw Dinah bobbing along behind him and supposed she would do. She, and later Grace, would become more entourage than family.

Brother Willis was in a hurry to begin his lesson. He removed the announcements, including the prophecy, from his lectern and stuck them in the back of his Bible, thinking he would read them out to the class before the second bell. But, he and a visitor began wrangling about whether or not the Bible allowed humming in church, and he forgot.

Thursday morning, as he walked into his office, his Bible lay on his filing cabinet. The forgotten announcements jutted accusingly from the black leather. He stepped to his secretary's door.

"Sylvia, did you keep copies of those late announcements yesterday?"

Sylvia Meadows looked over her half-mast, computer glasses, "Sure, do you need them?"

"No. Thanks."

He tossed them in the trash.

\* \* \* \* \*

It had taken Mrs. Trenton Townsend, Sr. three days to get her stubborn old man to see a doctor. By then his kidneys had shut down, and, by that Saturday, he was dead.

# 5

# Give Me Liberty or Give Me Death

6:30 A.M. WAS EARLY—too early for a Sunday morning, but, true to his name, Grit clamped his jaws and willed his six-foot-three-inch, sleep-deprived body out of bed. He had started his internship at the Bennettville Sentinel in addition to his job at The Dive, and Sundays were his only day to sleep in. But somehow, in spite of, or maybe because of, last night's late date with Grace, he would keep his promise to attend two church services and a dinner, all before his usual Sunday wake up time.

Though he would never admit it, Grace was a sweet addition to Grit's black-coffee world and the main reason he had sought out the internship at the paper. She was the sort of girly-girl that could elevate his aspirations. But that paradigm shift was totally unconscious. In his conscious world, Grace was an unanticipated complication—playful and cheerful, knowledgeable and gentle—but a complication.

Grit was smitten, but he continued to take his coffee black and his life sugar free. Being dumped could do that, take a perfectly good, warm heart and knock it cold.

Last night's gathering at the Michaelsons' had not wound down until one in the morning, but the occasion was somber; New Jerusalem College President Newell Post Lawson had fired the entire communications department: Troy, Amber, and Ricky. Grit shared the former teachers' anger and was fearful for Kale, Maggie, and Buddy, who could face dismissal. Not only that, without teachers, the communication majors would not be able to complete their degrees.

The friends lamented, harangued, threatened, encouraged, and, by the end of the evening had formed a plan to strike the head of the monster, soon.

Around one, Grace reminded Grit of his promise to attend church where her father preached; Bible School started at an ungodly 9:00 AM.

Grit hated Thomas Willis' sermons. The argumentative, everyone-else-is-wrong flavor at The Bennettville One True Church left a bad taste in Grit's mouth and gave him an even greater appreciation for Deep Water.

As he and Grace left the Michaelsons', Ricky ran out of the house. "Hey, Grit! I've got a minor emergency. Can you run sound at Holy City this morning? Mike check is 8:30."

Ever willing, Grit said, "sure," and Ricky went back into the house before Grit spotted Grace's disconcerted face.

"Oh crap, Gracie, I'm sorry." Grace frowned and Grit back-pedaled. "Listen, the Holy City broadcast is over at 10:00; I can still be at your dad's church in time for worship service."

Grace was silent on the drive to her apartment, assuming her silence would prompt another apology, but Grit was clueless—anticipating the rapidly approaching goodnight kiss. He parked, walked her to her door, and bent for his kiss. She looked accusingly into his pale blue eyes.

Something clicked, and Grit realized it was time to make love or war. He nuzzled her ear and whispered in his sexiest voice, "When your mom asks me to stay for Sunday dinner, I'll say, 'yes.'"

Grace laughed, "You must be getting serious if you're ready to try Mother's cooking." She kissed him sweetly.

Grit pulled her close and kissed her passionately.

Grace pulled away, said a quick, "Good night," and ducked into her apartment, but her cheeks were flushed, and, in spite of it being well past two in the morning, she had a hard time getting to sleep. If she had known that four men, including Grit, were scheduled to die before the day was over, she wouldn't have slept at all.

\* \* \* \* \*

Grit slapped his alarm and reached for his cargo shorts and a t-shirt. He might be headed for two sermons heavily seasoned with Old Testament legalism, but he didn't have to dress like it. He was hoping the Christian tattoos visible on his arms and legs would raise eyebrows. His only nod to convention was a quick shower, a shave of his face and head, and a bit of attention to his teeth. If he were going to offend, it wouldn't be with odor.

Both of the congregations he would be joining expected solemn ritual, Sunday dress, and traditional behavior. Grit believed that guilt-induced church attendance and "Sunday dress" reflected a primitive need to appease the gods. But occasionally he wondered, *Am I claiming superior knowledge and insight? Am I just as misguided? Am I guilty of the sin of pride?* And concluded, *Probably.*

He slipped out the front door for his Sunday paper, squinting against a beautiful but unwelcome sunrise. Back inside, he found his latest story—page two, Metro section:

## FOOD POISONINGS

One has died and two remain hospitalized after nine attendees at the Rainbow Unity Picnic, Saturday, May 22, were diagnosed with salmonella poisoning. Mr. Trenton S. Townsend, Sr., eighty-four, died of complications at Bennettville Memorial Hospital, Friday. Six others remain under doctor's care.

Two are being treated at Bennettville Memorial Hospital: The Reverend Bishop Reverend Bishop of Greater Bennettville First Methodist/ Episcopal/ Baptist/Holiness Alpha and Omega International Tabernacle and a two-year-old whose name has not been released.

Doctors report that Mr. Townsend, Sr.'s advanced age contributed to his death.

The illness seems to be confined to attendees who ate from a chocolate, cherry cake, origin unknown. Both the toddler and The Reverend Bishop Bishop are recovering and should be dismissed Monday.

The Reverend Bishop's Commandment Sunday sermon, "Thou Shalt Not Steal" will be replaced by a special prayer service on behalf of the food poisoning victims and their families.

*Not bad,* Grit thought. *Maybe next time I'll get a by-line.*

\* \* \* \* \*

Today was the "Commandment Sunday" Grit had mentioned in his story: the Memorial Day weekend observance instigated by Bennettville politicians to woo the votes of conservative Christians.

Ostensibly, asking area preachers to pick a commandment and deliver an appropriate sermon fostered Christian unity and bolstered the resolve of city fathers to keep two ancient stone tablets on the grounds of the Courthouse, in spite of legal challenges. In practice, uncooperative One True Church preachers resisted the observance, calling it ecumenical. Unitarians decided it was too Biblical, and Pentecostals could not allow anyone but the Holy Spirit to determine what would be preached on any given Sunday. Episcopalians and Catholics had their own liturgy to follow, so the mainline Baptists, Methodists, and Lutherans picked up the flag and carried the day.

Since then, most Bennettville churches had fallen into line, and a sermon on one or more of the holy ten was pretty much expected over Memorial Day—the tie-in being that American fighting men and women did not die in vain as long as the good citizens of Bennett County could observe the Ten Commandments—if only at the courthouse. It was rarely mentioned that the contested monument was donated by Colonel Jubal Lee Cornrow after a particularly splendid Confederate victory.

Grit turned to the published sermon titles before reading the funnies. Commandments were assigned at the first of the year, giving Bennettville clergy plenty of time to twist the Old Testament admonitions past recognition by adding perennially favorite exclusionary church doctrines. Pastor Newell Post Lawson, for example, was preaching on "Thou Shalt Not Commit Adultery: God is Faithful to the Jews." Grit fully expected an eschatological tirade beginning in Genesis and ending in Revelation explaining current historical events as the prelude to the end of the world.

Brother Willis' title was "Thou Shalt Not Bear False Witness: Strange Worship," which left Grit with the distinct impression that he was in for another spirit-dampening lesson on why Christians should not use musical instruments, or choirs, in church services. *Oh well*, he thought, *listening to see if I'm right might keep me awake.*

Grit checked the clock, downed the rest of his coffee, and skipped the funnies; Pastor Lawson would be standing at the pulpit waiting for mike check precisely at 8:30, and Grit had a twenty-minute drive—if all the lights were green.

He sped past his mailbox. Late or not, he rarely checked his snail mail. This was one time he should have. The letter inside read:

THE PROPHET SPEAKS
Honor Your Father and Mother.
If a man has a stubborn and rebellious son who does not obey his father and mother and will not listen to them when they discipline, he is profligate and a drunkard. The Prophet of his town shall stone him to death and purge the evil. Deuteronomy 20
**YOU HAVE THREE DAYS TO REPENT!**
The high walls in which you trust will fall. Deuteronomy 28
Just as it pleased you to dishonor your parents and your God, so the Prophet will rain dishonor and death upon your head.

By the time Grace picked up Grit's mail on Wednesday, it was too late.

\* \* \* \* \*

Grit got lucky and was pulling into Holy City's parking lot at 8:25. The only vehicle in sight was a large, unmarked, gray van near the church's side entrance. Choir members and church staff were parked in the rear. Within minutes, 800 vehicles would fill the empty spaces and surrounding streets. Latecomers would have to risk being towed from neighborhood sidewalks, driveways, and posted areas by presumably non-Zionist Christian tow trucks.

Grit pulled up next to the van, hauled his large frame from his compact, hurried through the delivery door, and sprinted to the sound booth high in the second balcony. Behind him, a deliveryman, in a cap and cover-alls, placed a large basket of red and white carnations, draped in star-spangled ribbon, to the left of the massive, stainless steel pulpit.

Pastor Lawson entered from his office and set his "preaching Bible" and a full glass of water on the pulpit. He leaned into the mike, adjusted its height and intoned, "Testing, one, two, three. Test, test."

Grit slid into the booth and flipped on the console.

"In the beginning was the Word," Pastor Lawson crooned.

Grit watched his gauges and slid the treble up, careful to keep the sound modulated for proper transmission. Too much bass and Pastor Lawson's natural resonance would dissolve into a growl. Too much treble and the robust beauty of his God given instrument would be muted.

"And the Word was God."

The gauges arched, and Grit lowered the volume.

"And the Word became flesh and dwelt among us."

"We're good, Pastor," Grit spoke into his headset.

Lawson opened his Bible to the morning's text and retreated to his office, leaving the well-worn book on the pulpit.

After marking the position of the soundboard switches, Grit looked down into the sanctuary where he noted a second flower arrangement to the right of the pulpit. Even one was unusual. Early in the church's history, it became apparent that the concrete and metal interior overwhelmed anything natural, even most people. Grit watched amused as the flower deliveryman tested both baskets for water, came up dry, and looked over at Pastor Lawson's handy water glass. With a bit of useless stealth, the driver commandeered the glass, poured the contents into both baskets, replaced it on the pulpit, and beat a hasty retreat.

Other preparations buzzed throughout the building. From the second balcony, Grit had a bird's-eye view as early arrivals in fashionable dress found seats in the cavernous auditorium; choir members took their places in an acoustically perfect amphitheatre to the left of the pulpit, and deacons in dark suits and ties marched ceremoniously to reserved chairs on the elevated dais. Somewhere in the bowels of the behemoth, nursery attendants greeted their diapered charges and apron-clad matriarchs filled coffee urns.

* * * * *

Ever vigilant for her husband's wellbeing and public image, Martha Elizabeth Lawson, from her front row pew, noticed the empty water glass and went into battle mode.

To those who did not know Martha well, and no one did, including herself, she projected an image of complete competence and modesty; the nondescript, beige hen to Newell's showy rooster, comfortable in his large shadow. But, as the wife of Bennettville's most prominent Zionist Christian pastor, she was frequently forced to meet and greet, host and preside, comfort and cheer—at funerals, weddings, retreats, conventions, and revivals. Newell ignored her reticence and thrust her to the fore, hoping she would eventually take to prominence with his own robust fervor. She did not, and he became increasingly impatient. Her coping mechanism was an exaggerated politeness with very little charm and the didactic, matter-of-fact manner of a pleasant, no-nonsense, sixth-grade teacher.

But Martha was devoted. Devoted to God and Newell Post Lawson with a frightening passion. Lawson's natural charisma and pew-shaking bass voice stirred her spiritually and physically. She relished the admiration given to him by friends, disciples, peers, and strangers. He was her sun, and she counted herself most blessed of women to call him husband. What God had joined together, Martha Elizabeth Lawson would defend to the death.

Her immediate mission was filling the water glass. Trying not to attract attention, Martha approached the pulpit slowly, reached over her head, slipped the glass down, and hurried to the nearest faucet—only seven minutes to airtime.

* * * * *

Pastor Lawson joined the deacons on the dais. Maggie and Kale took their places behind television cameras. Grit could hear their chatter in his earpiece as they hailed the floor director, "Camera one up," Maggie signaled. "Camera two," Kale echoed.

Tom Dixon, a senior Radio and TV major, checked his monitors. "Check, One and Two, set your light levels. Maggie, one is running dark. Probably on its last legs, so bump it up a little; just be careful. Don't aim at anything too bright; you could wash out completely. Kale, good job last week, but you're smearing. Watch your pans. And keep—" Tom broke off as unusual activity and ominous silence caught his attention.

Troy, Amber, and Ricky stood in silent protest in front of the pulpit. At their feet a large sign read, "Freedom of Speech, Freedom of the Press, Freedom of Religion." No one breathed, and seven hundred sets of eyes watched in anticipation. Three minutes to airtime.

# 6

# Payment in Full

"TRUST THOSE HELL-FIRE FUNDAMENTALISTS to think they can park any damn place they want just because they have a fish on their rear end!" Victoria Sellers was raising Old Ned on the telephone. Actually, she was waking Bart Crutcher, which was about the same thing. Despite the fact that Sunday was a lucrative day of the week for his business, Saturday nights were busy into the wee hours, and Bart always waited for that first call to climb out of bed.

"'Lo, do ya want a tow?" Bart's voice sounded like morning breath.

"Of course I want a tow; I didn't call for pizza! There's an oversized, overpriced Ocean Liner blocking the drive at 1370 College, and this house has to be open to buyers by ten. Where are people going to park?"

"Sundays are double."

"I don't care if they're triple; whoever parked this boat is going to pay. Get down here and move it!" Victoria replaced the receiver in a decidedly unladylike manner and went back to sweeping the porch of the craftsman style bungalow she was showing.

When Victoria started in real estate twenty-five years ago, her husband Clark had just been diagnosed with kidney failure, and Bart's wife, Meta, had been Victoria's best friend.

Meta and Clark had died within weeks of each other, but Victoria's relationship with the Crutcher family ended when Bart began drinking. She doubted that Bart would remember her.

Shortly after losing both her husband and best friend, Victoria opened a real-estate agency. Though it prospered, medical bills and her children's educations made it impossible to catch up. Sorrow, debt, family obligations, and a heavy work schedule put a kink in her tail. The once smiling, energetic, community volunteer was now an impatient, moody business owner.

But she retained a smidgen of optimism. Lately, with an empty nest, a bit more time and money, she was testing her wings. She and a few like-minded speculators had bought ten dilapidated relics within walking distance of the New Jerusalem campus. All were fundamentally solid and architecturally promising. Nine were in various stages of restoration.

Victoria's, directly across the street from Holy City, was the first finished. A poor showing at this open house could doom the entire project. She and her fellow investors had bet heavily on this neighborhood. She personally stood to lose her home if the investment soured.

And sour it would, if Newell Post Lawson and his cronies could make it happen. Over the years, as area real estate values fell and NJC grew, the college bought homes bordering the campus. The few brave souls who had refused to sell, in spite of new, variegated neighbors, were now retirement age and ready to seek green pastures, but New Jerusalem no longer had the funds or the imperative to expand. Regardless, Lawson wanted those properties, and he wanted them at pre-restoration, slumlord prices.

He and the New Jerusalem board were pushing to have the area around the college rezoned to allow multi-family rentals. This would serve the school in two ways. First, the few homes New Jerusalem still owned could be rented to students. Secondly, property values for single-family homes, no matter how beautifully restored, would fall.

But today Victoria refused to believe that Lawson and his yes-men would prevail. She inspected her Galatea with well-earned pride and justifiable hope; every polished copper porch light shone; every beveled window glass sparkled. Freshly sand-blasted, limestone steps and porch pillars glistened, and a substantial wooden swing hung from the porch ceiling.

Inside, hard wood floors, built-in cabinets, and detailed woodwork spoke of an elegant era and a work ethic remembered and practiced by few. If they ignored the late model sedan blocking the drive and the architectural monstrosity across the street, potential buyers could sit on this particular porch and imagine a Sunday eighty years ago.

But Victoria was contemplating the next six hours. Six hours that would put her in the money or in the soup. She needed help. She wondered if her tirade on the phone had put her temporarily out of God's calling area, but she decided to try the line. "Oh, Lord," Victoria looked up sheepishly. She noticed a cobweb in the corner, but continued, "God, you know you made all of us out of dirt. I ask for your forgiveness and for some home buyers." She thought of a bargaining chip. "I'll tell you what," she stopped praying and started negotiations, "if I get three serious lookers before 11:30, I'll pay to have that boat towed back here for your blessed church-goer."

Victoria herself was what Baptists refer to as "backslidden," still saved, but away from the Baptist church. She and her late husband, who had been "One True Church," could not agree on a denomination, so they had compromised and attended none.

"You know my word is my bond," Victoria continued, "even if you and I can't shake on it." Satisfied she had sealed the deal, Victoria grabbed her broom and attacked the cobweb.

* * * * *

Bart Crutcher and his son Buddy climbed into their new, six ton, hot orange tow truck and drove toward campus. It was more truck than Bart could afford, and Buddy didn't want to know where the money came from. Across the hood, in large black letters, were the words, "**Here Comes Crutcher**," written backwards to be seen from a rear view mirror. Of course, the back of the trailer read, "**There goes Crutcher**."

"Buddy, target, two o'clock." Bart indicated an older, well-polished Oldsmobile parked in an inconspicuous spot two blocks from Holy City. "Soon as we get the Caddy back t' the lot, bring the Varmint back here for that'n."

Buddy stared out the passenger window.

"D'ja hear me, boy? I'm talkin' to ya!"

"Yeah, Dad."

"Well?"

Buddy had removed himself from the criminal half of Bart's business after his conversion three months ago, and Bart had been relentlessly cruel since.

"I'm tellin' you t' git back here 'n pick up that peach."

Buddy turned, "And I told you, I'm not into that anymore."

"Yer into it all right! Yer damned near up to yer neck in it. Yer in it, and yer going to stay in it!"

"No, Dad." At twenty-one, Buddy still felt awkward going against his father. Whatever his father was or had done, Buddy would never feel completely comfortable contradicting him. "I can help you with your business, but I won't be a part of that anymore."

"Well 'that' is my business as much as anything I do. You and those God bless-ed Zionists!"

When Buddy was a senior in high school, aiding and abetting a felon began to look like a bad idea. One of his teachers, a member at Holy City, approached her Bible Class about a scholarship for the bright young man with a dim future, and he enrolled at New Jerusalem to pursue Communications—a course of study that fit him as well as a formal tux would fit a shovel.

"I let you go to that school because they paid yer way," Bart screamed, "but I didn't think you'd turn on me."

Bart pushed hard on the accelerator and made the first of several turns required to detour the New Jerusalem campus. The heavy truck lurched. Buddy fell against the door. Houses passed in a blur as the truck skidded around another turn and veered toward a dark blue sedan.

"Dad, watch the road! Slow down!"

The truck jolted to a stop, trailer rattling.

"So yer a Christian now." Bart sneered. "What exactly have these Christians done for you besides leave you high and dry? That hot air balloon of a preacher, Lawson, has fixed it so you can't graduate. Hell, he's fired the whole department, and you won't graduate before the judgment."

Buddy didn't have an answer.

\* \* \* \* \*

Victoria heard a tentative knock, turned toward the front door and caught her first impression of the now grown Buddy Crutcher. Surrounded by the heavy doorframe and silhouetted by the morning sun, Buddy's dark shape invoked images of invading aliens or newly resurrected saints. At closer range, however, he became a totally earthbound, wiry, not so tall, uncomfortable, young man in a mechanic's jumpsuit.

"Ma'am?" Buddy, who was looking at Victoria's shoes, did not recognize his mother's friend, nor did she see the connection between this slim mechanic and the seven-year-old she had known fourteen years ago.

"Well, it's about time!"

"Sorry, Ma'am." Buddy didn't raise his eyes. "I hate to bother you, but could you please show me the car you want towed?"

Victoria would have let loose with a few cuss words and a comment on his eyesight, but the young man's diffidence brought out her motherly instincts.

"Let me show you." she lilted, "It's the one in the drive."

She walked out the door and pointed—no Queen Mary. The full-sized, cream colored, Caddy, was gone. "But I . . . It's gone. I didn't hear it start up." She had been vacuuming. "I'm sorry you came all the way here for nothing." Victoria was about to add, "What do I owe you?" when a much older, much rougher version of the kid in front of her came charging up the steps—Bart Crutcher.

"Hold on, Lady! I'll be damned if your gonna git me outta bed on a Sunday morning and send me home with nothin'! You owe me!"

This Crutcher Victoria remembered, but barely. He had lost several teeth and nearly all of his hair. His skin, creased with the spider webs reserved for life-long smokers, clung to his bones like shrunken leather.

The look on Buddy's stricken face kept Victoria civil. "No problem, I'm sorry to trouble you." She forced a smile. "How much?"

"Sixty dollars!" Bart waived his arm toward the truck. "I can't pull that rig out a' the garage fer less than that."

No time to protest; she had to get these people off the porch and that truck gone before the drive-by lookers, *please, Lord, buyers*, showed up. "Come on in out of the sun. I'll get my check book."

Bart didn't move, "We don't take no checks, lady. Too many a' them bouncers and stop-payers."

*Oh Lord, I don't have time for this!* It took ten precious minutes to dig all the bills from her wallet, find thirty dollars in her brief case, retrieve about eight dollars in change from her car's ashtray and make Bart and Buddy Crutcher go away. Victoria shut her eyes and sighed. What else could go wrong?

She checked herself in the entry mirror; sweaty Kewpie Doll curls plastered her face, and make-up melted into her wrinkles. She blotted with a tissue and moved to the window air-conditioner. She was standing squarely in front of it, arms raised and pits exposed to the breeze, when her first prospect looked in the open door.

* * * * *

By the time Bart had remembered who Victoria was, he had shown his tail and was too ashamed to acknowledge the connection, so he blustered his way through and cursed all the way home.

First, he cursed Victoria for waking him, then Buddy for refusing to steal the "peach," then Buddy again for not cursing him back.

Buddy kept his temper by thinking about his mom. He remembered birthday cakes, and walks in the woods, and prayers at bedtime. All that had ended when Meta died and Bart started drinking. Buddy was five. Somewhere along the line, he fell into his father's lifestyle. It was hard not to. You don't grow up "normal" and law-abiding if you believe no one will ever love you, and you constantly wonder when and how you will get another meal. You do what makes people act like they care and what you have to do to eat.

Around his dad, Buddy could still get angry enough to use any and every surly word Bart had ever taught him, but he was trying to stop. Deep Water, where Buddy had been converted, didn't do much teaching against "cursing," but Buddy was a natural philosopher. He reasoned that every religion taught reverence for God. And most everyone, religious or not, agreed that loving your neighbor was a good thing. It followed that, if you believe in a Creator, you should revere His name; if you do not, you should respect your neighbor who does. Vulgarity on the other hand, showed a lack of respect for yourself and humanity in general. Words intended to insult, intimidate or offend were the weapons of the cowardly. Bart's cursing made it clear that he loved neither God nor his neighbor. He was everything that Buddy did not want to be.

As soon as they reached the house, Bart dumped Buddy and parked the tow truck in the barn behind. The Crutcher place was located in the middle of several acres of salvaged autos; no neighbors, but Bart was still cautious. He checked the main road for cars before he pulled the Varmint out of the barn. The Varmint, a moving van about the size of a large U-Haul, had two mud tires under the cab and four double sets under the trailer. Bart and Buddy had rigged it with four-wheel drive and a diesel engine that could haul a circus. The only identification was a counterfeit, New York state, commercial plate on the back bumper.

Buddy watched as the Varmint turned down a rutted path and disappeared into the woods. By the time it reached pavement, about ten miles west of Bennettville, anyone who saw it emerge from the woods would not know its origin or ownership.

Bart put on dark sunglasses, pulled a ball cap down to meet them and rolled up his deeply tinted windows. Next stop, that peach. He needed to get his business done before Holy City turned out. With clear streets he could pull up, open the van, lower the ramp, Slim-Jim the lock, hot wire the car, drive it into the truck and be gone in less than six minutes. In less than five more, he would be on a nearly deserted rural highway, and in twelve he would be back in the woods. That '88 Cutlass, sold for parts, would bring more than a newer car sold whole.

As soon as Bart was out of sight, Buddy slid into his rattletrap pick-up, pulled on to the state road and drove back toward town for some unfinished business of his own.

# Tongues of Fire

FOUR DECADES AGO, at 29, Newell Post Lawson was the youngest minister and the only Zionist Christian minister pastoring a church in Bennettville. Every Sunday, his fiery rhetoric, slathered with buttery intonation, alternately singed and soothed the rapt attendees at his many revivals. Hundreds slid down the aisle at every altar call. His Holy City Zionist Christian Church grew from a few dozen members to over 600 in three scant years.

Pastor Lawson rode the crest of the baby boom and kept his eye on the accompanying Christian youth movement. With the help and blessing of prominent Zionist Christians throughout the state, Lawson founded New Jerusalem College as a youth outreach of Holy City.

New Jerusalem's statement of purpose was a lengthy harangue denouncing secular education, punctuated with reminders that young Christians needed to find mates among their kind, an oblique acknowledgement that NJC was, first and foremost, segregated. Segregated from all but white, conservative, Zionist Christians and consequently an insular, non-challenging, suitable institution of higher education.

As other Christian colleges adopted more lenient dress codes, denounced chauvinistic academic practices, and accepted benign cultural changes, NJC remained an island, both figuratively and literally, of mid-twentieth-century mores and behaviors. Initially surrounded by the upscale homes and gardens of Bennettville's finest, the campus was now bordered by an iffy lot of inner city poor, hopeful do-it-yourselfers and greedy, real-estate speculators. When "white flight" hit Bennettville in the late 70s, the tender Caucasian neighbors were routed like Southern belles in front of a Yankee assault.

And New Jerusalem was slipping: Slipping from an all time high enrollment of over 3000 in 1975 to the current low of 900. Slipping from its fingernail hold on fifty-year-old sensibilities, and slipping from the all-powerful hands of Newell Post Lawson. Lawson's hold on NJC was being challenged from many quarters—the most recent, the three communication teachers now picketing his pulpit.

Grit didn't move. Three minutes to airtime, three demonstrators posted directly in front of the pulpit; one garish protest sign prominently displayed. The air seemed to crackle. Kale and Maggie turned their cameras away from the sign, but, Grit wondered, when Lawson's eight-thousand-plus, back-slidden or bed-ridden viewers tuned in the "Holy City Zionist Christian Hour" (in two minutes and counting), would all Heck break loose?

As four deacons and Pastor Lawson rose to confront the protestors, quiet, unassuming Martha Elizabeth entered from the side door carrying the blessed vessel of water. Intent on her task, head down and hurrying, she did not notice that, as the only body moving, she was now the center of attention. All eyes followed as she crossed to the back of the pulpit and climbed onto the riser. She carefully reset the glass then noticed the figures below her.

"Oh, dear," she gasped. "You can't stay there. Pastor Lawson will be speaking in a minute. You need to take your seats!"

Troy, Amber, and Ricky had anticipated every scenario but this. Martha's helpful tone and clear instruction were irresistible. The trio sat down hastily on the front row as two ushers removed the sign, and Tom signaled the choir director to hit the downbeat. For now, God was in His heaven and, to the viewing audience, all was right at Holy City.

The usually unflappable choir managed to settle down by the end of "Soldiers of Christ Arise," and Pastor Lawson launched into a particularly energized exhortation for Christians to rise up in support of God, country, and Israel. Looking down, Grit saw the pastor's carefully sprayed, white comb-over swaying hypnotically with the ebb and flow of the sermon. As the practiced orator warmed to his message, his voice became a deep, brass instrument, resounding from the walls and sending Grit back to his gauges.

At a particularly dramatic moment, the charismatic, visibly aging leader paused. He took a long drink from his glass then slapped his open

Bible. "Thou shalt not commit adultery!" Another pause. "The Rapture is only the beginning, children!"

Troy, Amber, and Ricky stood to exit, moving into the camera frame. Tom switched cameras to Maggie's close up of Lawson and signaled Kale to change angles. No one outside of Holy City would see the insubordination.

Pastor Lawson did not miss a beat; his basso profundo rang out con brio in march time, "It won't be very long 'til this short life shall end! It won't be very long 'til Jesus shall descend! And then the Bride of Christ will meet him on that shore,"

Andante, "You won't want to be in this world any more."

A whole rest, four long beats during which the protestors exited. Lawson glanced their way and slapped his Bible again, disguising the sound of the large wooden doors swinging shut.

"Woe! To the drunkards, the harlots, and the whoremongers." And again, "Woe! To the fornicators, the adulterers, and the hypocrites."

He switched instruments; his words, low and powerful, shaking his listeners like the growl of an idling, full-bore engine; his tone and pace a rumbling, irresistible sotto voce. He spoke directly into the microphone, confiding to his audience earnestly, "Only God knows what is in store for the sinners left behind." Pause. "Left behind to suffer."

Piano forte, "Left behind, caught on the wrong side of the battle between the God of guns, guts, and glory and the ancient enemy, Satan." Another dramatic pause, another long drink, this one emptying the glass.

Lawson hit the accelerator and began climbing through the gears. "There will be weeping," first gear. "And gnashing of teeth," second. "The heavens will open and . . ." he double clutched into fourth. "The mountains will tumble! Gibraltar may crumble." Now in overdrive, "They're only made of clay!"

Roaring down the straightaway, "The fires of Hell—" Pastor Lawson wiped his brow, faltered and began again, "The fires of Hell—"

An incongruous smile lit his red, sweating face. His motor overheated. He clutched his chest, looked straight up at Grit and giggled. "The Rapture! Oh, the Rapture!" Newell Post Lawson laughed in ecstasy as he hit the floor, dead.

# 8

# The Campaign

MIZ DINAH WAS A BIT DISHEVELED but right on time for Ladies' Bible Class, even though, to quote the Bible, her "ox was in the ditch," (meaning she had an urgent need that might justify her absence.) She was expecting Amy Grace and Grit for Sunday dinner and had been cooking until early that morning.

If she had been late, both Brother Willis and the ladies in the class would have disapproved, even though Dinah had more than she could do in one Sunday: serving dinner, chatting, cleaning up, visiting the sick with Thomas and returning to church for evening worship. She would be lucky to be home by nine that night.

Her mind wandered. It was not as if she needed to be there; she had attended Ladies' Bible lessons on child rearing and husband pleasing at least weekly since Grace was a baby—twenty-two years and eight congregations ago. How those lessons could be relevant to the majority of the women in attendance, elderly widows, she did not know. She also resented the fact that lessons for men on fatherhood and "husbandry" were never deemed necessary. With a few such lessons, Thomas Willis might not have dragged her and Grace from church to church like presumably indestructible Samsonite.

She took a seat near the door, ready to leave as soon as the bell rang. She hated idle chitchat, and Ladies' classes were not the place to speak frankly. In Ladies' class, you and your husband were not near divorce. In Ladies' class, you did not hate your daughter's boyfriend.

Nor did a woman question One True Church leaders. If she complained, she was insulting the bride of Christ; if she questioned inequalities, she was "usurping authority"; if she expressed frustration with a cold or inattentive husband, she was not in "proper submission."

One True Church policies had also caused the Willises' financial problems; One True Church ministers, and by default their wives, were employed at the discretion of independent, autonomous congregations, each having its own criteria for assessing a candidate. Few provided insurance or retirement funds. Once hired, a minister could be fired for any number of reasons or none at all. The Willis family had moved fifteen times and gone through two bankruptcies. Grace had attended six different schools. Thomas had no retirement savings, and his life insurance would barely cover a funeral.

But his removal from twelve different pulpits was mostly his own doing. In each he had preached a strict, legalistic interpretation of the Bible, leaving no means of entry for the Holy Spirit or grace. Where the Bible spoke, he spoke, and where the Bible was silent, he shouted. To his way of thinking, any one who disagreed was in danger of Hell fire. When feasible he debated; when possible he coerced. Inevitably, each of his congregations shrank to those "true believers" who agreed with his particular interpretation of the Bible. When the members became too few to afford a full-time preacher, the Willises moved on.

For Dinah and Grace, each move was wrenching, but to Brother Willis each firing was a victory for the Lord. He had done God's work, revealed hidden heresies, saved the souls of those who recanted. He formed no lasting friendships, called no earthly place home.

After eleven forced moves, Dinah Lee adopted her husband's habit of keeping one's distance, but for her own reasons, and she acquired an odd assortment of minor disabilities—one of which was the inability to remember names. Among the two hundred or so members of The Bennettville One True Church, she had no friends. Grace, to the contrary, became garrulous and adaptable. Dinah failed to comprehend her daughter's rare gift of loving well and constantly.

On Wednesday nights Miz Dinah taught the Third through Fifth Grade Class. Nine, ten, and eleven-year-olds were at the prime age for introducing the concept of Hell and the need to avoid it. Baptism was the solution for sin, and Miz Dinah knew how to convince children that they had reached the "age of accountability"; from then on God was counting every misdeed against them. She was credited with the salvation of more than twenty youngsters in the last three years alone.

Ladies' Class was winding down. Dinah thought of little Rachel Albrighton, who, she was virtually certain, would respond to the Gospel invitation this morning. Hadn't the child trembled during the lesson on eternal torment? Wasn't she pale and wide-eyed during last Wednesday night's graphic description of crucifixion? Rachel's father, who hoped to become an elder in the church, was especially anxious for his daughter to become a "believer," as believing children were a requirement for the office.

For an extra push, Miz Dinah had called Greg Lindsey, the song leader, yesterday and asked him to sing all five verses of "Oh Why Not Tonight?" after the sermon. He protested that the song could only be sung at an evening service, but Dinah insisted, "It's for the children!"

During the break between Sunday school and Church, Dinah hurried to visit the dressing room off the baptistery to make sure all things were ready. Baptismal gowns, specially altered for Miz Dinah's small converts, hung on low hooks inside the dressing stalls. Stacks of fresh towels rested on shelves; combs, hair dryers, and handkerchiefs were arranged on a dresser near the sink.

Satisfied, Dinah Lee hastened to a seat. It was not her accustomed seat on a pew near the pulpit but another near the Albrightons' usual spot. She was hoping to catch Rachel's eye before the end of the fifth verse of the song of invitation.

She spoke perfunctorily to intervening members and visitors. Small talk frightened her; she invariably made some gaff regarding who was related to whom or which member had been relieved of which organ or spouse—too many odd looks and hurt feelings. No, best stick to women's clothes, hair, shoes or the weather. She rarely spoke to men.

But today, the church was abuzz with news of the very public collapse of Newell Post Lawson and speculation as to the cause. Dinah and others who had not heard were quickly told. Very few "One True Churchers" admitted to having tuned in The Holy City Zionist Christian Hour, but somehow the news traveled to and through this insular body. The general consensus as to cause became heart attack. A few leaned toward stroke.

Dinah sidled down the pew in front of the one in which Rachel and her parents, Dr. Raymond and Mrs. Tabitha Albrighton, sat. Dr.

Albrighton, forty-ish and stern, nodded. Dinah had a thought. She stopped, her face grave.

Dr. Albrighton spoke first. "Is there something wrong, Miz Dinah?"

"Oh, Dr. Albrighton," Dinah shook her head. "I'm sure you've heard. Wasn't that just horrible. I mean, a man dying—I mean, by all accounts he certainly looked dead—right there in front of God and everybody?"

"Yes," Dr. Albrighton answered, adding hastily, "I'm thankful we weren't watching."

"So tragic." Dinah continued. "So tragic. I couldn't help thinking of your patient, little Felicity Granger. She would have been thirteen today."

"Yes," Dr. Albrighton said, "I had forgotten. What a loss. She died so young and so suddenly!"

Miz Dinah added, "I just couldn't help thinking how, because she was a Methodist," she turned and looked at Rachel, "she wasn't baptized before she died."

Dr. and Mrs. Albrighton looked gravely at their daughter.

Rachel paled.

Miz Dinah took her seat.

# 9

# Shock and Awe

OUT OF HABIT, MAGGIE HARRIS kept her camera aimed at Pastor Lawson's laughing face and followed it down and down until he hit the floor. The sight of his lifeless eyes shocked her into reality. She let go of the heavy tripod-mounted camera. It nosed up into the lights, burning a permanent hotspot into the sensitive receiver and wiping viewers screens with a painful explosion of light. As she regained her composure and realigned the camera, bright streaks zigzagged upward suggesting Lawson's rapturous transport to realms of glory. Television viewers were mystified. Those with a touch of Pentecostalism believed they had witnessed the fall and miraculous ascension of one of God's saints and were never completely convinced otherwise.

As soon as Grit regained the use of his limbs, he shut off the audio, but not soon enough. Several terrified screams had hit the airwaves. Tom Dixon kept his wits. He threw the broadcast over to the "experiencing difficulties" screen and called through the head set for Kale and Maggie to shut down their cameras. When neither student responded, Tom personally shut down Kale's floor camera and told Grit to do the same for Maggie in the balcony, but she managed to flip the switch herself before Grit got to her.

In homes across the Bennettville area, friends called friends, neighbors called neighbors, and newly alerted viewers flipped on TV sets to see, "Sorry, we are experiencing technical difficulties." WBEN, a local TV station, and WNJC, the campus radio station quickly dispatched reporters. Other media scrambled to do the same.

Inside Holy City, traumatized worshipers sobbed and prayed. Several fled into the parking lot. Two doctors administered CPR as Lawson's color went from raging red to pallid green, and no one could detect a sign of life—not a twitch.

Two blocks down, Bart Crutcher arrived at his target and cased the quiet street. He pulled the Varmint up to the Oldsmobile, walked back to the car's driver side and inserted his Slim Jim. Suddenly, every phone in the neighborhood rang, and sleepy eyed, pajama clad, non-church goers wandered onto porches. In the distance Bart heard sirens. He looked toward Holy City where worried members stared in his direction. His open van sat like a huge, gray elephant, impossible to ignore, and approaching sirens meant police were on the way. Two television trucks drove past and parked in the next block. The sirens came nearer.

Bart cursed Lawson for shortening his sermon and wondered which way to run. Two ambulances sped past, sirens screaming. All attention followed them down the street. Unnoticed and unheard, Bart drove the Olds into the van, scurried back into the cab and started up the noisy diesel. He checked his rear-view mirror. Streets filled with media and on-lookers intent on the action at Holy City. He pulled out of view before anyone looked back.

* * * * *

Doctors summoned from the pews made heroic efforts to revive the unresponsive pastor. Martha Lawson remained frozen to the front pew, face ashen, skin clammy. With her eyes fixed on her husband's lifeless form, her mind wandered the back roads of a long and complicated marriage.

Disordered memories flickered like frayed celluloid on an unfocused screen: their wedding, Newell's charming smile; the shameless face of the first woman; the first miscarriage, Newell's tears; the second woman; charm school, cooking classes, exercise, church endorsed bowing and scraping lessons; Newell's scowl—and more women.

He never could have pulled it off without her. Could never have risen to prestige and power without her complicit silence, her public support. Even in private, Martha Elizabeth had poured herself into this man. Had fed his body, his cravings, and his ego. Without her, he would be, and now perhaps was, dead.

Her brain said, *No, the doctors might yet save him.* Her heart said, *I certainly hope not.*

When emergency personnel arrived, one confided to a colleague, "He's been to the ER twice with his heart. This must'a been the big one."

Regardless, EMTs made dogged efforts to bring him back from the dead. After twenty futile minutes, Lawson was loaded into an ambulance. The nearly catatonic Martha followed her husband to Bennettville Memorial in another ambulance, trailed by a funereal procession of praying Zionist Christians.

Two blocks from the church, the cortège passed a baffled choir member standing in the spot from which Bart had lately removed the peach.

\* \* \* \* \*

Victoria Sellers returned to her bungalow, walking hurriedly along streets filled with traffic. She had managed to place sales flyers on only six or eight windshields before she heard sirens and saw agitated members of the Holy City congregation swarming out into the parking lot. At first she wondered if she was going to be arrested for violating some ordinance, (signage? littering?), but no, the worshipers and neighbors mingling on sidewalks and lawns were not heading her way. Instead they gathered in troubled shoals, seemingly lost.

A few gawkers looked toward Victoria and the For Sale sign in the front yard. She waved, and walked inside. About 10:30 she heard sirens again—this time heading away from Holy City.

Victoria smiled. All in all, she decided, her open house should be quite successful.

\* \* \* \* \*

Troy's cell phone rang as he and Amber neared home.

"Did you hear about Lawson?" Ricky asked. "Tune in WNJC. We just announced he's dead."

Troy dropped the phone, "Wha . . . ?" He stopped the car while Amber recovered his fumble.

She saw his stark disbelief. "Here," she handed him the phone. "Put it on speaker."

"Troy, are you there? What happened?"

"Yeah." Troy's voice trembled, "Yeah. I had to pull over; I'm putting you on speaker, Amber's here. Repeat what you said."

"Sure. We just announced on WNJC that Pastor Lawson was dead when they got him to the hospital. He keeled over in the middle of his sermon. Everybody saw it. He just grabbed his chest and fell. But you can hear the details on the radio."

"Where are you?" Amber felt a need for fellowship.

"I'm at the station. I need to stay here through this, but you two might want to get over to Deep Water. I'm guessing some Divers will show up early tonight."

Amber's pleading look seconded Troy's decision, and he passed it on.

"Ricky?"

"Yeah."

"If anybody asks, we're at Deep Water."

* * * * *

Buddy pulled into Holy City as the ambulances left. Knots of church members huddled in the parking lot talking and weeping—compelled in their trauma to tell and retell what they had witnessed. A distraught lady approached and tearfully recounted the news before moving on to tell another.

Buddy sat stunned. He had come to confront Pastor Lawson. Now, he had nowhere to go and no one to talk to. He bowed his head, asked God for direction then pointed his truck toward Deep Water.

* * * * *

Mechanically, Grit, Maggie, Tom, and Kale shut down equipment, secured cords and microphones and locked up the control room. At this point, the four of them usually scattered to their separate obligations, but today even Grit, who knew he needed to keep his appointment with Grace, lingered in the balcony with the others.

Kale was the first to speak, "I don't know about you, but I need a stiff drink."

Maggie huffed in disbelief, "Kale!"

Kale defended himself, "It's not like I watch a man die every day!"

"We don't know that he's dead!" Maggie said through tears.

"Oh, he's dead alright." Kale looked spooked. "I've never seen anyone or anything look any deader."

Grit was thoughtful, "Did you see his face? He laughed all the way down!"

"Is that some sort of a Christian thing?" Maggie's question reflected her status as a new convert.

Kale laughed nervously.

Grit shot him a look and put his arm around Maggie's shoulders. "Awesome question. I never saw anyone die before. Tom, what do you think? Can someone literally die laughing?"

Grit was looking for help, but Tom didn't answer; he turned toward Grit, mouth set, eyes angry. Silent.

"Lawson's face just kind of creeped me out," Kale blurted. "He looked drunk, or high or something."

Maggie started to protest, but Tom cut her off.

"Pastor Lawson, it's Pastor Lawson, not 'Lawson.' Show some respect! You didn't show respect when he was alive; you could at least show a little respect for the dead!" Tom threw down the cable he had coiled around his forearm and headed for the exit.

"Hold on, Tom," Grit called. "You're right!"

Tom turned. "You just don't get it do you? I know about you and your little undercover church! You and the Michaelsons and Cruz! Well, you got what you wanted. He's dead." Tom shoved through the heavy double door and out.

Grit turned to Kale. "I could use a drink myself."

Maggie was crestfallen. "I just need someone to talk to."

Kale for once was serious. "Yeah, me too."

"I would join you," Grit lamented, "but I'm meeting Grace for church."

Kale couldn't stay serious. He poked Grit in the ribs. "Can you imagine what her mom would say if you showed up with liquor on your breath!" He laughed again. "Amy Grace Willis has you tied up in a big pink bow. I can't believe you're going to sit through another one of those 'One True Church' sermons!"

"Me neither," Grit agreed, "but it will probably do me more good than alcohol."

Maggie amened, but Kale had to finish his riff, "Yeah, Grit. Maggie and me will go remember a dead preacher while you listen to one."

"That's not funny!" Maggie protested.

Grit put a hand on Maggie's shoulder. "We all need to get our heads around this. I'm having lunch with Grace's parents, but we'll be at Deep Water later. You go on over." Grit handed Kale his key. "Order some pizza or something. Take it out of the collection."

"I'll buy the beer," Kale offered.

Maggie moved toward the door. "I can't make it," she said.

"Do you need a ride?" Kale offered. "My passenger seat is missing, but—"

"What?" Maggie seemed preoccupied. "I mean, no. I mean . . ." Maggie hesitated, but looked at Kale appraisingly. He was just under six-feet tall, plump, and sandy headed. He might be flippant and always kidding, but he never meant harm.

"So?" Kale offered again. "She's ugly as sin, but she runs like a grass snake!"

Maggie would trust him. "I need to go by my house first."

"Sure," Kale said, offering his arm.

Maggie took the cue, curtsied and adopted a proper British accent, "Thank you, kind sir. I will accept a ride in your carriage" Kale Edgar had smiled his way past her defenses. The two, arm in arm, started for the door.

Maggie stopped, "Grit, are you still leading the discussion tonight? The Fifth Commandment?"

Grit grimaced. "Yeah, I guess so. I'm struggling with that right now. I'm anxious to hear what I have to say."

The three emerged from Holy City into a darkening afternoon. Threatening clouds festered to the west. Scattered shafts of sunshine held out hope for clearing weather, but heavy winds spoke of an approaching storm.

Grit put his hand before his face to keep debris from his eyes while he walked to his pickup and squeezed in. "See you later," he called, and left for The One True Church and Grace Willis.

Kale and Maggie hurried, clothes flapping, across the parking lot.

At the sight of the contraption Kale called a car, Maggie bit her lip but laughed anyway. The front passenger door was welded shut, and the passenger seat was, as advertised, missing. Ragged patches of apple-green paint clung to the rusted body like algae on red clay.

"Go ahead, laugh," Kale said. "She's a funny car."

He escorted Maggie to the rear door, opened it ceremoniously and handed her into the back seat with a tip of an imaginary hat. To her surprise, the interior was spotless. Kale's textbooks were stacked neatly in the seat next to her, and his jacket lay in the back window, but all were clean and well cared for. If she ignored the missing front seat, she could imagine herself in an uptown taxi.

The old car did seem to run well as Kale started up. "Where to, m'lady?"

"My house is just two blocks away, but you have to circle campus to get there."

"Sure," Kale replied, "If I ignore my stomach, I'm not in any hurry."

"I . . . um. I need to check on my mom." Maggie felt silly talking to the back of Kale's head.

He caught a glimpse of her in the rear-view mirror. Something in her face made him stop the car and turn off the engine. "Do you need to talk?"

Maggie nodded. Kale heaved himself around and took her hand, "What's up?"

\* \* \* \* \*

After her talk with Kale, Maggie could have flown to her house on Twelfth Street. The trip in Kale's car took a little longer. At Thirteenth Street, he checked to see if Moses was in his usual place. The mysterious figure sometimes disappeared during really bad weather, but not today. Today, Moses leaned into the rising wind clutching a sign that read, "Honor Your Father and Mother," the title of Grit's talk at Deep Water. The coincidence seemed uncanny.

Maggie's neighborhood, half a block from the carefully tended landscapes and revered temples of New Jerusalem, was one of Bennettville's most neglected. Under the darkening clouds, the patchy dry grass and wilting houses faded to a weary gray. Kale's rusty orange and green car stood out like a psychedelic accent pillow in a funeral parlor.

At Maggie's house, Kale jumped out and opened Maggie's door. "I'm going in with you."

Maggie protested, afraid of what he would see, but Kale insisted, "You can't let your mother hide forever." Maggie went in first, to see if her mom was dressed. Loretta lay, mostly on the couch, half naked, belly distended, mouth open. She looked dead, but she was snoring. A pile of empty beer cans decorated the ratty carpet and perfumed the air.

Maggie picked up a tattered throw from the floor, threw it over her mother and motioned for Kale. The two of them checked the house. Only one burner on, no faucets running, and all cigarettes, for once, had been snuffed. Maggie was learning to let her mother suffer the consequences of her addiction, but she didn't want her burning down the house.

She shook her mother roughly. "Mom, wake up! I'm leaving, mom." Shaking rarely worked. She slapped gently at Loretta's face and hands. "Mom, you need to eat. There's a sandwich in the fridge, Mom." Loretta mumbled something about the grocery store and returned to her snoring. Maggie made one last attempt, "Mom, there's a storm coming, you need to wake up." Nothing.

Maggie closed her eyes, and "accepted the things she could not change," but this time she and God had a friend.

# 10

# A Watery Grave

The Bennettville One True Church's wide, one-story building had a low, sloping roof, plain windows, a gravel parking lot, and no steeple (no musical instruments equals no bell; ergo, no steeple). The building's aesthetic was not powerful, militant, beautiful, or reverent. It was heartless.

The Spartan design was not intended to inspire men or to glorify God. It was not intended to do anything, but it did plenty. It embodied the One True Church's strict adherence to spiritless, comfortless "denial of the flesh." A building was a "necessary expedient" to keep regimented Christians out of the elements while they performed their dutiful worship. Musical instruments, stained glass windows, art or displays of joy were non-Biblical, self-indulgent emotionalism. ("If such were allowed, next thing you know people would be dancing down the aisles naked!")

Grace waited for Grit in a small vestibule with a men's and ladies' restroom on either side (much debated innovations, finally conceded to as expedient for the sake of the very young and very old). She knew about Lawson's collapse, and was thinking that Grit might not make it when, true to form, he shot in the door at the last possible moment.

They hurried down the aisle looking for Dinah Lee. Plain, wooden beams arched gracelessly overhead. On either side, plain, wooden doors led to classrooms. Plain, wooden pews faced front in military precision.

Grit gave Grace a whispered account of the horror at Holy City. "Some medical people from the congregation got to him quick, but they couldn't bring him around. The EMTs took him to the hospital, but he sure looked dead to me."

Grace spotted her mom who had saved them seats. No time for greetings, just a peck on Grace's cheek; Greg Lindsey had climbed to the high pulpit and opened his songbook.

No one could miss the cue to find a seat and settle in for the hour-long service; the entire auditorium was arranged to raise whoever happened to occupy the pulpit to a place of preeminence.

Greg looked out over the congregation. "728b," he announced.

Dinah Lee sat at attention, songbook before her, ready to begin. She did not have a strong voice, but, after one particularly exhausting Sunday, she had confessed to Greg that of the five "required acts of worship" she was fondest of singing. "When the entire congregation stands to sing," she had babbled, "I feel as much like a full, participating Christian as any male. Why, if I wasn't afraid of becoming indecent and out of order, I might enjoy myself."

"Number 728b," Greg repeated, giving everyone time to turn the pages. 'Our God, He is Alive', 728b" He blew "do" on his pitch pipe, found the starting note, sang the alto, tenor, and bass intervals and beat out a full measure with his hand. Despite these efforts, he was singing solo on the downbeat, and only he and the sopranos sang the first three measures.

He kept singing but began to pray, *Oh Lord, please let the basses join in before the chorus.*

Without the rolling bass lead of the chorus, there would be huge gaps in the melody, but he needn't have worried. At the proper moment, every male in the congregation, bass, tenor or adolescent, attempted to sing the deep do, re, me, fa stair step, "There is a God." And the ladies echoed, "do, do, do, do, there is a God," from the upper staff. The mighty chorus finished all four verses, declaring their faith triumphantly then began another contrapuntal foot-stomper, "Ring It Out." This time, the ladies: altos, sopranos, et al hit the high lead, "Ring it out," and the basses echoed, "Ring it out." Voices were warming, and morning doldrums lifting just as the singing ended.

An imposing elder prayed gravely, then sat; a deacon read scripture and sat. For a moment, everyone sat. They sat until a low murmur began at the back of the auditorium. Finally, Brother Willis remembered that the elders had voted to move the weekly communion service from before to after the sermon. The reported purpose of the move was to make the Lord's Supper immediately available to anyone who, as a result of the sermon, had responded to the "invitation song" and been baptized. The actual purpose of the change was to keep a third of the congregation from slipping out the back door after communion. Law-keepers all, they knew that listening to the sermon was not one of the "five required acts of worship," and took advantage of this legal loophole weekly.

Brother Willis rose with a start, took two quick strides to the pulpit, stepped up on a small stool and began. "The Bible condemns strange worship." He intoned. "In the book of Leviticus Chapter Ten, we learn that strange worship is unacceptable to God and worthy of death. Chapter ten, verses one and two, 'Yea verily and therefore I say unto thee, that Nadab and Abihu, sons of the most high priest Aaron, did taketh their censers, and putteth fire in them and did addeth incense. The fire they did offereth before the Lord was strange and contrary to His command. So the Lord senteth fire from out His most holieth presence and did consume them, forsooth." Brother Willis put particular emphasis on the 'forsooth'.

"Webster defines the word strange as, 'unknown, alien or queer'." The congregation gasped. "Yes, queer, and I say to you that there are some very queer things going on in this city in the name of worship." He certainly knew how to get their attention.

Grit recognized Brother Willis' usual theme, the eventual damnation of every professing Christian not recognized as a member of the One True Church. But Grit had been wrong about the specific infraction; the sin *du jour* was "Drama in the Church." The target was the Presbyterian Easter service. Apparently male and female lay ministers had walked down a center aisle displaying symbolically colored scarves while the chorus sang appropriate psalms.

From Brother Willis' tone of voice and Sixteenth Century condemnations, Grit gathered that God did not care for such goings-on and was just itching to show those people how much.

As Brother Willis continued his harangue against drama, Grit's mind, and eyes, wandered. He noticed with amusement how much this One True Church service violated Brother Willis' own thesis. Hadn't Grit seen a lighted marquee outside advertising three weekly performances? Wasn't Grit holding a printed program in his hand listing the various actors and their roles? Wasn't that platform under the pulpit a stage, and the arch over it a traditional stage proscenium? Overhead, stage lights illuminated the performer and stage microphones amplified the sound.

Brother Willis, the featured performer, well-coiffed and appropriately costumed, was at this very moment subjecting his audience to a thirty-minute soliloquy in his best imitation of King James and Shakespeare.

Grit remained fascinated through the first two acts, each of which began with long Bible passages, carefully memorized and delivered on cue. Willis with his face toward the audience and in full light, showed the skill of a practiced thespian—not easy while using a blackboard.

(This last convenience had caused no little stir when Brother Willis moved it from one of the classrooms to the auditorium dais. The elders called a men's business meeting to debate whether using a blackboard was scriptural.

Brother Willis pointed out that Jesus had written words to illustrate a lesson when he handled the case of the woman caught in adultery, but others pointed out that Jesus was not conducting a worship service at the time. Some argued that the writing of scripture was restricted to Christ and his apostles, and had ended in the first century. All concerned eventually decided that a blackboard could be considered the Twenty-first Century equivalent of First Century dirt, and, as long as no one wrote scripture on it, it could not be labeled a "man-made innovation" and was therefore "expedient," if not actually commanded.)

The third and last act on the morning's bill reached its climax with a particularly splendid declamation of the entire second chapter of Acts. The denouement, an invitation to repent, confess and be baptized followed as the night the day. Brother Willis yielded the spotlight to Brother Lindsey who segued into "Oh Why Not Tonight?" with hardly any embarrassment but a surfeit of enthusiasm.

Dinah, barricaded behind her hymnal, snuck glances toward her left flank, where Rachel peeked from behind her own fortification. Near the end of the fifth verse, Miz Dinah grew worried. Rachel had shown no sign, other than a tightening grip on her hymnal, that she had been moved in any way.

It was time.

Miz Dinah turned toward Rachel and began to cry.

Heavy, despairing tears rolled down Miz Dinah's cheeks and dropped from her chin. All the solemnity she had exhibited when informing a classroom full of grade school children that they were eternally damned was directed at one child. Rachel uttered a strangled scream, dropped her head and ran down the aisle with Dinah Lee Willis in her wake.

Rachel landed, sobbing, on the front pew as the last notes of the invitation hymn faded. Dinah Lee lit behind her. Mr. and Mrs. Albrighton followed, taking seats to either side of their daughter.

Brother Willis stepped over, knelt and took Rachel's shaking hand. "Rachel, would you like to be baptized?" Rachel's head bobbed. Brother Willis led her to the microphone and conveyed her intentions to the congregation. "Rachel Albrighton has asked to be baptized. We rejoice with her and her parents." He motioned toward the dressing rooms. "Dinah Lee, if you would take Rachel and her mother?" Turning to his right, "Brother Lindsey, do you have a song?"

Brother Lindsey did. Rising to make his way back to the pulpit, he called out, "Number twenty-seven, number twenty-seven, 'Blessed Assurance'" (a soothing, thoughtful declaration of faith). Upon reaching the pulpit and opening his book, Greg discovered that number twenty-seven was not "Blessed Assurance" but "Jesus is Coming Soon" (a double-time ditty celebrating the destruction of the world.) *Oops!*

Greg swallowed and tried again; he must have gotten the number turned around. "Seventy-two, number seventy-two." He turned to the page. There the title, "Silent Night," brought tears to his eyes; One True Churchers did not sing Christmas songs at Christmas, much less at baptisms.

Greg prayed silently as he checked the index. *Oh Lord, please don't let anyone call a men's business meeting about this.*

He found the number then announced sheepishly, "Number 207, 207, 'Blessed Assurance'." *Well, I was close.*

In the dressing room, Rachel and her mother put a shower cap over her curls and located the smallest baptismal garment. Tiny Rachel removed all but her underpants before being wrapped in the heavy, ankle-length gown. Now fully and massively clothed, she felt cold and naked. No one spoke. Rachel shivered.

Brother Willis, in the next room over, removed his suit jacket, rolled up his sleeves, stepped out of his shoes and into large rubber waders that were hung on the back of the baptistery door. Once donned, the outlandish garment reached nearly to his chin; the ever-frugal elders had insisted on buying the largest size, in case their next preacher was a taller man.

When Rachel was dressed, Miz Dinah handed her a tightly folded handkerchief and one more bit of advice. "This will keep you from taking in a lot of water."

Rachel had not thought of this possibility. "But I . . . ."

Miz Dinah was reassuring. "Don't you worry, honey. Brother Willis will not let you drown."

Another unforeseen possibility.

"You're going to do just fine. Just don't think about all those people out there. When Brother Willis asks you to confess, you speak up into the microphone real loud so all of them can hear you."

*Confess? Confess what?* Rachel didn't want "all those people" to hear her confess anything. She turned and looked at the exit. *I could run, but where would I go? They have my clothes!*

Brother Willis, fully encapsulated, opened the baptistery door and started down the three steps into chest high water. By the second step, he knew that the waders had a hole in one leg. By the third step, he knew it was a large hole. He sighed in resignation, telling himself that he wouldn't melt. But he dreaded appearing in front of the congregation looking like he had just come out of a dunking booth.

He was smiling at his unconscious pun when the door opposite opened and Rachel appeared in her "garments white as snow"; her head haloed in silver plastic; her face bloodless.

Brother Willis whispered his exit line, "Angelic," reached to adjust the microphone and died, dramatically.

\* \* \* \* \*

At the coroner's inquest, witnesses were hard pressed to say which came first, the loud noise or the spectacular fireworks, but they agreed upon the sequence of nearly everything else. Brother Willis had grunted loudly, as if hit in the chest, then his body became rigid, his arms flew up and ragged streaks like lightning shot out of his fingertips. Everyone remembered the smell of singed hair and burning rubber.

Rachel's mother remembered pulling her daughter away from the arcing water. But Rachel remembered running for the exit, away from the baptistery where Brother Willis was taking his final curtain call and performing an encore, a six-minute, electrified, dance macabre.

It had taken that long to find someone who knew where the circuit breaker was, to reach it and to throw the switch. By then Brother Thomas Alexander Willis was far, far away learning about his need for grace.

# 11

# Death Comes in Threes?

THE REVEREND BISHOP REVEREND BISHOP soldiered on after Saturday's Rainbow Unity Picnic, but by Monday he was wretched, barely able to drive himself to Bennettville Memorial where his dehydration, uncontrolled diarrhea, and severe stomach cramps concerned the doctors; food poisoning could be lethal. Other reported cases were not virulent, but Bishop, an evidently healthy man, was severely ill.

In ICU, visitors and flowers were forbidden, but hundreds of Bishop's sheep and sundry dignitaries roamed the halls, and a garden of showy bouquets sprouted throughout the hospital—courtesy of The Reverend Bishop's many admirers.

By Sunday, both Bishop and little Honesty White had improved considerably. Honesty's doctor pronounced her healthy and sent her home. Bishop was moved to room 210 and finally allowed visitors. He had awakened hungry, as he had the last two mornings, but today he was allowed solid food—if oatmeal and Jell-O could be considered solid—and a TV. He dove into both with gusto, tuning in the Holy City Zionist Christian Hour to check out his competition.

Just as Bishop began to wonder at the iconic pastor's powerful delivery and hypnotic pacing, Lawson, in full close-up, began to laugh and slap at his heart, "Oh, the Rapture, the Rapture." Then he fell. The screen filled with Lawson's glazed eyes and gaping mouth. The Reverend Bishop Reverend Bishop lost his breakfast and was sentenced to one more night in Bennettville Memorial.

* * * * *

"Two large pizzas, one pepperoni with extra cheese, and one half ham and pineapple and half sausage and mushroom." Kale had raided the Deep Water cash box as per Grit's orders and was crushing the phone between his stocky neck and beefy shoulder as he searched the fridge for drinks. No need to shell out for beer if, as he suspected, there were a couple of cold ones on hand.

Kale figured two large would feed him, Maggie, and Buddy, who had been outside waiting for someone with a key when he and Maggie arrived. Kale could easily down a whole pizza by himself, but his weight was once again edging past stocky and heading toward fat. He had been "the jolly fat kid" as a child and knew, jolly did not necessarily mean happy.

But he was thankful for his genuine, cheerful nature. In spite of the grim events of the day—two dead men and Maggie's revelation about her mother—he had managed to lift Maggie's spirit. She had entrusted him with her deepest secrets, and, Kale marveled, *God used me to give her comfort*.

\* \* \* \* \*

Grit had not noticed Grace's nails digging into his arm during her father's unholy death scene, but now, as they waited in the ER for a report on her mother, he felt the gouges and recalled her horrified screams. Willis' electrocution lasted only minutes, but those minutes seemed endless as Grace, her mother, and two hundred congregants looked on, helpless. By the time someone turned off the power, Brother Willis' ordeal was over, but the ghastly spectacle continued; the body, loosed from electrically induced spasms, fell, lifeless and charred, face first into the baptistery. Dinah Lee Willis, pushed her way past Mrs. Albrighton's protective arms, took one look, fainted and fell into the water beside her husband.

Grace had collapsed, limp and sobbing, into Grit's arms, and he felt faint himself; he had witnessed two horrible deaths in less than an hour.

Grace remained slumped against him until they drove to the hospital where he left her in the care of several One True Church members while he stepped into the hall to call Troy.

\* \* \* \* \*

Martha Lawson was "resting comfortably," but it had taken some doing. Emergency personnel brought her back to consciousness with oxygen and warm blankets, and by the time she was assigned to room 208, her vitals were good, and she wanted to talk. She motioned to the nearest nurse.

"I want to see Reverend Bishop. I know he's here, and I want to see him."

Nurse Casey was astonished; Mrs. Lawson, had just witnessed her husband's collapse and did not know of his condition, but her first question concerned another man. She checked Martha's vitals again, thinking her patient might still be in shock. The heart rate was up and a bit erratic. Nurse Casey pushed the call button.

"Can I help you?" the desk queried.

Martha sat up and pulled off her oxygen mask.

"Mrs. Lawson!"

"You don't understand," Martha insisted. "I have to tell Reverend what's happened."

"I can't let you out of this room in your condition."

"Can I help you?" The desk called again.

"Yes, please send Dr. Clark to room 208."

Martha threw her legs over the side of the bed. Nurse Casey pushed the emergency button and tried to restrain her—a formidable task in any circumstance and nearly impossible at the moment.

"I'll see what I can do, Mrs. Lawson, but you will have to wait until you see the doctor."

Doctor Clark, a tall, rangy resident, stepped in from the hall.

"What is it Mrs. Lawson? Is there something wrong?"

"Yes. Tell this nurse to take me to Reverend Bishop. He's in this hospital, and I want to see him."

Dr. Clark was good with difficult patients. "That might be possible, Mrs. Lawson, but first I need to check your heart." He summoned his most soothing bedside manner, positioned his stethoscope and gave a conspiratorial nod to Nurse Casey before addressing the patient. "The Reverend Bishop may not be able to have visitors. You wouldn't want to harm his health would you?"

Martha shook her head.

"Ok, let's have a listen."

The heartbeat was still abnormal. Dr. Clark wrote out a prescription for a sedative while he continued to placate his patient. "I'll see what The Reverend's doctor says about visitors and give you that information. Until then, you need to rest." He would order an EKG later if necessary, but the immediate course of treatment was stress relief.

The good doctor's beeper summoned him to the ER . Outside Martha's room the hall was full of hospital staff in excited chatter. Dr. Clark gave a quizzical look to a nearby orderly who filled him in on the buzz: a second minister's wife, Dinah Lee Willis, had witnessed her husband's death and was in the ER .

"You're kidding!" Dr. Clark remonstrated. They were not. His beeper jangled again loudly and he hurried on to his next patient.

Nurse Casey monitored Martha as she fretted in her sleep and repeated softly, "Reverend, Reverend, Reverend."

\* \* \* \* \*

"Oh, God!" Troy wasn't swearing, he was praying. He could barely believe Grit's report; Grace's dad was dead, and her mom was hospitalized. He and Amber were in their van and had just pulled into the lot behind Deep Water. Buddy's truck and Kale's excuse for a car were parked nearby.

"What is it?" Amber knew it was bad.

When Troy explained, her first thoughts were for Grit and Grace. "We can't leave them at the hospital alone," she insisted.

"You're right." He jumped out of the van. "I'll let Kale and Buddy know where we are and why. Do you want to go in?"

"No," Amber picked up the cell phone, "I'll stay here and call Ricky."

\* \* \* \* \*

When Troy and Amber arrived at the hospital, they found Grit and Grace in the waiting room. Doctor Clark came over to report on Dinah's condition.

"Your mother is distraught, but out of shock." He said. "We're going to keep her overnight, just to let her rest. I've given her a sedative, and she should be asleep shortly. If you want to see her, you should go in now."

Grace clung to Grit's arm as they took the elevator to the second floor and walked down the hall to her mother's darkened room. Grit stopped, silhouetted in the doorway.

"Tommy, Tommy," Dinah Lee whispered. "Oh, Tommy."

"It's me and Grit, Momma."

"Gracie! He's gone! He's gone, Gracie!"

"I know, Momma. I'm here now, and we're going to be okay."

Grit moved to a darkened corner.

Amy Grace climbed up in the bed, lay down beside her mother and stroked her hair.

"We're going to get through this, Momma. God is good, Momma."

"God is good," Dinah repeated. "The Lord giveth and the Lord taketh away. Blessed be the name of the Lord."

Dinah Lee sat up. "But Gracie, you saw, Gracie! You saw it! You saw . . ." Dinah Lee laughed hysterically. "You saw your father in those ridiculous waders; right up under his chin. I had Rachel ready when— Oh, God!" Dinah shouted at heaven. "Thomas reached up . . . and . . ."

"I know, Momma, I know. I saw."

"Oh, Gracie!" Dinah clutched her daughter in a ferocious hug. "Your father! Your father! I screamed and screamed. And I couldn't do anything! I just hung onto Rachel's hand. And the smell! Oh, Gracie! I'll never forget the smell. Burned rubber and . . ."

Grit moved toward the bed as Grace struggled to reach the call button. Dinah fell back crying, exhausted, and Grace fled to Grit's arms as her mother, at last, succumbed to the sedative and slept.

Grace too was exhausted and crying, but thankful to be drawing strength from Grit's quiet presence. She had planned to tell him just how much he meant to her after dinner with her folks, then this. She would wait—wait until her life returned to some semblance of sanity.

In the ER waiting room, a truly remarkable congregation of One True Churchers, Zionist Christians, sheep from the flock of The Reverend Bishop, and Deep Water Divers mingled in ecumenical prayer.

At Grit and Grace's appearance several in the crowd rose to offer comfort. Mrs. Albrighton, who had brought little Rachel to the ER after finding her hysterical in the church parking lot, was the first to approach.

"Grace, I'm so sorry, is there anything we can do?"

Grace spoke faintly. "Excuse, me, I'm . . ." she withdrew, pulling Grit aside. "I can't do this right now. Could you tell them? Just tell them I love them, but I need to rest. Ask them to go . . . Ask them to pray and . . ." Grace swayed and caught herself against the wall.

Grit pulled her to him, picked her up in his arms and hailed the nearest nurse. "I think we have another patient."

"I'm fine," Grace protested, but the nurse prescribed a chair and some nourishment.

Fortified with food and coffee, Grace's mind cleared, only to fill with pain. Memories of her father, unbidden but not unwelcome, overwhelmed her heart. Grace had always lived in his shadow. Without him, she felt exposed, like a child, alone and far from home. She needed to be near her mother, so she arranged to have a cot put in the room.

Grit stayed until Grace fell asleep. He ached to lie next to her, hold her close and make her pain go away. He ached until his body burned and the heat of his anguish turned the bitter ice in his heart to an emotional flood. He needed to clear his head. Leading the devotional at Deep Water tonight would give him something to do and something to feel other than pain.

He asked Troy and Amber to watch over the two Willis women until he returned.

"You don't have to go," Amber assured. "Tell him, Troy."

But Grit insisted, "People are counting on me. Ricky did a power point. Grace took refreshments. Maggie decorated for hours."

Troy objected, "That's just it. They'll do just fine without you."

"They don't have to have a speaker." Amber continued. "God knows they have plenty to pray about."

"What about the audio?" Grit asked. "And I need to check out the computers."

"Kale and Buddy can take care of all that." Troy said.

Grit clamped his jaw, and Troy got the message. He shot a "don't worry, it's okay" look to Amber and backed off. "Hey, you're right. You need to be there. I'd like to be there myself, but do you need to go now?"

Grit did; he still had not prepared his lesson—another soggy mound of procrastination he had piled in his own way. Some of those piles seemed insurmountable: his unfinished degree, his relationship with Grace, his lack of direction. As his parents reminded him at every opportunity, he needed to budget his time and set attainable goals, and he was determined to do so—later.

\* \* \* \* \*

Every Sunday after church, Bennettville Memorial Hospital was resplendent with high-heeled ladies and well-heeled pastors ready to "lay on hands and pray." This Sunday, the hall outside Reverend Bishop's room was particularly notable; a gaggle of colorful ladies— each in an eye-catching suit, shoes dyed to match, and an unforgettable, custom-made chapeau—had formed a line outside the reverend's door. They carefully guarded their places and talked loudly despite signs for QUIET.

Sister Whyneatta Wilson and Sister Immaculata Jones stood closest to Bishop's door, having skipped the last half hour of church service to be the first (as per hospital regulation, two-at-a-time) visitors. The other sisters shifted their eyes with obvious disapproval, but the news that had them all clucking was not the erring sisters but the very public deaths of two prominent preachers.

When visiting hour began, Sisters Whyneatta and Immaculata sashayed hurriedly into Bishop's room. He was not surprised but thoroughly dismayed that these particular ladies had managed to find their way to the head of the line. For one thing, he had convinced each of them (and every other lady in the congregation) that she was his favorite—a task that became trickier when the ladies traveled in pairs. For another, they each bore a basket of goodies. (It would be a cold day in a bad place before he ever again took a bite of home cooked gifts.)

Bishop made appropriately flattering comments on the ladies' impossible hats then smiled through gritted teeth as they launched into a full account of all they knew about the macabre news of the day—with embellishment.

"Guernicka Jackson's niece is 'One True Church'," Whyneatta avowed, "and she said you could smell that preacher cookin' on out in the street. All the peoples there went home and washed they's clothes and took a bath. It was that bad."

Immaculata would not be outdone, "I don't think they're gonna have church in there Sunday. Why, the whole fire house is down there now scraping what's left of Thomas Willis off the bottom of that baptistery." She held out her basket. "Would you care for some of my special Bar-b-qued ribs, Reverend Bishop?"

Bishop pushed the button for the desk.

"Could I help you?" an aide responded.

"Yes, would you please send a nurse with a bedpan?"

He had been making his way to the bathroom by himself for days, but the ploy worked; the ladies adjourned for the day, and Bishop quickly hung the "no visitors" sign back on his doorknob.

The gory recital had done nothing for the poor Bishop's stomach, but more than his digestion was troubled. Something wasn't right. He remembered the note left on his door a week ago—the clipping about a car theft ring and the handwritten warning. He had taken it as an attempt at blackmail, but no one had claimed credit or asked for money. Who could it be? No one, outside of Bart Crutcher, could link him directly to any of that, and he had Bart in a pretty tight corner.

But two preachers were dead—on Commandment Sunday! The coincidence seemed prophetic, like the fulfillment of some Biblical curse. *But God doesn't work that way, does he?*

Had the note, the single handwritten phrase, "Thou Shalt Not Steal," been a threat? *Is my life in danger? If so, is my death to come today?*

Bishop snorted at his own foolishness. *Faulty wiring results in electrocutions, and driven men die of heart attacks. The fact that both victims were preachers and both died on the same Sunday was simply coincidental. Wasn't it?*

# 12

# Where Was Moses When the Lights Went Out?

AT DEEP WATER THE MOOD WAS SOMBER but not yet resigned to mourning. Maggie and Kale tried to stay busy checking out equipment, but there wasn't much to do; someone had set up already (Troy? Ricky?) Ricky had definitely been there; his Power Point was loaded, and, Buddy noted, someone had added anchors to the bottom of the largest speakers.

"We have beer." Kale pulled out two bottles and a six-pack of coke. He held up the latter, turned and called, "Maggie?"

Maggie stood on a folding chair checking an overhead monitor. At Kale's call, she lost her balance.

Buddy turned, yelled, "Careful!" and ran.

Maggie reached to steady herself on the monitor. It swiveled, and she clutched at space.

Buddy caught her at the waist and scolded as he lowered her to the ground. "Holy crap, Maggie!" Buddy blushed and apologized. "Excuse my language, but you could have been hurt, or even worse!"

"Yeah, you could have broken the equipment!" Kale did not get a laugh, in spite of the six-pack of cokes he dangled unconsciously at the end of his arm. When he noticed, he reminded himself not to open them any time soon.

Maggie hung her head.

"I'm sorry for yelling," Buddy apologized again. "I thought you knew where we keep the ladder. Don't ever hang your weight on one of those monitors. It could come down and do major damage to anyone near it."

Someone knocked. Kale answered the door and returned with two pizzas.

He opened the first. "One pepperoni," he drooled. He opened the second and whiffed, "Ah yes, one flat folding chair, half Maggie and half television."

This time Buddy laughed. But Maggie started crying.

Male instinct told Kale and Buddy that, no matter what had caused the tears, they were responsible. Each began apologizing for anything and everything short of criminal activity.

Kale came up with, "Whatever it is, it's my fault; I'm sorry, and I won't do it again!"

Maggie smiled weakly through tears and insisted, "No, no, it's not you, it's this day. It just hit me; Pastor Lawson is dead; Grace's dad is dead. It's just too awful!"

The two men sobered and agreed. Outside thunder signaled that the storm had prevailed.

Buddy led Maggie to a chair. Kale grabbed napkins and drinks. It was three o'clock and well past time to eat. Hunger and emotional exhaustion cracked their defenses. Dark thoughts of the day seeped in. Kale and Buddy wondered aloud about graduation. Now that Lawson was dead, would Troy, Amber, and Ricky be reinstated? Something would have to be done or he and Buddy would have to finish their degrees elsewhere. Elsewhere for Ricky and Buddy meant nowhere.

Maggie had her own dark thoughts. She was thinking of Thomas Willis. Now that he was dead, would the shadow he had cast over her and her mother disappear or darken?

* * * * *

Grit was half way to Deep Water when the events of the day caught up to him. He stopped and pulled over. Just breathing was too much; driving was impossible. In the last two hours he had watched two men die and seen hundreds of people he cared for suffer. He was tired past words and still had a lesson to present. Maybe Troy was right; he should blow it off, go home and crash.

*Where do I come off teaching about honoring parents anyway?* His last visit to his parent's home ended in a total meltdown. When he told them about dropping out, everyone, even his brother, started screaming. His mom cried. He was one huge disappointment. *How could they think anything else? They sacrificed to keep me at New Jerusalem, and I threw it in their faces.*

The glowering sky that had threatened rain all day let loose. Noisy raindrops flopped and splattered on the windshield just in front of Grit's face. He put his seat back, closed his eyes and relaxed for the first time in days.

He began to cry, or was he praying? Whatever it was, it felt good—God reaching into his heart and throwing out great, sodden handfuls of guilt. Grit prayed for over an hour. He prayed for Grace and Dinah Willis. He prayed for Mrs. Lawson and himself. By the time he got around to praying for his parents, he knew he was ready for Deep Water—not to preach a sermon but to confess his sins.

* * * * *

Amber slipped into Mrs. Willis' darkened room. Dinah Lee was sleeping peacefully, but Grace sat up and put her feet on the floor. She was hungry and needed company. She left to have dinner with Amber and Troy and to stop by the "preacher's house" to pick up the "sitting-with-the-sick" bag Dinah kept packed in the front closet.

When they pulled up to the house, Grace couldn't make herself go in; she half expected to meet her father in the hall or to hear one of his thundering sermons resounding through the house. Thomas Alexander Willis had dominated Grace's life for nineteen years and would haunt her forever.

* * * * *

A little thing like food poisoning did not stop Reverend Bishop Reverend Bishop. He had begun working on his upcoming presentation to the Bennettville City Council as soon as he was able to sit up—earlier, if you counted his thoughts as he lay nauseated and fevered in his hospital bed. He put the final touches on his plea for a "non-profit" casino in Bennettville, but the presentation was a mere formality; the outcome was a given.

State gaming laws had heretofore kept Bishop from achieving his goal, but he was counting on a loophole; gambling was allowed on the Mississippi—an exception held over from the Nineteenth Century when riverboats and riverboat gamblers plied her waters. The Mississippi was four hundred and fifty miles to the west of Bennettville, but no matter, Bishop knew he had the clout to flout.

A lovely, old, paddle wheeler, the regal River Queen was a national treasure harkening to an era of leisure and wealth, the last all-wood passenger vessel to travel inland waters. But time and FEMA had caught up to her. She had, since the early nineteen-fifties, required a special dispensation from federal authorities to circumvent fire regulations. Now, newly empowered bureaucrats were flexing their muscles, and the Queen would not be given an exemption.

Politicians on all levels were in Bishop's debt and drooling over possible payback, so Bishop was sure of financing—a government grant, if not full federal subsidy. The River Queen, piece by piece if necessary, would be moved to and anchored in the Bennettville municipal reservoir. Her three decks and large parlors would be refitted to house a small but lucrative casino.

All of Bishop's well-oiled locals were "on board," and, as soon as he delivered his speech, they would know their talking point, "It is all for education."

\* \* \* \* \*

Grit listened to the WNJC weather report as he pulled in to the lot behind Deep Water; thunderstorms and possible hail were expected off and on all night. The Dive, surrounded on three sides by dirt, would be a good place to ride out a storm.

He parked as close as he could to the door, ducked his head and ran through the pelting rain. Inside, he greeted Kale, Maggie, and Buddy, and they offered him the last piece of pizza. The smell had hit him at the door. He had not eaten since breakfast.

He gulped it down and did one last check of the equipment while the others cleaned up the remains of their meal. Everything checked out. Instruments and mikes were hooked up to amplifiers; amplifiers were plugged into the wall of speakers; the computer was linked to the monitors, and the whole mess was plugged into two crowded power strips attached to an extension cord which was plugged in upstairs. It was an invitation to an overload. Grit knew this, but the only wiring in the hundred-year-old basement was two pitiful light sockets.

"Great job guys," Grit congratulated. "I may let you do this by yourselves from now on."

"It was nearly all done when we got here," Maggie said.

"Yeah," Kale looked at Maggie, "all but the folding chair."

Maggie shot daggers at Kale, and Grit decided to ignore the comment, considering the source.

He went upstairs to The Dive and opened the street door. For the next two hours, Divers, guests, and visitors wandered in and dripped down the candlelit stairs.

At the bottom, in the hall leading to the meeting area, Maggie had hung several large "family" photos. The first was a giant print of Grant Wood's "American Gothic" labeled "Dad and Mom?" Other huge portraits, among them the Simpsons, the Osbournes, and Prince Charles and Camilla, were similarly labeled. Maggie hoped the rogues' gallery would help make anyone's family situation, including her own, seem doable by comparison.

Divers mingled in the meeting area, greeting visitors and serving refreshments. Ricky kept an eye on the computer as his video played soundlessly on the monitors overhead. Scenes of gamboling lambs, flying geese, feeding lions, etc. suggested a run-of-the-mill nature documentary. When the service began at six, Ricky turned up the sound. Twenty seconds later, the crowd was laughing; Ricky and a few of his students had added raucous voiceovers and wild music to the staid documentary. Incongruous rock music played as starlings complained about getting up early to feed their chicks; rebellious lambs rocked out and ewes and rams bleated about the noise; lionesses roared resentment of their lazy mates and young lovebirds were grounded for billing and cooing. Ricky hoped the humorous video would set-up Grit's lesson on parental respect.

The soundtrack segued into the evening's devotional music. Stage lights came up, and the noise level came up with them. Ricky punched up a music CD. Grit pounded his jungle drums and sang. The crowd joined in: singing, clapping, humming, and hammering on the tables.

By the last song, an instrumental, Grit was into worship and feeling good. *God is good,* "BOOM!" *God is a God of comfort,* "BOOM!" *God will comfort Martha Lawson,* "BOOM!" *God will comfort Grace and Dinah,* "BOOM, BOOM!"

The burden of guilt Grit had carried for the last two years was gone. "BOOM!" *I did not dishonor my parents when I took my own path.* "BOOM!" *I dishonored them when I did not trust their love.* "BOOM, BOOM!" *I dishonored them,* "BOOM, BOOM!" *and cheated myself,* "BOOM!" *by assuming they did not care,* "BOOM, BOOM!" *that they would not,* "BOOM!" *or could not,* "BOOM!" *understand or help.*

"BOOM, BOOM, BOOM!" He was ready to apologize, to say to his parents and to God, *You love me and want the best for me. I love you and I trust you.* "BOOM, BOOM, BOOM, BOOM!"

The music ended, and the final drumbeat reverberated from the concrete walls. Grit, full of the Spirit, stood to testify. He smiled, shaded his eyes and squinted into the darkened basement. "Any body out there?"

Grit's friends called out, "Yeah, brother," "Amen," etc. from the shadows.

"Ricky, turn on the house lights, please." Grit stepped off the low platform.

"Pop—pop! Pop—pop!" four quick flashes—explosions—two at the bottom of the largest speakers and two more near the ceiling. The bulky equipment quaked, toppled and began to fall. The last thing anyone saw before the lights went out were two dark walls of sound and video equipment tumbling toward the stage.

* * * * *

Bishop finished writing his presentation around nine thirty and reached to turn out the light over his bed. A nurse entered.

"Reverend Bishop Bishop, your doctor thought you might be ready for something to help you sleep after all the excitement."

Bishop swallowed the pills gratefully, switched out the light and fell asleep.

He woke with the return of his severe nausea and stomach cramps. He rang for the nurse then tried to reach the bathroom. Minutes later the nurse found him slumped over the toilet and incoherent. Doctors worked for the next hour, but the deadly botulism was unstoppable; every organ in the retching man's body was shutting down and bleeding. Shortly before midnight, the powerful politician and religious leader was placed on life support—technically alive, but most irrevocably, dead.

# 13

# Let There Be Light

SOMEWHERE IN THE SUDDEN and complete darkness at Deep Water, Maggie was screaming, "Grit! Grit!" and others cried out for light. Kale felt his way around tables, found the exit door, ran down the hall and two-stepped up the candle-lit stairs to see if the extension cords had been disconnected. No. He did so.

He dropped his head, panting from the unaccustomed exercise, and considered the situation. The problem had to be a fuse. Any number of things could have overloaded the makeshift system: overheated equipment or a surge from lightning certainly. Either could have caused the explosions and knocked out the lights.

He grabbed a couple of candles from the stairs and followed sounds of panic back to the unlit chaos. Someone had a flashlight. Several others held up cell phones. Glowing shreds of luminous green licked eerily at the fallen mound of speakers, mikes, and monitors, casting dim reddish shadows. Grit lay, his head cradled in Maggie's arms, near the bottom of the pile.

Kale and Buddy lifted the largest speaker off Grit's left side. "Call 911," Buddy yelled into the darkness, and at least three people did, adding to the six or so who had called as soon as the lights went out. Maggie checked for bleeding. Grit was scraped but not bloody, breathing but unconscious.

Kale pulled Buddy aside. "Have you seen Ricky? I'm pretty sure he knows where the fuse box is and the main power switch."

"He was just here," Buddy replied and then called, "Ricky?" No answer. "Somebody find Ricky and get him to check the fuse box,"

Just as it became evident that Ricky was not in the basement, the lights came up. Sparks shot from cords and outlets, and a frightening concert of popping noises elicited screams of fear. Sirens neared. Buddy quickly unplugged the power strips, leaving one bare bulb overhead to relieve the darkness.

The harsh light revealed two blessings. First, most of the fallen equipment lay exactly where Grit had been before he stepped off the stage. That one step had saved his life. Second—praise God—no one else was hurt.

\* \* \* \* \*

Troy, Amber, and Grace were on their way back to the hospital when Grace's cell phone rang. Grit was on his way to the ER with multiple injuries. Unbelievable!

Stunned into emotionless efficiency, Grace called Grit's parents. They would leave immediately and should arrive sometime Monday.

Grit was admitted, X-rayed, CT scanned and stabilized. Finally, doctors reported: The CT scan revealed a concussion with minimal swelling. X-rays showed a broken right collarbone and no breaks in his left arm, just a bad strain. They did not detect any brain damage, but, when Nurse Casey went off duty at midnight, Grit was still unconscious.

Sometime after two that morning, Troy and Amber escorted Grace back to her mother's room. Flickering, fluorescent light shrouded the empty, echoing hallway and reminded the trio that everyone around them was suffering.

"You don't really need to stay here tonight," Amber whispered. "You would sleep better at our house."

Troy had come to the same conclusion, but Grace still wanted to stay.

"I need to be here if Grit comes to," she said, "and Mother will need me. I'll be fine." They said good night.

Grace saw no need to wake her mother; Dinah would learn of Grit's accident soon enough. Sufficient to that awful Sunday was the trouble thereof, and Monday was here with its own troubles.

Grace fell heavily onto the folding cot, its one bed-slat banging against her ribs. She counted fourteen clicking, flickering or beeping lights before closing her eyes to techno music as restful as the "Anvil

Chorus." Breakfast and Dinah's doctor arrived just as she fell into her first real sleep. She gave up and groggily greeted the dawn.

Dr. Clark found Dinah doing better. She could go home that afternoon. Grace, not wanting to upset her mom more than necessary, told her very little about Grit's accident, but Dinah reacted with alarm.

"Are you sure he's going to be all right?" she asked. "Where is he?"

"He was in ICU last night, but he should be in a room this morning."

Dinah knew where Grace wanted to be. "I'm doing fine," she assured. "Go check on him."

"Are you sure?" Grace asked. "You need to pack."

"Don't worry about that, packing will give me something to do. Go!"

"OK," Grace agreed, wondering at her mother's new found acceptance of Grit's existence. "I'll be back around noon to drive you home."

At Grit's door Grace heard moaning. The room was dark, drapes pulled, lights out. Grit tossed wildly.

A pain-and-terror-induced nightmare had him running, stumbling, falling. *Two men are dead. Someone (something?) started screaming. Maybe my alarm? No, someone is screaming . . . someone . . . I'm screaming!*

Grit's eyes flew open—dim light, an unfamiliar room, drumming in his head. *Somebody, kill that drummer!* Another scream formed at the back of his throat. A face emerged from the darkness. *Amy Grace. Thank God, Gracie.*

"Grit, honey? It's Okay. I'm here. It's me, Grace."

*Her eyes are swollen. Her face is covered in tears, but she's smiling?* Grit remembered; *Grace's tears began before this pain.* "Why?" he groaned. "What?"

"Don't talk, baby. You've been in an accident. You're in the hospital, and you need to rest."

Grit groaned again and tried to raise a hand to his aching head. His right arm protested, and his left didn't move at all.

"Lie still," She bent down and kissed his forehead. "Shh, shh. Does it hurt?" She stroked his cheek. "I'll call the nurse."

But there was no need; at the sound of Grit's screams several nurses had headed that way. They were almost pleased; at least he was regaining consciousness. The first to arrive cautiously examined the bandages on Grit's arm and head. In his semi-conscious, terrified state Grit found her kind attentions threatening. A nest of venomous expletives swarmed out of his mouth, buzzing and stinging.

Grit fought to clear his head. He did not want to be shouting curses; he wanted to ask about Grace's tears. *And two men are dead, but who and why?* He could not form the words.

\* \* \* \* \*

Bart Crutcher rarely read the Sentinel, or anything else for that matter, but Monday morning he came into town before sunrise to get a paper and check the obituaries. He found a pile intended for a hard working carrier, helped himself and confirmed that both Lawson and Willis were dead. *Good riddance.*

Bart's dislike of preachers in general was long-standing. His dislike of Lawson in particular had grown each time his son's regard for the man had increased. Now that Buddy's regard for Lawson and New Jerusalem was fading, Bart's anger grew in concord with his son's disappointment.

As for Brother Willis, just reading the name raised Bart's blood pressure and unleashed his most irreverent vocabulary.

Shortly after the Willises had arrived in Bennettville, Bart saw a new marquee outside the One True Church touting their new Minister, Thomas Alexander Willis, and the sermon for the upcoming Sunday: "Will You See Your Loved One in Heaven?" The question gave Bart pause; Meta, who had been a devout Pentecostal, was in heaven, Bart knew; but would he make it there to see her?

That Sunday, he rose early, dressed and headed for the One True Church, thinking, *Meta would be proud.* And he sat through most of Brother Willis' sermon.

Willis strutted and preened, shouted logical proofs and syllogisms, and, in summation, proved, to his own satisfaction, that anyone wanting to go to heaven had to be baptized in the One True Church. According to Willis, if Bart wanted to see Meta again, he would have to see her in the fires of Hell.

* * * * *

"Good Morning, I'm Victoria Sellers, owner of Sellers Realty." Victoria had missed the last two meetings of the monthly Bennettville Entrepreneurial Breakfast due to pure cussedness, but one more absence from the networking group of small business owners would give her membership to the next realtor on the waiting list, so she put together a three minute sales pitch and a reasonably professional outfit and hauled her occasionally lazy assets out to the six a.m. meeting. Why not? She had pictures of her two-bedroom, one-bath, baby to show.

She drove down Crown Street, crossing Thirteenth one block east of Moses' corner. Five thirty in the morning and there he was, his sign clearly visible even at a distance. "Thou Shalt Not Steal."

"Amen," Victoria said. "More power to you."

The Entrepreneurs were out in force. Many, like Victoria, had missed a few meetings in the deep of winter and needed to show up for the rest of the year to keep their places. Plumbers, contractors, architects, nail artists, party planners, car salesmen, etc.; the club membership encompassed forty-eight trades. After introductions, the tradesmen and women lined up for Wally's, All-You-Can-Eat Down Home Buffet and "networking." But the shmoozing this Monday morning was about the two deaths on Sunday. Every member had a question or a bit of information about either Brother Willis or Pastor Lawson or both.

"Did you see it?"

"I was there."

"Did you know . . . ?"

Pepper Knutt of Current Electric said insurance inspectors had found rat droppings inside the baptistery water heater at the One True Church, and the wires were chewed through.

Victoria interjected what little she had witnessed, but she quieted suddenly, along with the rest of the crowd, when Ralph Bruiser, the club's cosmetologist, mentioned Reverend Bishop Reverend Bishop.

"Yes," he said, "they put him on life support last night."

A sort of mass hypnotic suggestion silenced tongues and stopped forks in midair.

"My cousin, the nurse," Ralph continued, "wasn't supposed to tell me, but Bishop is definitely brain dead."

*Dead?* they thought, *Dead!* and then, *Good Lord, there were three!*

Ralph Bruiser's "cousin-the-nurse" had just enlightened the entire city.

# 14

# The Prodigal

GRACE PICKED HER MOTHER UP Monday morning and drove her home. Neither felt like talking. Grace dreaded the ghosts that would greet her, but Dinah welcomed them. In the "preacher's house" she would be near familiar things, doing familiar chores. Even without Thomas, it was home.

Grace parked outside the open garage at the side of the house. *Mom and Dad's cars must still be parked at church*, she thought, one more thing to take care of. She walked to the back of her car and pulled her mother's heavy bag out of the trunk, "Oh, Lord, I'm tired."

"Grace!" Dinah stood behind her, aghast.

"Sorry, Mom. I wasn't talking to you."

Dinah didn't fume for long; she had nearly uttered the same flippant prayer herself when she pulled her aching bones from the car.

Grace lugged the suitcase to the porch, unlocked the door, and Dinah went wearily upstairs to rest. Grace watched, remembering the first time she had looked up those stairs, the day they moved in. Her father had stood on the landing, looking like a tintype portrait of a hell-fire revivalist as he designated the sunny room overlooking the back garden for his office and the corner room with two large windows for his and Dinah's bedroom. The darker, interior room he left to thirteen-year-old Grace.

That was the first, but not the last time Grace wondered at her father's selfishness. *Who is this man?* she asked herself. And the more painful question, *Does he truly love me?*

She and her mother sacrificed for Thomas' profession without question: doing without while he bought books for his library, pulling up roots and leaving friends because of his caustic theology while Thomas Willis' feet of clay left muddy footprints across their self-esteem.

Grace shook off the bitter memories and followed Dinah up to her room.

"Would you like some help with those?" Grace indicated Dinah's suitcase, laundry bags and assorted hospital debris.

"No. Thanks," Dinah said. "I'll get to it later. I just want to rest."

As much as Grace dreaded spending the night in this house, she did not want her mother to be alone. Truth be told, Grace did not want to be alone either. "Would you mind if I crash in my old room?" she asked.

Dinah bit her lip, but the tears came anyway. "Please do." she said.

Grace put her arms around her.

"I didn't want to ask." Her mother said, "You have your own life, but I need you to stay—at least until after the funeral."

"Sure," Grace said, wishing she could say no, but added, "I love you."

Dinah wiped her eyes and went to the bathroom to blow her nose. "I have an extra toothbrush and a nighty," she called back. "You can go home and get the rest of your things in the morning."

Grace went down to the living room to collect her thoughts and nap—no need to see her old room until she had to. At the bottom of the stairs, near the front door, Grace saw her mother's address and appointment books lying next to the telephone and realized there were still people who needed to be notified of her father's death. She checked the clock. It was nearly three; she would begin canceling appointments immediately and call family and friends after business hours.

Dinah's appointment book was a mess. Hurried notes in barely legible script filled small calendar squares. Grace recognized most of them: Mother's Day Out, Prayer Meeting on Wednesdays, baby and wedding showers, a rare hair appointment. Grace called her mother's beautician and made an appointment for Tuesday.

One notation scribbled in on a Saturday looked like, "Abe," something, something, "8:00 AM, Rev." something. She checked several months ahead, finally finding an entry she could read, "Abigails, M/B/E/H, 8:00 AM, Rev. Bishop." That was one appointment she would not have to cancel, but what was her mother doing at Greater Bennettville First M/B/E/H Alpha and Omega International Tabernacle every Saturday morning? She made herself a note to ask.

Thomas' only family was a sister in Indiana and her two sons, Grace's cousins. Grace called, but her father had not stayed in touch, and they likely would not come.

She finished her phone calls and went into the kitchen to find something to eat. She expected to find the meal that Dinah had prepared for Sunday's dinner, but the refrigerator was full of food left by the ladies of the One True Church. Thanks to her Christian sisters, who believed in and practiced only one spiritual gift, the gift of "casserole", her mother would not have to cook for weeks.

Grace heard a noise and looked out the back door. Dinah was emptying trash into the container at the back of the yard. Grace called her in for dinner. She came in, and Grace showed her a list of the phone calls she had made.

"Thank you," Dinah said, reaching for Grace's hand. "I hadn't thought about all of that. I guess I'm still in denial."

They sat down at the kitchen table with plates of warmed up casserole and homemade bread.

"The funeral home called." Grace said. "We need to be there tomorrow at 1:30. And you have a hair appointment in the morning."

Dinah put her head in her hands.

"It's hard, Mama, but we can do this together. God is good."

"God is good." Dinah nodded.

Grace would not ask about the Abigails tonight.

Dinah located the new toothbrush and an old nightgown. Grace went to bed, grateful for a real mattress and for the soft tick of an old-fashioned clock.

*And thank you, God,* she segued, *for saving Grit and letting him heal.* She lapsed into wordless supplication and eventual sleep, thinking of her mother, of Martha Lawson and of her own sorrow.

\* \* \* \* \*

New Jerusalem College Provost Albert Chessman had, in consideration of President Lawson's death and the dismissed faculty, cancelled all classes until further notice. Students, who needed to finish another week of classes and take exams, wondered how and when they would get credit for their courses. Some took a holiday and went home, but most stayed, waiting. Ricky's radio students pulled their shifts at the station regardless. So did Ricky.

WNJC stayed on the air, mostly live, broadcasting tributes and some of Lawson's most famous sermons. Even Ricky, in spite of run-ins with the old goat, praised the pastor's charismatic ways in a short, but cushy puff-piece.

Ricky stayed without pay, round the clock, catching naps in the lounge. He could not imagine a better opportunity for his students to get a taste of real journalism. He would stay and teach until someone dragged him out.

About eleven PM Monday night, Grant Perrish, III, owner of the largest, oldest, and most Zionist Christian funeral home in Bennettville, called the station. Maggie took the call and handed Ricky the phone. "It's the funeral home." She said, "a Mr. Perrish."

"This is Cra . . ." Ricky cleared his throat. "Excuse me; this is Ricky Cruz. How can I help you?"

"Mr. Cruz, this is Grant Perrish with Grant Perrish and Sons Funeral Home." His cool, even voice perfectly suited his profession: slow, unwavering, soothing. Ricky found it creepy.

"One of Pastor Lawson's last requests was that his preaching Bible might be placed in his casket," Perrish lowed.

Ricky shivered.

"I have spoken with the custodians, with the facility manager, and with the church secretary."

Ricky expected Perrish's next words to be, *You are becoming sleepy—very sleepy.*

Instead, Perrish cooed, "I am ashamed to say I have even disturbed Mrs. Lawson. Each agrees that Pastor Lawson had the Bible in question at the podium Sunday morning, but no one seems to know where it might be found."

Ricky shook himself awake. "I'm sorry, Mr. Perrish; I don't think I can help you. I wasn't even there Sunday."

"I just spoke with Albert Chessman." Perrish purred. "He seemed to think someone in the communications department might be of help since they were the last ones out of the building."

All Ricky heard was "Albert Chessman." *Oh, Crap!* Up till now he had managed to stay off the Provost's radar.

"Excuse me," Ricky said. "Would you please repeat your question?"

Perrish did, and Ricky thought of Tom Dixon who had been the floor director during the taping of Lawson's last sermon. "I'll call you back." Ricky said.

Ricky picked up the phone, but he didn't need to bother. Before he could dial, Dixon and Chessman charged into the office leading two campus security guards. Apparently Perrish's call had reminded Chessman that he had no faculty left in the communications department. When he turned on the campus radio station and heard the supposedly dismissed Ricky holding forth, he called the only replacement he could think of, senior assistant, Tom Dixon.

Now Chessman, a rotund, ruddy-faced sixty or so, stood panting in front of Ricky's desk. He pulled out a handkerchief and wiped his face. His suit coat fell open revealing an uncustomarily crooked tie. His off-kilter belt hung dejectedly outside the last loop like a base runner who had missed third.

"Mr. Cruz," Chessman puffed. "What are you doing here? These students need to be in their dorms!"

Tom smirked, walked over to the master switch and put WNJC off the air.

"You have ten minutes to vacate the building." Chessman said.

Ricky knew it would be counter productive to argue. He stood, grabbed an empty box from the storage room and began gathering his meager belongings—three tattered communication texts, his framed diploma, and twelve outlandish neckties—each worn once to some campus event then thrown in a studio corner. Tom sat down at Ricky's desk triumphantly.

"It did not have to happen this way." Ricky said. He indicated the two guards, "I didn't intend to fight anyone for this job. I just knew someone had to be here."

Chessman lifted himself to his toes, "If you return to campus without prior authorization," Chessman said, lowering himself with a blubbery bounce, "you will be prosecuted for trespassing." He smiled.

The jig was up. Ricky didn't stay to down-load or delete, just picked up his box and turned to leave, praying Tom would forget to cut off his access to the campus computer system. His files were not incriminating, but they were private. If this coup was personal, Ricky did not want to leave ammunition behind.

He balanced the awkward box under one arm and attempted to open the door. Neither Tom nor Chessman offered to help.

He put down the box and faced them. "I won't beg for this job," He said. "But I will beg for my students. Don't deprive them of this opportunity. Let them learn what they are here to learn."

Tom and Chessman did not respond.

Ricky pulled the door open, held it with his foot and bent to lift the box. His rear end was the last thing Tom or Chessman saw of him.

On his way home, Ricky's fury took the form of too much speed, but he slowed past Moses' corner and read the Prophet's admonition, "Thou shalt not bear false witness." He thought of Tom's glee and wondered how many other sad faces at New Jerusalem hid happy thoughts. Lawson's death would dramatically affect academic and personal freedom, but how?

At WNJC Tom surveyed his newly acquired fiefdom, thinking of the many changes he would make—none of which involved freedom.

* * * * *

Ricky parked in his usual spot, carried his belongings to his front door and fumbled with his keys. He took a deep breath and steeled himself before confronting his constant roommate, loneliness. He opened the door and glanced at his secondhand furniture and nonexistent décor. Disheartened, he cleared the stack of mail from his keyboard, accessed the New Jerusalem computer system, downloaded and deleted. Before he called it a night, he updated his resume'.

* * * * *

Not all of Bennettville's sidewalks rolled up at midnight, just most. Downtown, where private investors had built the world's first indoor forest, tourists thronged. A substantial segment of the world's population preferred to experience nature, minus anything that might bite, in air-conditioned comfort. Gradually, restaurants, museums, theatres, and other moneymakers had sprouted, turning the derelict, Bennettville riverfront into a thriving tourist destination in less than a decade.

A mile from there, near the railroad yards, investors were not interested in long-term gains, and did not mind sweating.

About one o'clock Tuesday morning, an unmarked van rolled slowly down South King Street with the windows down. Its headlights shot a wide stripe past corner street lamps and other vehicles behaving similarly. Half-clad women huddled in small groups or leaned into cars. Hyperactive men caromed from corner to car to corner, exchanging insults and cash.

A bone thin, haggard woman with bad teeth sidled up to the passenger side window. "Whatever you're looking for . . ." the woman noticed she was talking to a female, but she continued, "I've got it."

"I'm here to give you what you need," the passenger said.

"Whatever, It's going to cost you twenty."

"I have food, shelter, and the love of God for free, if you want it." The lady in the passenger seat handed a sandwich out the window.

The prostitute was too far-gone to care. "I don't need no sermons, lady." She shoved the packaged food back in Haley Philben's face.

Joe Uptain, Grit's boss, drove on to the next corner. "You'll get used to it, Haley," he said. "Not everyone is ready. You know how hard it was for you to accept help when you came to us homeless and pregnant."

# 15

# The Bottom of Things

GRIT'S MOM, SUZY, in her squeezable middle age, was about half Grit's size and full of energy. She spent Monday afternoon and night in Grit's hospital room brooding over her chick, but, when he showed improvement on Tuesday, she devoted the rest of the day to cleaning his apartment—determined to seek and destroy several strange smells that Grit's father, Clyde, had met when he crashed there Monday. She also hoped to find Grit's Bible. Grit had mumbled something about it Monday night, just after squeezing her hand and asking about Grace. Suzy took the mumble as a sign that Grit had indeed returned to Christianity, and she wanted to make sure he had his sword. When the book was not found in Grit's hospital room, she decided to go to his apartment, throw caution to the wind and look under his bed.

She located dirty socks and underwear, old pizza boxes, and empty beer bottles but no Bible. She had, however, worked off most of the fear and anxiety of the last two days and triumphed over the evil axis of odors. Given another day or two, she would do something with Grit's dilapidated couch. Calling it "used" was a complement. Something about the shredded upholstery and exposed stuffing reminded her of a cheap stripper.

Clyde wisely stayed out of Suzy's way—but busy—talking with doctors and insurance providers. He also contacted Grit's employers. The Sentinel was obliging, assuring him that Grit's position was safe. And, Clyde was less than happy to learn, Grit could also return to work at The Dive as soon as he recovered. He and Suzy did not approve of alcohol, but Grit's choice of occupations had moved way down the list of their concerns. No part of this unplanned visit, they agreed, would be given to argument.

When Grace called his hospital room Tuesday, Grit answered. He still had some memory loss, but his left arm was working, and he could feed himself. More importantly, his stupor was gone, and his language was the proper color.

"Are you up to visitors?" she asked.

Grit could not let himself say how much he needed to see her. "Yeah, sure."

"Are you bored? Can I bring you anything?"

"Just yourself. Mom smuggled in junk food. I've got magazines and my cell phone. I've text messaged 'til my thumbs hurt."

"My mom is coming home today, and we have to um . . . we have some things to do." They would be making arrangements for Thomas' funeral. "Afterwards, I'm going back to work, but I'll see you about six."

\* \* \* \* \*

Grace was baffled when Dinah insisted that Thomas should be buried in Texas. The Willises had lived there when Grace was very small, but to Grace's knowledge there was no other connection.

An open casket was out of the question; no amount of post-mortem sorcery could make Thomas presentable after such a death. After two hours of ghastly decisions, Grace grew numb. When the funeral director, Mr. Hershell, suggested cremation, a disembodied voice inside her head responded, *Why not? Electrocution did half the work; maybe we can get a discount?*

"Transportation costs will be much lower." Mr. Hearshell added.

That choice and similar unthinkable options took another hellish hour.

\* \* \* \* \*

No one had yet stuck a fork in Reverend Bishop Bishop, but every other test proved Bishop was done. Bennettville Memorial CEO , Jerry Elkins, was not happy; The Reverend Bishop had been on life support since late Sunday; today was Tuesday and the hospital had yet to find a next-of (or distant) kin or a living (or not) will.

*Why were doctors so quick to put the man on life support?* he thought. If Bishop were "dead" dead, not just brain dead, the only question would be who pays the bill. But now, if the hospital did not come up with a next-of-kin, the questions of removing life-support and inevitably the disposition of Bishop's body would become the hospital's responsibility. Any misstep involving the high profile minister could end up in court and the national news.

Hospital lawyers with the ethics committee, the hospital board, and Bishop's church would discuss the options, but it boiled down to this: Without a legal claimant, the fate of Bishop's remains would be determined by the hospital ethics committee. Bennettville Memorial was standing in a rising pile of potentially hazardous possibilities.

*God help us!*

\* \* \* \* \*

Zephonia Summer had been Reverend Bishop Reverend Bishop's personal secretary for fifteen years. When Bishop hired her, she was tall and willowy. Now she was tall and refrigerator-y. But Bishop had not replaced her with another willow; Zephonia knew too much, and she could pin him in two moves.

All of those years Zephonia wondered what person or persons actually owned the Greater Bennettville First Methodist/Baptist/Episcopal/Holiness Alpha and Omega International Tabernacle and all of its holdings. The question was moot as long as everyone in The Reverend Bishop's circle, from janitor to Senator, was reaping benefits, but The Reverend, as Zephonia had come to call him, was no longer able to sign the checks, and the question had become a matter of conjecture among the general populace.

Wednesday morning she dug through church archives, mostly to find out if she was going to be paid and if so how. She started in her own office, but moved on to long-neglected files in a dusty storage area two halls down.

Cobwebs and dust clung to her leopard print skirt and accessorized the matching shoes. Her midnight blue nails were scratched and flaking, and the inset rhinestones, which had not come cheap, were, Zephonia estimated, at the bottom of a file drawer somewhere between M and Q.

She leaned over to search the V-Z drawer, but the consequent breeze up her skirt chilled her nether regions and made kneeling the better option. She lowered herself to her knees. Her office phone rang.

Zephonia pulled herself up with a groan and tottered, as fast as possible on her stilettos, down the hall and around two corners to catch the phone on its last ring.

"Greater Bennettville First Methodist/Episcopal/" Zephonia puffed, "Baptist/Holiness Alpha and Omega," she took a deep breath, "International Tabernacle, Zephonia speaking."

"Hello?" Jerry Elkins was confused. "Is this First M/B/E/H?"

"Yes. Zephonia—" she caught her breath, " . . . whew!" She wiped her face, "speaking. May I help you?"

"Ms. Whew?"

She didn't bother to correct him.

"This is Jerry Elkins, CEO at Bennettville Memorial Hospital. May I ask how you are associated with Reverend Bishop Reverend Bishop?"

"I was his personal secretary."

Elkins noticed the "was." "We are trying to locate someone to handle his affairs. Does he have a lawyer or any family that you know of?"

"I'm just lookin' to find that out myself," she said. "Is The Reverend still hangin' on?"

"I'm sorry, I'm not at liberty to say." Elkins responded, wondering, *How much does this woman know?*

"Don't you worry, honey," Zephonia answered his unspoken question. "I know you have to find a next of kin before you shut him off."

*So much for HIPPA.* "I assure you," he said, "it would be in The Reverend's interest for you to furnish the hospital with anything you might find."

"What exactly am I lookin' for?" she asked.

"Any family records or any legal documents signed by his lawyer. Any names or addresses of relatives."

She thought of Reverend's Bible; she had seen a family tree and some addresses in it. "Did you check his Bible? He always had it with him."

"I have looked through his personal effects," Elkins said. "There is no Bible."

Zephonia was puzzled; Reverend always had his Bible. "I'll see what I can find, and I'll call you." She said. But she had her own ideas about what she was looking for and what she might do when she found it.

She found incorporation papers, insurance policies, architectural blue prints, and several deeds. All were prepared by the same, unfamiliar, Washington D.C. law firm, and all bore the same two signatures, Reverend Bishop Reverend Bishop and Dr. David J. Morgan.

"Doctor who?" Zephonia asked the empty office.

She would find out; she had "found" Reverend's computer passwords long ago—just in case. The need to get Bishop legally dead and buried would justify any future indiscretions.

Searching his personal files without legal authority risked more than her manicure, but who would prosecute a poor church secretary just trying to be helpful?

\* \* \* \* \*

Grace's boss agreed to let her come in that afternoon only after she insisted, "I need the distraction."

With Grace out of the house, Dinah paced Thomas' office, imagining every "worst case scenario" possible and mentally selling, giving away or packing all of her worldly goods. She would "fret not" and "consider the lilies" only after a long afternoon of "walking by sight." No amount of faith could change the facts: "Preacher's Wife" was not a paid position, and a "preacher's house" housed a preacher.

*Surely,* she thought, *they will let me stay until another preacher is hired—at least long enough to harvest the garden?*

She tried to remember what she and Grace had decided at the funeral home. All she could think of was the fact that Thomas' life insurance would barely cover the cost of his cremation and burial.

At work, Grace's grief knocked around her insides like an alien parasite. Coworkers, afraid to stir up her pain, hesitated to talk, but a few tried. Their I'm so sorry!s and What can I do?s were comforting. Maggie, God bless her, just listened.

Grace left at exactly 5:30, and nearly ran to her car. It wasn't far to the hospital, but she wished the drive were shorter. She needed to see Grit. At Ninth Street, a scattering of white petals floated past her window and skittered across her hood like silken snowflakes. Spring had arrived. She detoured onto Tenth Street and its canopy of ornamental pear trees. Snowy blossoms showered the street and joined their fallen comrades in swirling drifts. Beauty, whimsy and hope stuck a wedge between Grace and her grief.

At the hospital, she stopped in the gift shop and bought several balloons. The thought of them tied at the foot of Grit's bed caused her to smile for the first time since Sunday. She was still smiling when she walked into his room.

"Hi," he said, smiling back. He was sitting up.

Grace gave him a joyful kiss. "You look so much better." She kissed him again for good measure, tied the balloons on the footboard and sat, ready for happy chitchat.

But, as soon as she was settled, Grit asked about the two men in his nightmare. "Who are they? Who died?"

Grace sobered and told him all she knew about Lawson's heart attack, explaining that, since she had not been there, all she knew, ironically, Grit had told her. Grit remembered very little—single moments like video clips: Lawson pounding on his Bible, Lawson turning red, Lawson drinking from his glass, Lawson falling. A heart attack, surely.

Grace sat silent for some time, staring at her lap, her hands clasped tightly. She looked up, cleared her throat and stood beside the bed. "And . . ." She grabbed Grit's hand.

He waited.

"And my father . . ." she paused and started to cry. "Daddy died of electrocution."

Grit gasped.

Through tears, she described the accident, sparing him the grotesque details, but breaking down at the last. She fell to her knees sobbing in a firestorm of emotion, lack of sleep, joy at Grit's recovery, and the horror surrounding her father's death.

Grit too was crying. He stroked her hair, moved beyond his ability to express. He loved this woman, but his damaged heart recoiled in fear. Loving Grace would mean drawing close to the intense heat of her pain, love, and sorrow. He was not ready to rush into the flames.

Instead, he held her hand and continued to stroke her hair as her crying subsided. When she stood, he patted a spot next to him on the bed and she scooted in. They sat quietly, her head resting on his broken collarbone. Neither of them noticed. They were kissing when the phone rang.

Grace sat up and listened to Grit's side of the conversation.

"Yeah, Mom." * * * "No?" * * * "Did you look under the bed?" * * * "Well, thanks, anyway." * * * "Yeah, I'm doing better." * * * "Grace is here." (Grit laughed.) * * * "I'll see you in the morning. Good night!" * * * "Me too, tell Dad I love him too."

Grace thought she knew what Suzy had been looking for. "Did she find your Bible?"

"No. How did you know?"

"You asked about it yesterday, I assumed someone would find it at Deep Water."

"Of course!" Grit remembered. "I haven't been thinking; I had it with me that night."

"I'm staying with Mother tonight. I'll go by Deep Water and get it on the way. That way I can bring it to you in the morning."

Grit hesitated. "I don't know, Gracie. You didn't see the damage, and I don't really remember. Who knows what sort of mess you might get into?"

"I'm not going to move stuff around. I'll just take a look."

"But it's late, and you don't have a key," Grit reminded her.

"The Dive is open until 12; I'll go in the front door," Grace countered. "Besides Ricky made me a copy of his key last week when I was decorating."

Grit still didn't like it. "You shouldn't go by yourself," he said.

Grace was determined. "There are plenty of people around as long as the bar is open; if I need any help, I'll just holler."

"And if nobody hears you?" he asked.

"I've got my phone."

Grace considered the matter settled. So did Grit, but he didn't like the settlement.

"By the way," Grace asked. "Has anyone checked your mail?"

\* \* \* \* \*

At the Dive, Grace caught Joe's eye and waved before heading down the stairs. At least one person would know where she was.

The switch at the bottom of the stairs turned on a bare bulb in the hall and another in the meeting room. The ineffective glare did little more than cast confusing, angular shadows over the chaos. Grit had been right, the mess looked dangerous. It even smelled dangerous. A faint eau de electrical fire hung in the air along with . . . Grace sniffed; something that smelled like firecrackers. Is that gunpowder? She stooped near the stage, looking under the wreckage.

"Lady?"

Grace turned, startled.

A bus boy stood at the door brandishing a towel as if to shoo her away. "You're not supposed to be down here. My boss says nobody can touch nothin' 'til the insurance people take a look." He was young—about seventeen—cherub faced and totally harmless.

Grace stalled. "I'm sorry, I didn't mean to cause any trouble. It's just that my b . . . (She had started to say "boyfriend.") My friend, who was here Sunday, is in the hospital and asked me to see if I could find his Bible."

The boy looked scared and spoke haltingly. He did not want to "cause trouble" either—especially not for this girl who's wavy, dark hair transformed the stark overhead light into a chocolate halo.

"Well," the boy considered. "I guess you can look around a little and leave out the back." His thoughts came slowly. "I'll tell my boss you're gone." He started to leave then turned to apologize, "I'm sorry, I gotta shut off the lights." At the door he flipped the switch and whispered, "Don't touch nothin'! And don't make no noise!"

Grace did as she was told, stepping gingerly over barely visible speakers and cables until she decided to give up the search; one black Bible would have to catch fire to be seen in this jumble.

The thought of fire reminded her, *I definitely smell gunpowder!* She sniffed closer to the floor; the smell was stronger. She followed the scent to an ugly, mottled stain on the floor. Breaking her promise to the bus boy, Grace took out her handkerchief and wiped up a finger full of oddly colored soot. The sound of footsteps coming down the hall sent her quietly but quickly out the back door.

# 16

# The Old Switcheroo

WEDNESDAY MORNING GRACE picked up Grit's mail on the way to the hospital. She could not visit with Grit for more than a few minutes; visitation for her father's funeral would begin at four, and she needed to tend to her mother before, after, and during. She hoped Grit would be willing and able to attend, but she wouldn't ask; he might feel obligated, and Pastor Lawson's funeral was scheduled at two.

Her father's memorial service, tomorrow, would be held at the funeral home; the One True Church building was unusable. The auditorium smelled of burned flesh and the baptistery bore jagged, fire-etched streaks. Tonight's Bible classes were canceled, and Sunday's special prayer service would have to be relocated. Something might eventually remove the unholy stench from the building, but nothing would exorcize the evil memories.

Grit and his parents were packing his things when Grace arrived.

"I was just about to call and tell you to meet me at my apartment," Grit said, "but I'm glad you're here." He carefully waved his damaged arm toward his parents, "You met mom and dad?"

"Yes, I did." Grace replied. "You were unconscious."

"We would like to go by the funeral home and give our condolences to your mother." Clyde said.

"Yes, of course. Thank you." Grace answered.

Grit added, "I could stay there, if you need me."

Grace sensed his ambivalence. "Church people will be there, and a few cousins."

"What I mean is, I want to be there."

She smiled and said exactly what she felt, "That would be wonderful!" She was tired of playing games. If he couldn't take it, she would look elsewhere.

She put his mail in with the cards he was taking home, gave him a kiss and said goodbye, forgetting the stained handkerchief in her purse.

* * * * *

Tom Dixon spent two days on the telephone locating someone, anyone, to man the equipment at Holy City for the broadcast of Pastor Lawson's funeral. The regular crew of communication students and alums were still angry at the firings, so early Tuesday afternoon three of Tom's friends from local media and a few desperate students, including Maggie, who needed extra credit and extra cash, were at unaccustomed posts, nervously awaiting instruction—an inexperienced crew handling unfamiliar equipment. This broadcast was Tom's first solo production since taking over the department. He had personally checked every knob, lever, and button, but thirty minutes from the two o'clock start, the possibility of disaster loomed large.

Maggie stood behind the heavy black console in the sound booth high over the sanctuary, praying she would remember everything Tom had told her. She went over it again. On the wall to her left was the on-air switch, to pull when Tom signaled. He had pre-set the sound controls in front of her so she would have only two switches to deal with in addition to the master: the first, in the middle of the board, toggled between two sound feeds. Thrown to the left, it accessed a wireless mike used by the various eulogizers; to the right, it picked up the mikes in front of the choir and the digital feed from the electronic organ. Her only other concern was the master volume, a white lever on her right.

"You won't be hearing the broadcast through your headset," Tom had said. "I'll keep track of that through the PA. Just listen for my instructions and watch this dial." He pointed. "If the signal goes into the red, turn the volume down. If it goes below the blue line, turn it up."

She checked the TV monitor overhead; it showed a test pattern. She pictured the first dignitary standing at the pulpit and Tom's voice telling her to throw the on-air switch. She mimed that action, checked to make sure the toggle switch was to the left for the portable mike, mentally adjusted the master volume to the reading on the dial, took a deep breath and waited. The first three minutes of the broadcast would be a pre-recorded introduction that Tom controlled from the floor.

* * * * *

Grit and his parents ordered pizza, propped their feet on Grit's secondhand coffee table and switched the TV to the local cable access where they heard somber canned music and saw, "Stay tuned for the Pastor Newell Post Lawson Memorial Service, Two o'clock." They might have considered more formal demeanor if they hadn't been desperately hungry and tired. Funerals are for the living, and these living needed to eat and relax before meeting Grace at her father's visitation.

Precisely at two, the Griffins and half of Bennettville were treated to a prerecorded video of Lawson's body lying in state and long lines of mourners. The funereal soundtrack and deep shadows reminded Grit of black and white horror films that had terrified him as a child. At the climax of a particularly scary minor chord, the picture faded to a wide-angle, exterior shot of Holy City. A cathedral pipe organ version of "A Mighty Fortress," heavy and morose, faded in as the camera entered and panned ponderously from harsh metal surface to hard corner, to angular shadow, then into the sanctuary to focus on Lawson's now closed, dark granite vault. (Church deacons had decided that displaying the impressive fifteen hundred pound sarcophagus in front of the pulpit was worth hiring a tow truck and removing a door. The ostentatious display was all the more egregious considering that Martha had Newell cremated immediately after the viewing.) Picture and sound faded to black. Lights came up on the assembled mourners. On the second row near the pulpit, two women in full mourning held black handkerchiefs under veiled, wide-brimmed hats. Neither "widow" was Martha Lawson. She sat on the front row; legs splayed, head wobbling. Tom switched to a close up of Provost Chessman standing at the pulpit.

The Griffins stopped chewing to listen. Chessman gestured toward Lawson's vault, apparently speaking, but the only sound was coming from the mike near the off-camera choir. To the mourners in Holy City, the PA system sounded fine, but to viewers at home, Chessman's speech was barely audible. Tom had switched the feeds: the toggle was left for the choir and right for the speaker. Grit, along with every other viewer, turned up the volume.

Maggie, in the booth, was flying on instruments; she too turned up the volume. The result, in Grit's apartment and in homes across Bennettville, was a picture of the somber Chessman accompanied by sounds of chairs

scraping, choir members coughing and pages rattling. Sounding as if he were somewhere in the far distance, Chessman introduced the governor.

The wide-open microphone in front of the choir picked up an alto whispering to a tenor, "I can't believe they asked that old windbag to speak," and the tenor's response, "We'll be here forever!"

As the governor waxed eloquent in the echoey distance, the "chorus," as in classic Greek theatre, added uncomplimentary comments. The Griffins settled in for an hour and a half of high comedy.

* * * * *

"Mom?" Grace called up the stairs. "We need to be at the funeral home in twenty minutes."

Dinah appeared on the landing in a cherry red, satin dress. It was too small, too short, and decades out of date. Long, gold earrings jangled when she tossed her hair, which was teased and sprayed into a frightening heap. She wore bright red lipstick and tottered on black patent stilettos.

"What do you think?" she asked.

"I, ah . . . Where did that come from?"

"I've had it for years," Dinah pirouetted. "I wore it in a play the night I met your father."

"Ah . . . Well, ah . . ." Grace hurried into the kitchen. "Meet me at the car. I have to make a call."

Dinah jangled down the stairs and out the door. Grace dialed the Albrightons. Tabitha answered.

"Could you and Dr. Albrighton please meet Mother and me at the funeral home right away? I'm afraid she isn't well." Grace ran to her mother's closet, pulled out a long, dark dress, and low heels, took them out the back door and put them in the car trunk before her mother noticed.

At the funeral home, Grace and Dr. Albrighton gently persuaded Dinah that the navy dress would be much more suitable, but Dinah insisted on her noisy earrings and dangerous heels.

Visitation was an emotional ordeal. Grace thanked the Griffins for coming and stayed close to Grit. He, Grace and Dinah stood at the front of the chapel next to a small table holding Thomas' Bible, his urn, and the Willises' wedding picture. A long line of solicitous friends and church members filed past, offering condolences. Their reluctance to mention Thomas' manner of death resulted in stilted conversation or deafening silence. Dinah became withdrawn and incoherent.

Grace signaled Dr. Albrighton. He and Tabitha took Dinah to a private mourning room. Grace, with Grit by her side, spoke with the last few visitors.

Afterward, Doctor Albrighton and the funeral director approached Grace. "I don't believe your mother is up to a funeral tomorrow." Dr. Albrighton said. "I gave her some sleeping pills to take when you get her home, and I made her an appointment with a psychiatrist in the morning."

"But what about . . ." Grace began.

"We really can handle tomorrow's service without either of you." Mr. Hearshell assured. "Your friends and loved ones will understand. I've spoken with the cemetery in Texas; there is no time limit on your father's burial."

Grace looked at Grit questioningly.

"Do what you need to do," he said.

Grace took a deep breath, dropped her head and relaxed her shoulders. When she looked up, her eyes were damp. "I really don't think I can do this again." Grace said. "If you really think it will be OK?"

"Don't worry about anything." Mr. Hearshell said.

Grace closed her eyes and sighed. "Thank you"

She said good-bye to the Griffins, assuring Grit she would be fine. "I'll call you in the morning."

At the house, Grace gave her mother a sleeping pill and helped her dress for bed. She didn't bother to undress herself, just unhooked her bra, took the phone off the hook and crashed until morning.

\* \* \* \* \*

Clyde and Suzy took Grit to dinner then back to his apartment and called it a night. Grit lent them his one bedroom. He would take the couch.

A pile of unopened mail lay on his kitchen table. *Might as well sort through it.* The bills went into a pile; ads went in the trash, but he opened the get-well cards. Most of them were intended to be humorous. He held back guffaws, not wanting to wake his parents, but could not help groaning at several horrible puns. The last, plain, square envelope contained a typewritten letter.

"The Prophet Speaks," Grit read.

*Okay,* he thought, another gag. He continued reading, waiting for the punch line.

"Honor Your Father and Mother."

Grit checked for a signature. *Nothing.*

If a man has a stubborn and rebellious son who does not obey his father and mother and will not listen to them when they discipline, he is profligate and a drunkard. The Prophet of his town shall stone him to death and purge the evil."

*This isn't funny.*

"YOU HAVE THREE DAYS TO REPENT."

Grit felt prickles on the back of his neck.

"Deuteronomy 28: The high walls in which you trust will fall."

The prickles moved to the top of Grit's head.

"Just as it pleased you to dishonor your parents and your God, so the Prophet will rain dishonor and death upon your head."

Grit dug the envelope out of the trash and checked the postmark— May 27—*four days before my accident.* He sat down, shaking. There were two possible conclusions: either this "prophet" had truly foretold the future, or someone had tried to kill him.

Grit got up, ready to wake his parents, but sat down and took a deep breath. Clyde and Suzy planned to start home after the Willis funeral on Thursday. If they thought Grit was in danger, they would stay and get mixed up in whatever was going on. Grit put the letter back in the envelope and stuck it in his desk. It would wait. He turned out the light, lay down on his pitiful couch and closed his eyes. He did not sleep.

He tried to make sense of his scattered memories. He had seen Pastor Lawson and Brother Willis die, but the memory was fragmented. He knew, along with all of Bennettville, that Reverend Bishop Bishop died the same Sunday as Lawson and Willis. But only Grit and a few others knew that his own brush with death could be factored into the equation.

His damaged mind, unencumbered by distracting "facts" or presumed causes of death, saw Sunday's events as simple arithmetic: one Sunday plus two "accidents" minus three preachers equaled murder.

# 17

# Spying Out the Land

GRACE WOKE HER MOTHER at 7:30 and helped her pick out an appropriate outfit for her appointment with Dr. Marvel. She would not leave that task to her mother for a while. She followed Dinah outside where the empty driveway reminded her that she needed to get her mother's and father's cars off the church parking lot. But not today.

She left a key under a flowerpot for Tabitha, who had volunteered to keep an eye on the preacher's house, "so robbers who scanned the obituaries could not rob the place." Rachel would come too. (After her near-death-experience, she was loath to have her mother out of arm's reach.) Unbeknownst to her parents, she was considering alternatives to water baptism. Methodist sprinkling or even Pentecostal baptism in the Holy Spirit was looking very attractive. Until she chose one of her options, she tried to remain sinless.

Grace and Dinah's drive to Dr. Marvel's office was strained. Dinah stared ahead, not speaking but sighing deeply at irregular intervals.

Grace tried to reassure her, "Visiting a psychiatrist is pretty routine after trauma," she said. "I'm making an appointment to see a counselor myself."

"Goodness!" Dinah exclaimed, "Words won't help!"

Grace was about to argue but stopped when she looked toward her mother. Dinah was pointing out the window. On the corner, Moses held a sign. "Thou shalt not kill."

"Why is he staring?" Dinah asked. "Why is he staring at me?"

\* \* \* \* \*

The "preacher's house," a small, half-timbered, brick cottage built in the 1920s, was purchased as living quarters for preachers after the One True

Church building was built next door in 1963. Rachel had never been inside, but the gabled outside promised explorable nooks and crannies.

Tabitha located the key and gained entrance with undue excitement. She had never been in the Willises' home without supervision. She settled Rachel and her summer reading books in a second floor bedroom and went on a tour.

*Church members are obligated to make sure church property is well cared for*, she rationalized.

As soon as her mother left, Rachel, forgetting the danger to her unshriven soul, snuck back down the stairs, out the front door and around to the back yard. She walked through Dinah's newly planted tomatoes and beans to check out the strange, dark, plants standing sentinel at the back—nothing but a few more beans. She wasn't interested in beans. She opened the back door and walked into the kitchen. It looked like an old magazine picture: no dishwasher, a small rounded refrigerator and chrome edged counters. The cabinets smelled like fresh paint. Starched white curtains hung at the windows. She opened drawers and cupboards and peeked in the small refrigerator but found nothing tasty.

She ventured down the basement stairs. An incongruous mix of smells—moist, moldy air and laundry detergent—wafted to Rachel's nose. Half way down, spider webs at eye-level draped ancient plumbing and dirty basement windows. The wispy slaughterhouses full of fresh victims and eight-legged diners stopped her cold.

She scanned the depths from where she stood. Decades of church leftovers: revival banners, Vacation Bible School pictures, even piles of discarded lumber, lay tucked into corners and scattered on shelves. Gardening tools, bags of seed, and several huge cooking pots leaned against the back wall. Nothing she saw was worth venturing into the damp, buggy cold to explore.

She clambered hurriedly back to the kitchen and meandered through the living room to the entry hall where she found an oddly shaped door under the stair. It opened into a deep closet whose musty interior enticed her with dark, soft shadows and the smell of mothballs.

She reached into the darkness, stroked the mysterious softness and breathed in slowly, letting the camphor tickle the back of her throat. Giddy with sensation, she leaped headlong into the unknown, landing among heavy coats, old dresses, shoes, hats, uniforms, and graduation gowns.

Tabitha confined her search to the upstairs. Thomas' sunlit office and desk were well ordered, but his shoes lay in a jumbled heap in the closet floor; cobwebs hid behind doors and baseboards needed dusting.

The Willises' bedroom was also in disarray. Scattered piles of family photos covered the unmade bed, and Dinah's night things lay on the floor.

Tabitha riffled through the pictures and looked under the bed. She pulled out a well-worn box—more pictures, the Willis family plus one, a doe-eyed, blond girl the spitting image of Thomas. The most recent picture in the box was of that same girl, about four, holding a red parasol over a dark haired infant, clearly Grace.

* * * * *

Grace sat for an hour in the waiting area while her mother spoke with Dr. Marvel. An aide appeared.

"Miss Willis, Doctor Marvel would like to see you, also."

The Doctor was succinct, "Dr. Albrighton has described some of your mother's symptoms to me," he said, "what have you observed?"

Grace described her mother's unusual costume and near collapse at the funeral.

"I cannot make a full diagnosis when the trauma is so recent," he said, "but I suspect your mother is suffering from Post-Traumatic Stress Disorder. An intense reaction such as hers usually indicates a history of trauma. Was she exhibiting any strange behavior before your father's death?"

"Not really."

"Has she suffered any other trauma?"

Grace sighed. "I guess you could say we both were traumatized by our constant moving. But we've lived in Bennettville longer than we've lived anywhere, and we're pretty settled."

He handed Grace her mother's prescriptions for sleeping tablets and anti-anxiety medication. "Right now," he said, "she needs relief from her fear and anxiety. She is fragile. Someone needs to stay with her day and night for the next two weeks while she adjusts to this medication." He wrote out his phone number and extension. "If she shows any radical changes in behavior or exhibits any physical symptoms other than a little drowsiness, call me immediately."

"Thank you." Grace stuck the prescriptions in her purse.

She and Dinah got back to the house around noon after stopping at the pharmacy. Grace checked her watch and thanked God she did not have to go to her father's funeral, which would start in a couple of hours.

Dinah climbed to the porch more slowly than usual, opened the front door and stopped short. Rachel popped out of the stairwell closet blushing and stammering. Dinah glowered, turned away and climbed the stairs to her room.

Tabitha, still holding the mysterious photograph, closed the Willises' bedroom door and stepped onto the landing directly into Dinah's path. She stuck the photo behind her back and froze. Dinah huffed and quickly went back down stairs, passing Rachel on her way up. No one spoke.

Rachel zipped back into the bedroom and opened a book before her mother had a chance to scold. Tabitha sighed and followed Dinah to the living room. Dinah turned a chair toward the window and sat down stiffly.

Tabitha took the upholstered chair near the door and surreptitiously stuffed the incriminating photo behind a pillow at her back. She waited for the bereaved widow to speak. Dinah did not. Tabitha attempted the weather and failed, then gardens.

"Have you had a chance to work in your garden this year?" she asked, speaking to Dinah's back.

"Yes." Period, end of sentence.

Tabitha tried again. "Have you had any trouble with pests?"

"No."

Clearly Tabitha was floundering. "Um a . . . We have the cutest little rabbits and squirrels in our yard. Rachel just loves them."

"I shot two yesterday," Dinah said

Tabitha's mouth fell open but nothing came out. Grace walked in the front door. Tabitha mumbled something incoherent then managed, "I think we need to go." She hurried up the stairs calling, "Rachel? It's time to go!"

Rachel was in the attic, transfixed by a trove of forgotten household goods that stretched before her like Ali Baba's loot. She caught sight of a red silk parasol poking from an old toy box.

"Rachel!"

"Coming!" Rachel closed her eyes and forced herself to turn away.

* * * * *

Doctor and Mrs. Albrighton (sans Rachel) came back by the house after Thomas' funeral. They delivered several potted plants, Thomas' urn and the Willises' wedding picture. Tabitha carried a casserole. Grace took it to the kitchen and put it in the fridge with the others. Dinah placed the urn and the picture among several bouquets on the mantle and sat down wordlessly.

"The funeral was lovely," Tabitha said. "Elder Baker preached a wonderful Gospel sermon."

Dinah rested her elbow on the arm of her chair, put her chin in her hand and looked away.

"Brother Lindsey was in good voice," Dr. Albrighton added. "He led the congregation in all four verses of 'When the Saved Get To Heaven'."

Dinah snorted.

Tabitha excused herself and went to the kitchen to get Grace. Grace came as soon as she was beckoned, but Tabitha stopped just behind Dinah's chair. She pointed to the back of Dinah's head, rolled her eyes, shook her head and mouthed, "We have to go."

Grace walked out to the porch with the Albrightons and related Dr. Marvel's warning that Dinah should be watched.

Tabitha immediately volunteered to stay two days a week if Rachel could come as well.

"I really do need some help." Grace said. "Thank you."

As the Albrightons drove off, Tabitha called back, "Let me know when you need me."

Grace found Dinah in the kitchen, arms crossed, staring out at the garden. "You didn't ask that Tabitha person to stay with me, did you?" she asked.

"Yes, I did and she said . . ."

"I don't care what she said, I don't want that woman or her snoopy little girl in my house. Rachel tramped down two of my tomato plants and got into my mole beans."

"Thank goodness!" Grace said. "It's good to hear you complaining. I thought you had lost your voice!"

Dinah didn't smile.

"I don't know what else to do, Momma. I can't stay with you everyday. I would lose my job."

Dinah fumed. "I will have to keep an eagle eye on both of them!"

Grace prayed silently then remembered: Maggie was not taking classes this summer. "Mom, could you stand them for a day or two?"

"I don't know." Dinah pursed her mouth. "I suppose I could lock up anything I don't want them getting into, and I could warn Rachel about the garden, but," Dinah huffed and shook her head, "it would be a lot of trouble!"

Grace gave her mom a hug. "Thank you." She pulled three nondescript casseroles out of the fridge, hoping she had a meat, a vegetable, and a dessert. She put a large dollop of each on a plate and stuck it in the microwave. "I'll get Mrs. Albrighton to stay tomorrow and Friday," she said, "and I'll arrange something else before Monday."

The microwave dinged and Grace handed the plate to her mother. "See if any of that is edible, and don't forget your pill." Dinah took an experimental bite as Grace got her cell and called Maggie.

"I can use the extra money," Maggie said, adding, "I'm supposed to meet Grit and Kale at the coffee shop later. How about we meet at your place instead! You shouldn't have to miss out just because you're sort of quarantined."

"Hold on, I'll ask. Mom's not crazy about Deep Water." The phrase "Mom's not crazy" echoed in Grace's head.

"Your friends won't bother me," Dinah said. "I'll be upstairs boxing up things and hiding them in the attic."

Grace decided her mother's medication must be kicking in.

Maggie called Kale. Grace called Grit.

* * * * *

Grit was on the line with his boss, Joe, and did not answer.

"I'm sorry," Joe was saying, "There's nothing I can do. My insurance company has been pissing up a storm about me letting you meet down there."

No one at Deep Water had thought of insurance.

Joe got to the point. "You could have burned my place down, and I wasn't covered. As it is, I'll have to pay someone to clean up that mess. And," Joe continued. "I have to ask; are you planning to sue?"

"What!" Grit had not even considered it. "No! No! Of course not!"

"Well that's good, because I'm not covered for that either. You're a good, dependable employee, and I don't want to lose you, but there is no way in perdition that I can let Deep Water meet here again."

"I totally understand," Grit said. "And don't worry about the mess. We'll clean it up."

"I don't think so." Joe said. "No one can stick their noses down there without insurance. I hired professionals."

Grit thanked him for the call and said, "Let us know what it costs. We'll find some way to pay you."

Grace beeped in again, "Maggie said you and she were getting together with Kale and might meet here so I wouldn't miss out. Where are your folks?"

"They left earlier than they planned after . . ." Grit hesitated, but continued. "After you decided to stay home with your mom instead of going to the funeral."

The mention of her dad's funeral did, as Grit had feared, cool the conversation, but Grace was determined to carry on.

"Maggie's calling Kale."

"Good thinking. Listen, I just got some pretty important news. Would it be too much for your mom if I invite the Michaelsons?"

"You might as well call Ricky and Buddy while you're at it. I need the company if Mother doesn't. We won't disturb her if we keep it down."

* * * * *

Troy and Amber parked their van in the driveway next to Grace's Malibu. Kale and Ricky parked on the street. Maggie, who walked over, was standing on the Willises' porch when Grit pulled in—last as usual—and parked behind Ricky.

Several neighbors saw the Divers arriving and assumed they were family members. A line formed at the door. Each neighbor offered condolences and brought food: homemade cake, pie, bread, and yet more casseroles. Grace thanked everyone without correcting the misconception. When asked about her mother, she simply promised to pass the messages along. Upstairs, Dinah wondered why the doorbell kept ringing and just exactly how many friends Grace had invited.

Grit could not get the meeting started. Grace jumped up every two minutes to answer the door. Maggie helped in the kitchen, and the others, especially Ricky and Kale, stayed busy sampling the endless buffet.

Grit looked around for an ersatz drum, spotted an empty trashcan and called the meeting to order with a couple of whacks to its bottom.

Grace jumped at the noise. "Shhh!" She pointed upward.

"Sorry." Grit looked sheepish.

Everyone stared at the ceiling and held their breath as if Dinah were about to poke her head through. After a second, they inhaled, and Grit continued, "I'll get to the bad news later, but the first order of business is, someone tried to kill me."

# 18

# Moses and the Law

GRIT HAD EVERYONE'S ATTENTION, but before he could elaborate, Ricky interrupted. "I was the one who set up the speakers and lights. If anyone is responsible for the accident, I am."

"I don't think so," Grit said.

Buddy too felt guilty. "Kale, Maggie and me worked some Sunday. We could have crossed wires or something."

Grit pulled out the threatening letter. "No, I checked that set-up when I got there. I didn't see any problems. Besides, I have reason to believe it was not an accident." Grit showed them the letter and pointed out the postmark; it was obvious; someone had caused, or at least predicted his accident.

"There could be fingerprints." Buddy ventured, calling on his own criminal experience. "You need to put that in a bag or something."

Grace got up to get a baggy from the kitchen then remembered the handkerchief in her purse. She pulled it out and showed the black stain.

"I found this when I went back for your Bible. I wiped it up from the floor near the stage. I think it's gunpowder residue."

"Whoa!" Ricky said. "You mean someone triggered the explosion?"

Grit sniffed the hanky. "It certainly smells like it."

Maggie was incredulous. "Who would want to kill you?"

"I don't know," Grit said, "but it had to be someone with access to the equipment, and someone who was there Sunday night."

This last statement was more than disturbing as the Divers began making mental lists of friends and fellow Christians who had been at Deep Water that night. Grace returned from the kitchen, handed Grit two Baggies and went back to her chair near the door.

"We should call the police." Troy said. "Grit could still be in danger."

Grit agreed, "Three other preachers died Sunday. I believe I was supposed to be number four."

It made sense—unbelievable, perfectly logical, stunned-into-silence sense. A shiver rounded the room.

Grit was the first to shake free. "Grace, do you work tomorrow?"

"Yes, I won't get off until five. After that, I have to relieve Mom's sitter."

"OK," Grit said. "I'll take your handkerchief to the police in the morning."

Grace wriggled uncomfortably, reached behind her and pulled out a stiff piece of paper by one sharp corner.

"I'm sure they will want to question you," Grit continued. He looked around the room. "I guess they will need to question all of us."

Grace stared at the small, square that lay in her hand.

"Grace," Grit nudged, "did you hear?"

"Yes? I mean, No." She looked up, "I'm sorry."

"The police will want to question all of us." Grit repeated.

"OK," Grace said mechanically.

"What is it?" Grit asked.

"Nothing. Just a picture." She stuffed it in the pocket of her jeans and refocused.

"They will want to see the crime scene." Ricky said. "And I do too." He was excited. "Let's meet there tomorrow night and check it out!"

"That," Grit grimaced, "is the bad news."

Grit's sense of humor was off tonight.

He continued, "We can't meet there tomorrow, or ever. Because of the explosion, Joe can't get insurance if we meet down there."

Not as dire as predicted but still unfunny, and mention of Sunday's explosion was not going to get a laugh out of this crowd.

After a thoughtful silence, Amber offered, "We can meet at our apartment Sunday."

Everyone but Kale remained somber as they accepted her invitation.

He pointed to his well-filled plate, "What ever you do, Grace, bring the rest of this chicken casserole and the carrot cake!"

\* \* \* \* \*

First thing Friday morning, Grit walked into the Bennettville police station. A female officer sat behind an ancient but imposing counter reading. The nametag over her pocket read "Davis."

"What is this concerning?" She didn't look up.

Grit's answer, "I think someone tried to kill me," got her attention.

When she stood, her dark blue uniform amplified her generous curves, and set off the blonde braid caught to the back of her head with a dark clasp.

"I, um . . ." Officer Davis gave Grit the once over. "I guess you will need to see Detective Hunter. I'll see if he's in." She punched a button and informed the detective. After a short exchange she turned to Grit, "He'll be with you in a minute."

She filled out a form with Grit's name and address, waved her arm in the general direction of a hallway, then bent her wrist and pointed. "Take a seat around the corner."

Grit wandered to a dingy, windowless room furnished with dilapidated folding chairs. A simple sign, "Waiting Area" assured him that he was in the right place, and a look around assured him that his public-safety tax dollars were not being spent on frivolities.

He passed the time wondering exactly how to explain to the police that the three preachers who died Sunday were murdered. Technically, only two had died, but all of Bennettville knew that Reverend Bishop Bishop was no longer among the living.

Officer Davis appeared at the door and summoned. Having observed Grit's hesitant meander to the waiting room, she thought it prudent to lead him to Detective Hunter's office.

"Detective Hunter, this is Mr. Truman Griffin," she did the honors.

Manfred Hunter, balding and fortyish, stood when she entered. He couldn't help it. His chivalrous behavior teetered on the edge of political incorrectness but was incurable. It had taken years to break him from calling her "honey" or "girl," and Hunter was the only fellow officer who occasionally slipped and called her by her given name, Sandy.

Hunter extended a friendly hand, and asked Grit to take a seat. As Grit had predicted, the detective, after seeing the letter and the handkerchief, wanted to interview anyone who had been at Deep Water Sunday night, especially anyone who might have handled the equipment. Hunter

also called Joe Uptain and arranged for forensic specialists to examine the scene.

He hung up the phone and leaned over his notes. "Is that all you have to tell me?"

Grit did not want to sound like a nut, but Detective Hunter had taken him seriously to this point. Grit took a deep breath and cautiously tipped his can of worms.

"You know, of course, that three other preachers died Sunday."

Hunter did, but he sat up and looked into Grit's troubled face. "Yes," he said, "Pastor Lawson died of a heart attack; Thomas Willis died of electrocution, and Reverend Bishop Bishop died of food poisoning."

"And if I had died, my death would have looked like an accident, too." Before Hunter could react, Grit dumped the entire can. "I think they were murdered. I don't know how or why or who, but I think someone is murdering pastors."

"We don't have any reason to call these deaths anything but coincidental," he said.

"But. . .," Grit waved the letter and handkerchief.

"Yes, someone tampered with the equipment at your meeting, but the Dive is hardly a church, and you are hardly a pastor. It seems to me that someone took exception to you personally.

Grit resented Hunter's characterization of Deep Water but let it pass. "Who could hate me enough to want me dead?"

"You never know," Hunter said. "What about ex-girlfriends or rivals?"

Grit had not considered Haley.

"Do you have an ex?"

"She left for parts unknown with persons unknown."

"Do you have a current girlfriend?"

"Yeah, Grace, Grace Willis."

Hunter frowned, "Thomas Willis's daughter?"

"Yeah."

"Were you at the One True Church when Willis died?"

Grit sat up and squared his shoulders. "Yes."

"Did you ever have a run-in with Willis?"

"Never." Grit leaned forward. "He gave Grace a hard time about coming to Deep Water, but I never confronted him."

"You aren't connected with Newell Post Lawson are you?"

"I was a student at New Jerusalem College for two years. He expelled me."

Hunter looked at Grit closely.

"Were you at Holy City when he died?"

Grit saw the direction Hunter's questions were leading, but answered truthfully. "I was running sound in the balcony."

Hunter cocked an eyebrow. "What about Reverend Bishop Bishop? Did you ever have words with him?"

"Never laid eyes on him, except on billboards."

The detective relaxed and steered his questions in another direction.

"What do you do for a living?"

"I'm a server at the Dive, and I work part-time as a reporter for the Sentinel."

"You must meet plenty of unsavory characters."

"A few."

"Anyone challenge you—quarrel?"

Grit remembered Tom. "I had a run in with someone Sunday morning—Tom Dixon. He's sure I'm going to Hell for starting a church in a bar. He confronted me at Holy City Sunday morning after Lawson died. But he's never been to Deep Water."

"Do you have an address or phone number on him?"

"He lives on campus, but he would never want to kill Pastor Lawson, and I doubt if he knew Willis or Bishop."

"We're not talking about anyone but you. There are perfectly reasonable explanations for the other deaths."

"But they were all preachers, and they all died on the same Sunday."

Hunter dismissed the whole notion, "I read the obituaries. At least forty people die in this county every week. Over half are Baptists; all the men are vets. Two weeks ago, six retired teachers died. It just so happens this week it was preachers."

*So much for the police,* Grit thought, but asked, "Will you let me know what you learn at the crime scene?"

"Sure! In fact, I want you and your girlfriend there tomorrow. Bring a list of anyone else who was there that night."

# 19

# Tattled Tales

MAGGIE WASN'T SCHEDULED to take over Grace's hours at the dealership until Monday, so on Friday Grace left Tabitha and Rachel (after tactful instructions to refrain from snooping) with her mother and went to work. On her lunch hour she drove to The Dive to meet with Grit and Detective Hunter. Two police cars and a dark van sat near the back door. Grace pulled in beside them, and Grit pulled up behind her.

He was early. She had planned to stay in her car until he arrived so she would not have to face Detective Hunter's questions alone. His early arrival was a pleasant surprise. She walked across the crunchy gravel trying to think of a way to congratulate him without letting him know how surprised she was. She took his hand and settled on the truth, "I'm really glad you're here."

"Me too." He said.

He put his healthy arm around her waist and led her into the dim, cluttered basement where two fire inspectors, officer Davis, a photographer, and Detective Hunter swarmed around the collapsed equipment like ants on a dead bird.

Officer Davis stood to the right of the stage. She pointed behind a fallen monitor.

"I've got broken metal here," Officer Davis said.

The photographer maneuvered to the spot and snapped a Polaroid.

Grace was fascinated, but she needed to be back at work in less than an hour. "Could I see that picture?" She asked.

Detective Hunter raised his head. "I didn't see you two come in." He walked over. "This must be Grace." He introduced himself and called to the photographer, "Ansel, show him your photos."

Grit and Grace flipped through them.

"You can see," Hunter said, "we haven't found any evidence of gunpowder. Plenty of broken equipment and a little blood near the stage . . ."

"Mine," Grit said.

"But . . . ?" Grace questioned.

"No gunpowder." Hunter finished.

Grace picked her way to the spot where she had seen the dark stain. "It was right here."

Grit joined her. "Someone fastened a new anchor to the bottom speaker right there."

"Did you see it?" Hunter asked.

"Yes. It was screwed to the floor and strapped to the woofer. There was another one just like it on the other side of the stage."

Hunter, Grit, and Grace searched the vicinity. No black stains or screw holes.

Grace couldn't believe it. Not only had someone caused an explosion, apparently that same someone had removed the evidence. She said as much to Hunter.

"I suppose that's possible." Hunter agreed. "But freshly patched concrete would show. Nothing has been screwed in this floor."

Hunter mumbled under his breath, "People are stranger than anybody."

To Grace it sounded like an accusation. What if Hunter thought all this was a hoax? That someone at Deep Water had written the letter and staged the "accident"?

Grit was baffled. "I see that equipment in my sleep, frozen exactly where it was just before the lights went out. I know this is the right spot!" He looked around again. The oversized woofer lay about two feet back from its customary spot. He pointed. "That speaker was sitting right where I'm standing. There's no way it could jump back two feet just by falling." Still examining the speaker, Grit shouted, "Look! Look at that!"

Linear abrasions marched around the bottom of the big box like white stripes on black asphalt.

"Those weren't there before," Grit said. "It had to be caused by a strap."

Hunter stooped for a closer look. "It certainly looks like it. Check the other one."

It too bore the telltale damage, but the evidence left the original question, where were the screw holes?

Grace had an idea. "The screw heads Grit saw were just that," she said, "screw heads. The anchors were only fastened to the speakers; they didn't really hold anything to the floor." She stopped herself. "Well, they did hold the gunpowder."

"Could I see that last picture again?" Grit asked. "The photo of the metal fragment officer Davis found."

Hunter handed him the stack and Grit shuffled.

"This is it. Look." Grit handed the photo to Hunter. "That's a piece of the bracket that held the overhead monitor. And that black stain on the end could be gunpowder. Whoever took the rest of the evidence missed that piece."

The fire officials left their searches and carefully hurried over.

"Let's see that picture," one said.

"Where's the real thing?" the other asked.

Hunter checked the number on the back of the photo.

"San . . . uh, Officer Davis," Hunter summoned. "Would you please show these gentlemen number eighteen?"

The inspectors followed Sandy to the flagged fragment, stooped and sniffed and confirmed that gunpowder had indeed been used to topple the equipment. Grace returned to work, satisfied that she had aided the investigation.

Grit stayed to give Hunter a list of people who had been at The Dive that night: Ricky, Buddy, Maggie, Kale, three of Ricky's students, two of Kale's dorm mates, and two girls, Julie Washington and Tanya Hancock, who had shown up looking for Grace. Grit had obtained the last two names from self-appointed girl-greeter, Kale. Grit vigorously defended everyone on the list that he knew and suggested that the detective consult Ricky, Kale, and Grace concerning the others, but, as he told Grace later, he left the interview feeling like a snitch.

\* \* \* \* \*

This should have been Zephonia's payday, but, according to the bank, no one was authorized to sign checks on the Greater Bennettville First Methodist/Episcopal/Baptist/Holiness Alpha and Omega International Tabernacle account except Reverend Bishop Reverend Bishop or the heretofore never seen Dr. Morgan. In other words, to paraphrase a Munchkin, until Bishop was "not only merely dead but really most sincerely dead," Zephonia could whistle, stomp or click her heels for her wages.

Something smelled. Beyond a $46,000 past due account at a high-end men's store, a $3000 per month lease on a Bentley, and credit card receipts from questionable "business" trips, Zephonia had found evidence of a for-profit business run with church funds. What she did not find was the name of an accountant or any record of tax payments—not sales tax, income tax or payroll tax. Phone messages to Bishop's presumed law firm were not returned.

Her next call was to the IRS .

* * * * *

In sickness or in health, tired, cramping, or in labor, Dinah Willis had pulled herself together, tended to her family, and showed up at a One True Church somewhere every Sunday morning for twenty-six years. Within days of giving birth and after her father's death—post partum or post mortem—she had sat, front and center in her pew, composed, if not smiling.

This Sunday was different; Dinah was observing a long needed Sabbath in "The Church of the Holy Comforter." Grace was next door attending the "The Church of the Inner Spring"—two separate denominations with the same basic belief system.

The rest of the Bennettville One True Churchers were wearing uncomfortable clothes and sitting in uneven rows of battered folding chairs in a long-abandoned, unair-conditioned storefront, having leased the first available space, not daring to risk the fires of Hell by missing the weekly requirements of singing, giving, praying, communing, and reading scripture.

Rachel sat with her parents on the back row and squinted into dark corners where empty store fixtures reached toward her like hungry beggars. Behind her, the door was open to let in a bit more light and, by the Grace of God, a breeze. So far God had not sent that particular blessing. Rachel waved her bulletin in front of her face for relief.

Greg Lindsey had braved the malodorous OTOTC building to retrieve songbooks for today's service. He rose grandly from his rickety front row seat, turned to face the faithful and began the service.

"There should be a songbook on the floor under each chair," he announced, smiling broadly.

One hundred would-be singers dived floorward, fumbled around each other's ankles then stood, books in hand. "Please turn your books to number thirty-eight," Greg said. "'Where the Roses Never Fade'."

Obedient church members opened books and rustled pages, releasing a vile stench that triggered grisly flashbacks of Willis' death. Several in the crowd began to cough. Rachel thought she might throw up. Without debate, the congregation closed the books and put them back on the floor. They would sing from memory.

Two more songs, "The Lily of the Valley" and "There is a Balm in Gilead" failed to sweeten the air or to ameliorate the ill-chosen sermon title (taken from II Corinthians 2), "The Smell of Death."

Half way through the visiting preacher's admonition to live a life offensive to the enemies of God, a heavenly breeze wafted through the open door bearing the scent of fresh-brewed coffee; whereupon, all but the terminally pious gave up religion for the day and adjourned to Starbucks across the street.

At the Willises', Dinah and Grace sat in the sunny kitchen wearing PJs and drinking instant.

* * * * *

The Holy City Zionist Christian Hour was shoved into homes across twelve counties via a network affiliate whose engineer had witnessed Tom's debacle at Lawson's funeral. This Sunday, that engineer checked every piece of equipment and every cable connection in the building.

The church board of directors and deacons conducted the service as if Pastor Lawson were alive and well; the only difference being that

140

he appeared from the great beyond by way of video. The broadcast transitioned seamlessly from live feed to canned sermon. The few viewers who did not know Lawson was dead would see his incongruous St. Patrick's Day tie but remain clueless.

Judging by the reaction of church members and the home audience, the pretence that nothing had or would change at Holy City soothed the faithful and bought the leadership time to hash out political and doctrinal differences in a more deliberate manner than Lawson's precipitous death might have demanded.

Over the next few weeks Provost Chessman would determine who was loyal to the dead pastor and who was not. Whichever party prevailed, Chessman would position himself to take over without a ripple—preferably with Lawson's sycophantic faculty, coercive policies, and stagnant faith intact.

\* \* \* \* \*

Grit worked all day Saturday at The Dive, but not at his best. By the end of his shift he had spilled two drinks and forgotten an order, but he had also decided on a strategy to find the killer; he would ask his editor to assign him to the story—just the explosion, the letter, and the police report. Once he was given the assignment, he could follow the trail wherever.

Sunday morning, as he did whenever possible, he slept late. When he woke, his mind was clearer, and his arm felt stronger. He was hungry. The accident had not affected his appetite.

Grit's first meal would also serve as lunch, so he prepared a "real man's" breakfast. He pulled out a skillet and filled the coffee maker, reminding himself to thank his dad for directing his teenage self to the kitchen and instructing him in stove operation. "Every man should know how to fry sausage, scramble eggs and make pancakes," he had admonished.

Grit finished eating his sixth and last pancake around eleven and spent the next five minutes "cleaning" his apartment—clearing dirty laundry off the couch and pitching overflowing garbage—preparing for Grace's visit after the meeting at the Michaelsons'.

* * * * *

Worship service at the Greater Bennettville First Methodist/Baptist/Episcopal/Holiness Alpha and Omega International Tabernacle on the Sunday following Reverend Bishop Reverend Bishop's "death" was a shambles.

Seventy-year-old Deacon Jefferson stood near the front of the church wondering how to start. The choir could not sing: the altos and sopranos could do nothing but sob, and the tenors and basses could not carry the melody. The organist and the choir director, both female, were at home, prostrate with grief.

He looked out over the congregation. Every lady over the age of sixteen was dressed in black, from pointed toe to feathered hat, and wailing like a murder of dying crows. The children, taking their cue from the mommas, wailed as well.

The obviously disconcerted speaker, who had simply shown up and volunteered to preach, could not be heard over mournful cries of "Oh Lord" and "Dear Jesus."

When the preacher gave up, Deacon Jefferson decided, at the very least, someone should take up a collection. He looked under the communion table and found the collection plate in its usual spot, but full of money from the previous Sunday. No one had taken it to the bank. The Reverend Bishop had handled financial matters. Bishop had handled every matter.

The helpless deacon returned to his post in defeat and watched eight hundred Methodist, Baptist, Episcopal, Holinesses sit, united by confusion, until one by one they trickled out of the building like a slow leak.

* * * * *

Grace looked out the kitchen window as she did the breakfast dishes. Dinah was in the garden cutting and burning. For the first time since Thomas' death she looked relaxed and happy. In her garden, she could pull weeds, poison pesky insects and, though she broke several laws in the process, shoot four-legged pests. She decided what to plant, when to fertilize, what lived and what died.

Grace thought of other spring afternoons—her mother coming in through the kitchen door glowing with sweat and sunshine and carrying a basket of newly sprouted lettuce and green tomatoes. Dinah would wash the garden off her hands, start dinner and call Thomas down from his study.

Grace wiped her eyes and finished drying the dishes. She would pretend for as long as possible that all was well and that certain questions did not need to be asked. But eventually she would have to know: Why did Dinah want Thomas buried in Texas? What had she been doing at the First M/B/E/H Tabernacle once a month? And who was Abigail?

At two-thirty, when Tabitha and Rachel arrived to mom-sit, Dinah pulled Grace out of Albrighton earshot and began to fuss.

Grace did not want to argue. "I'm going to spend some time with Grit after the meeting," she stated flatly. "I'll be home by eight."

Dinah made a face.

"This is the last time you have to put up with them, Momma. I promise."

# 20

# Testimony

ONE OF THE THINGS VICTORIA liked least about the real estate business was working on Sundays, but she didn't know why. Like most Gentiles she confused Sunday with the Old Testament Sabbath. She tried to keep all the other shalt and shalt nots, including not coveting her neighbor's wife. So why is it okay to work on Sunday? The omission gave her a vague sense of guilt, as if some unacknowledged Jewish ancestor were shaking a finger.

She had no choice today; she had to make a sale soon or miss a payment on her bungalow. The showing last Sunday had gleaned three offers, but all were pending. Victoria knew the prospective buyers, or she at least knew their families. Any of them could readily obtain a mortgage, so the problem wasn't the buyers. *Could something planned at New Jerusalem be affecting property values? Is Lawson's plan to rezone all of the school's residential property to multi-family still in the works? Surely not.*

She was almost sure of a sale today; she was showing a tiny, ultramodern, downtown condo, exactly what Martha Lawson had requested, "No guest rooms, a small kitchen, and a one-car garage. Close to shopping and hiking and wired for Internet." Martha would never again entertain random evangelists or dignitaries; no more church committees or showers, no voracious hoards of visiting youth.

Victoria had no difficulty locating the Lawson estate on its unnaturally well-groomed street in the overly planned Bennettville suburb, Shangri-lot. She had seen the house in some frankly frightening pictures. The reality was worse.

A pair of rampant English lions flanked each end of a circular drive. In the center, a feverish, tiered, stone fountain performed water aerobics. The house, a three-story, pseudo-Queen Anne-party of pink and fuchsia, looked like Barbie's birthday cake. White, beaded gingerbread ornamented every inconceivable nook, and plastic tulips grew from plastic boxes under each window.

To Newell, whose taste in churches ran to mighty fortresses, this outlandish dollhouse represented domesticity, femininity, and womanhood in general.

Martha put it on the market two days after Newell died.

When Victoria arrived, Martha stood at the front door wearing faded, "mom" jeans, a vintage T-shirt, no make-up, and sneakers. Her long, fine hair fluttered around her shoulders like wind-blown spider webs. When she clambered into the back seat, Victoria caught a whiff of whiskey.

Victoria drove onto the street, and checked her side mirror. The lions snarled behind her. She pushed the accelerator harder than she should have, and Martha swayed.

"Excuse my appearance," Martha tittered. "I've been packing up Newell's things for the Good Will." She did not wait for a comment. "I can't wait to see what you found for me. I've seen those condos in 'Architectural Digest.'" Martha pulled a small thermos from her purse and took a drink. "I know this is going to be perfect. It's right on the river and close to a bowling alley. You would not believe how much I love to bowl! I haven't bowled since I was a kid in Jersey. Have you ever been to New Jersey?"

This was not the Martha that Victoria knew only by reputation: reserved, aloof, imperious.

"Did you see the funeral?" Martha hiccupped. "Wasn't that something! Nice funeral." She closed her eyes and leaned against the window, still talking. "But we never found his Bible. We looked an' looked."

She sat up, tapped Victoria on the shoulder and offered her a drink. Victoria shook her head, and Martha drank up. "Did you know he wanted that Bible buried with him? Me too." She smiled. "That Bible made me hate him. Just like I told Reverend Bishop, Newell read it and pounded on it and slammed it on the pulpit, but he didn't believe it. Newell Post Lawson broke the commandments every day," Martha held two fingers in front of Victoria's face, "and twice on Sundays!" She settled back in her seat, laughing then seemed to fall asleep. Her mouth was open.

Victoria began to wonder about the ethics of selling to someone in Martha's condition, but turned onto River Street, still headed for the condos.

Martha fell over, hit her head and resumed her monologue, eyes closed. "I told the Abigails too." She sat up and opened her eyes. "I said, 'Newell Post Lawson is an adulterous pig who will burn in the fires of Hell'." She giggled. "I never liked a big kitchen. Did you ever see my kitchen?" She swayed as she held her hands wide. "Big? Lord, you could have held a bowling tournament in there! You would not believe how much I love to bowl. I used to bowl in Jersey, New Jersey, when I was a kid. Have you ever been to Jersey?"

Victoria made a U-turn and headed back toward the lions; she could not sell a condo to Martha today, not without breaking at least one commandment.

* * * * *

All the regulars, Kale, Maggie, Buddy, Ricky, Grit, and Grace were supposed to be at the Michaelsons' by three. Grit arrived at two thirty.

"You're early, "Troy remarked.

"Yeah," Grit laughed. "I thought I'd try it.

Troy directed him into their small den where Amber had chips, dip, and fresh vegetables spread on the coffee table.

Kale arrived next with Maggie. Both saw Grit and exclaimed, "You're early!"

"Yeah," Grit said, thinking, Is it really that big a deal?

When Amber ushered Ricky into the den, he too reacted in disbelief. Even Buddy when he arrived let out a loud, "You're early!"

Kale laughed. Grit felt a bit defensive, but figured he deserved at least some of the incredulity.

Only Grace failed to comment. When she arrived, she simply smiled and accepted Grit's welcoming hug.

After a short devotional and prayer, the Divers settled into the comfortably shabby furniture and listened as Grit related his interview with Detective Hunter.

"He doesn't think the deaths of the other ministers are connected to the explosion, but he insisted that whoever rigged it had to be at The Dive that night."

No one spoke, and Grit saw fearful looks on several faces.

"I don't think so," Grace said.

Grit was abashed. "Which?" He asked. "That the deaths were related or that the murderer was there?"

"I've been thinking since our last meeting."

She does that a lot, Grit thought.

"I don't believe my father was murdered."

Grit was about to argue, but wisely shut his mouth.

"And, if we limit the suspects to the people who were at the service," Grace continued, "that cuts it down to Kale, Maggie, Ricky, Buddy, and a few visitors. Troy, Amber, and I weren't there, and the list of visitors isn't very long: I've talked to Julie and Tanya; Ricky spoke to his students, and Kale checked with his friends from the dorm. So far as we can tell, none of them had laid eyes on you before that night." Grace paused. "Think about it," she said. "Who in this room would have reason to kill you?"

Grit looked at the worried faces of his friends and slumped back into his seat. "God forgive me," he said. "I can't believe I've been so stupid. Of course, none of you had anything to do with it!" Grit shook his head. "I never realized the implications."

Suspicion and fears lifted. Ricky dropped his arms from a protective self-hug and reached for a handful of chips. Maggie's face went from a guarded mask to a wide grin, and Buddy loosened up as if he had been shot with WD40. Kale snickered nervously.

"There are plenty of ways to detonate an explosion from a distance." Troy ventured.

"But how would they know when to set it off?" Maggie asked. "He couldn't just set a timer. He must have had some way to see what was going on."

"Um . . ." Buddy examined the rug. "Maybe Troy and I could look into how the murderer set off the explosion. Or . . ."

"I could work on the timing," Maggie interrupted then apologized, "I'm sorry, Buddy. You were saying?"

"Did you want to add something?" Grit encouraged.

Buddy looked up briefly. "No, I'm good."

"We can meet here to compare notes," Amber said. "At least until we find something better," She scanned faces, especially Troy's for assent. He nodded.

"Does anyone mind if I volunteer as secretary?" she asked.

Nobody else wanted the job.

Grace had a request, "I'm going to be holed up with Mom for the next two weeks at least." she said. "Could we please meet at the preacher's house instead?"

No one offered a veto.

"How about Tuesday night?" Grit asked. "Seven?"

Again, no problem.

"Good," Grit said.

"Before we leave the subject," Amber said, "eventually, and I hope soon, we are going to need another permanent meeting place. I make a motion . . ." Kale guffawed but Amber continued, "that we all look for another meeting place." She faced Kale. "I know you think Robert's rules of order are too formal, but a little order helps keep things moving."

"I second the motion, "Troy said.

Kale stopped snickering long enough to vote aye with the rest.

Grit reclaimed the floor. "I'm asking my boss at the paper to assign me to the explosion story, and I need input."

"I'll ask Julie and Tanya if they saw anything unusual." Grace offered.

"Hold on," Kale protested. "You help with something else! Investigating girls is my job!"

Kale got another laugh, and Grace granted his request.

"But what about the other murders?" Troy asked. "We can't just look into the mess at The Dive, we might miss something."

"True," Grit said, "but whoever tried to kill me, killed Lawson, Willis, and Bishop. If we solve one murder, we solve them all."

"But we have no proof that the other deaths were murders," Grace reminded.

"You're right," Grit said. "This investigation isn't going to be as easy as I thought. I'm going to need all of you to help."

"I'll ask the insurance investigator to check the wiring in the baptistery again," Grace said. "I guess it could have been tampered with."

"Good!' Grit said.

Grace looked stricken. "I don't think Daddy's death was murder."

"Sorry," Grit apologized, stumbling for words. "I mean, that's a good idea, checking the wiring."

"The original report was definite," Grace said. "The heater was shorted out by rats."

"What about motive?" Amber asked. "Why would the prophet want to kill these particular preachers?"

"We know why he targeted Grit," Amber added. "The so-called prophet spelled it out in his letter."

"Right," Kale said. "All that stuff about not honoring your father and mother."

"And that was your sermon topic." Maggie reminded.

The room grew quiet. The refrigerator humming from the kitchen mimicked the activity in the Divers' brains.

"Troy," Grit said. "Do you still have last Saturday's paper?"

Troy hurried to the back porch, dug into the recycling bin and pulled out the week-old religion pages with the list of sermons for Commandment Sunday.

"Here they are," Troy said.

He handed the section to Grit, and everyone but Ricky rushed in for a better view. He stayed at the far end of the room, pacing and thinking.

"Okay, let's see. Here's Willis'." Grit read out loud, "'Thou Shalt Not Bear False Witness: Strange Worship', so the Prophet must have thought that Thomas Willis was a liar."

"Well, he wasn't," Grace said.

"Of course not," Grit said. "But the Prophet is irrational; he could be reacting to anything."

"What about Bishop's sermon?" Maggie asked.

Grit scanned the list. "It isn't here."

"There goes that theory," Maggie said.

"Wait a minute," Grit was still looking. "I know I saw it somewhere." Grit turned the page. "Here it is," Grit laughed. "No wonder I remember seeing it; I wrote it myself. 'The Reverend Bishop's Commandment Sunday sermon, "Thou Shalt Not Steal" will be replaced by a special prayer service on behalf of the food poisoning victims and their families.' It's in the article about the Unity Picnic food poisoning."

"Isn't that how Bishop ended up on life support?" Grace asked.

"Yeah," Grit replied. "Health officials told me that everyone who got sick had eaten a piece of chocolate, cherry cake."

Kale, who was about to take a bite of a chocolate, cherry something, put down his fork.

"What about Lawson's sermon? Amber asked.

Grit scanned the article again. "Here it is, 'Thou Shalt Not Commit Adultery: God is Faithful to the Jews."

"Could this prophet person be anti-Christian or anti-Jew?" Buddy asked.

"Maybe," Troy said, "but the link between all of these murders is Old Testament prophecy. I think whoever killed these preachers is not anti-religious but super religious. He thinks he is ridding the world of hypocrites."

"Good luck with that one," Kale said.

Grit stayed on track. "I think Troy is right. The Prophet linked all of the sermons to hypocrisy and to Old Testament prophecy."

Ricky stopped pacing. "Grit?" All eyes went to the other end of the room. "Didn't you tell me you had lost your Bible?"

"Yeah."

"A funeral director called me at the station Monday night looking for Pastor Lawson's Bible. I don't think anyone ever found it."

"And?" Grit said, puzzled.

"Well," Ricky spoke slowly, "what if the murderer took a souvenir? What if he took Bibles from all the victims?"

"He couldn't have," Grace said. "Daddy's Bible was on the table next to his ashes at the viewing."

"Are you sure it was his?" Ricky asked.

"Yes, I opened it and read the inscription from my mom. It was the Bible he preached from."

"Have you seen it since?" Maggie asked.

"Actually, no. I left it there for the funeral."

"Try to track it down," Grit said, "I'll try to find out what happened to mine."

"Yours is still at Deep Water." Grace said. "We won't see it again until that mess is cleared out."

"Well, maybe," Grit said. "But I'm thinking Ricky is right; finding the Bibles could lead us to the killer."

Before the meeting broke up, each Diver had at least one assignment. Grit's first was to talk to his editor about doing a story on the explosions. Maggie was going to call The Greater Bennettville First M/B/E/H to find out if they had Reverend Bishop Bishop's Bible. Grace would check on the baptistery heater and call the funeral home about her dad's Bible. Kale would meet with Grace's friends, Julie and Tanya. And everyone would look for a permanent meeting place.

Outside, the afternoon had ripened, and bright sunlight lifted everyone's mood.

Buddy said, "Goodbye," and left hastily for Crutcher's Tow and Stow and a long work-night.

Ricky waved Grit down before he drove off. "Chessman has me barred from campus."

"Say what?"

"It's a long story. Can you get me a look at the Holy City video from last Sunday?"

"Probably," Grit said. "What's up?"

"I'm hoping whoever took Lawson's Bible did it on camera."

"Call me tomorrow," Grit said. "I'll see what I can do."

Grace stopped at the grocery to surprise Grit with a couple of small steaks, some baking potatoes, and a bagged salad. It would be better and cheaper than the pizza he planned to order.

Grit waited in the shade of the awning over his door. Sunlight slanted through newly leafed trees and speckled the grass with moving shadows. Honeysuckle sweetened the air. He thought of what he would do when Grace arrived and what he would like to do—two entirely different things.

Celibacy was not fun. Grit was a healthy, young male with just enough sexual experience to whet his appetite. He was tired of wanting and needing something that God prohibited outside of marriage, and he was not ready to marry—not ready to risk being hurt again and not ready to take on the responsibility. He knew the scripture, "It is better to marry than to burn," and right now, he was burning. Every hair was on fire, and he wondered if all this God business was worth the trouble. He would never force himself on Grace, *but what if she wasn't being forced? What if . . . ?* He was lusting, and he knew it. The best of him knew that Grace deserved better, but the best of him had not joined the conversation.

Grace, on the other hand, was as much female as Grit was male, younger, and probably healthier. She was not immune to warm breezes, flickering shadows, and sweet aromas, and, although she was a virgin and wanted to stay so until marriage, she was certainly not immune to healthy young males. She was hurting from her father's death and feeling tender toward Grit due to his injuries.

This afternoon's tryst would not be a clash between insistent male and implacable female, more like a volatile mixture of fire and gasoline.

# 21

# Passion and Poison

Dinah had kept Rachel and Tabitha under surveillance all day Friday. The only snooping Tabitha managed was to give the chair where she had hidden the mysterious "Abigail" picture a fluff or two, but Rachel had managed to go through Grace's old dresser when neither Dinah nor Tabitha was looking.

Sunday afternoon, when the two incorrigible nosies arrived at the preacher's house, Dinah was in her garden savagely pulling weeds. Tabitha approached just close enough to wave, then returned to the house and escorted Rachel upstairs. Rachel sat back against Grace's old bed, picked up "My Friend Flicka" and opened to page five—as far as she had gotten in a week. Tabitha closed the door, slipped across the hall to Dinah's room and peered under the bed.

Nothing. Not even dust bunnies. Dinah's dresser drawers held the usual underwear and nightgowns. Her bathroom was spotless; the medicine cabinet and vanity drawers were suspiciously empty. The linen cabinet behind the bathroom door had a shiny new lock.

Across the hall, Thomas' office was wall-to-wall bookshelves. Tabitha looked through his desk and opened a tall file cabinet. The only items of possible interest were his alphabetized sermon outlines, his bills, and tax records. But the entire congregation knew how much the preacher was paid, and Tabitha did not have to snoop to know how he had spent the majority of his salary; rows of expensive commentaries and Biblical reference works filled the shelves and spilled over onto the floor.

She despaired, went down to the living room, found the Sunday paper and took it into the kitchen. She laid it on the well-worn table and went to the cupboard for a cup and a tea bag.

Outside, Dinah bent over her garden humming contentedly; she had every single meaningful artifact in the house under lock and key.

Rachel eased off the bed and tiptoed to the attic door where she found a newly mounted hasp and padlock. Not a problem. She went back to Grace's dresser, opened the center drawer and pulled out a nail file. Unscrewing the hasp took all of five minutes. She did not regard her actions as sinful. Her mother would have done the same.

In the attic, Rachel dodged recklessly over and around broken furniture and unwanted doodads to the box sprouting the red umbrella. She grabbed her prize and pushed it open, ripping the aged silk and breaking two of the ribs. The umbrella's appeal immediately waned, and she tried to pull it shut. When she could not, she propped it over the back of a sorrowful looking rocking chair and began digging through the toys and papers still in the box. The toys, fluffy stuffed animals, and baby dolls, were interesting, but babyish.

At the bottom of the box, she found a frilly pink book. She picked it up and plopped herself cross-legged on the dusty floor. On the first page, a ragged envelope held a document that Rachel recognized as a birth certificate, very much like her own, but with "Abigail Faith Willis" typed on the "name" line and "Official Seal of the State of Florida" imprinted at the bottom. Rachel read the date of birth and subtracted. Abigail would now be twenty-four.

She turned a few more pages, past tiny footprints, locks of hair, and smiling photographs. She stood to carry the book nearer the window. A second official document fluttered to the floor. She held it to the light. It bore the same sort of seal as the birth certificate, but from Texas, and was bordered with delicate, black tracery. She read the intricate lettering with difficulty: "Certificate of Death." She tried to drop the frightful thing, but her fingers froze. Her eyes read on relentlessly and her agile mind did the math. Abigail Faith Willis died—at five years of age.

Suddenly, the musty toys and broken umbrella were not simple playthings; they were the personal effects of a real girl—a real girl, younger than she, and dead. Abigail's sleepy-eyed babies stared up at Rachel with accusing eyes. Her knees buckled, and she sank limply into the old rocker. Shreds of scarlet silk dripped over her shoulders and into her lap. She stifled a scream, shoved the certificate back in the book and stumbled, crying, down the stairs. When she closed the door at the bottom, the baby book was still in her hand. She dared not go back. She laid it on the floor of Thomas' office and pulled the nail file from her pocket. She could barely see to screw the hasp back into place.

Tabitha heard the commotion. "Rachel? Are you reading?"

"Yes."

"You sound like you've been crying? Are you all right?"

Rachel moved quietly to the bathroom. "I'm just blowing my nose." She grabbed a wad of toilet paper and did just that, loudly.

"What's wrong?"

"Flicka died," she said. She spent the rest of the afternoon finishing the book and praying she had not told a lie.

* * * * *

Grit's tiny kitchen, just off the equally cozy living area, needed cleaning. Before he and Grace could eat, someone had to wash at least two dishes. And something had to be done about Grit's charcoal-encrusted oven or it would activate the apartment's sprinkler system. Grit stayed close as Grace bent under counters and reached into cabinets. Grace felt her temperature rise and wondered if a sprinkler system might be just what the situation called for.

She went to the sink. Grit stood behind her and breathed down her neck. She tried to think of something, anything that might reboot her brain. Dire warnings that made perfect sense in Sunday school: shame, disease, loss of worth, pregnancy, were not doing the trick. *How about the fires of hell?* She remembered the oven. She grabbed a spatula and a garbage bag, handed them to Grit and sent him to the opposite side of the kitchen.

"Just scrape all of that burned stuff into the bag," she said.

She reached around the pile of dirty dishes and splashed cold water on the back of her neck.

"This is ridiculous," she declared, staring at the mess. "I'm not about to wash a kitchen full of dishes for a man who is perfectly able to do it himself." Her announcement rang with just enough anger to momentarily lower the temperature.

But Grit could not avoid brushing up against her on his way to get rid of the oven mess. He stopped, gave her a squeeze and whispered in her ear, "You look beautiful when you're angry."

Grace was in trouble. She lowered her head, close to surrender but caught a glimpse of Grit's filthy floor; a blessed jolt of indignation gave her strength to pull away and send him to clear and set the table. She stuck the potatoes in the microwave, put the steaks under the broiler and set the timer for three minutes.

Grit continued to find reasons to enter and leave the kitchen, always stroking Grace's hair or nuzzling her neck. She enjoyed every touch but did her best to keep her mind on dinner.

Grit reached into a cupboard over her head for something he had "forgotten" on his last four trips. Beneath his open arms, Grace emptied the salad into a bowl and turned toward the refrigerator. Her impractical heels caught in the tattered kitchen rug, and down she went. Her full weight caught Grit in the stomach, and the two of them landed heavily on the nasty floor—Grace on top of Grit and salad on top of both. The compromising position, full length in each other's arms, was exactly what both had been craving, but two painful circumstances rapidly cooled Grit's jets. First, the floor under his back was damp and gooey, and second, Grace had landed squarely on his injured arm. Tears streaming, Grit opened his mouth to scream.

Grace mistook Grit's tears for passion and planted her mouth on his, making screaming impossible. She proceeded to render aid until God's providence (in answer, no doubt, to forgotten recitations of "lead us not into temptation") intervened: the oven timer buzzed and the doorbell jangled.

Grace got up to deal with both, and Grit let out a howl.

Outside, Ricky pounded on the door, "Grit, hey, Grit!"

The oven continued to buzz.

Grit clamped his jaw and moaned, "My arm!"

Grace rose and ran toward the oven, looking over her shoulder. "Oh sweetie! Did I hurt you? I'm so sorry."

Grit groaned.

"I'm coming!" She grabbed a fork, turned the steaks and reset the timer.

"Grit!" Ricky insisted. Bang, bang, bang. "Grit!"

"I'm coming!" Grace yelled to anyone listening.

She opened the freezer, grabbed a bag of frozen vegetables and tossed them to Grit, who had moved to the couch. He caught it with his good hand, placed the makeshift ice bag on his upper arm and lay down.

Grace ran to the door, threw it open and went back to Grit.

Ricky walked in unacknowledged and examined the now peaceful scene: Grit stretched whimpering on the couch, Grace tenderly wiping his tears with a dishrag.

Ricky struggled to reconfigure the smirk on his face and asked what he could do.

"Just listen for the timer." Grace said. "When it goes off, turn it and the oven off and take the steaks out."

Ricky waited to announce his news until the steaks were done. By then, Grace and Grit had decided that his arm would need only ice and a couple of Tylenol.

"I've got the video," Ricky said.

"What?" Grit asked.

"The video of Lawson's death."

"But . . . ?"

"The office always makes one for the church in case members want a copy. I just called and asked for one!"

"Have you seen it?" Grit asked.

"Have I ever!"

Ricky pulled the DVD out of its sleeve and pushed it in the slot. "You've got to see this!"

Grit handed him the remote and headed for the dining table.

"Have you eaten?" Grace asked, hoping he had.

"Yeah." Ricky answered, his eyes on the TV. He fast-forwarded through the sermon while Grace filled two plates and cut up Grit's steak, insisting he rest his arm.

After watching Lawson fall, Ricky hit the pause button. The pulpit, centered between the deacons and the choir, stood empty, except for Lawson's Bible.

"Watch this!' Ricky said. "Kale's camera was running on closed circuit after the broadcast ended."

Grit laid down his fork. Grace did the same.

Ricky hit play. Stricken deacons and stunned choir members sat motionless until a tall coloratura stood, screamed an A above high C and fainted. Ninety-three robe-draped figures flapped their large white wings and rose en masse like a flock of frightened seagulls. Dark suited deacons waddled stiffly toward the camera, presumably to the aid of their fallen pastor.

"Okay," Ricky said. He pointed to a choir member kneeling with her back to the camera. "Keep an eye on her."

Madam X, without showing her face, rose deliberately and moved to the pulpit where her subsequent actions were hidden by long flowing sleeves.

"Kale's camera went off right about here," Ricky said, "but watch this last second."

Madam X stepped to her right, revealing the pulpit, sans Bible, just before the screen shredded to noisy gray.

"Did you see that!" Ricky exalted.

"Yeah," Grit said. "Show it again, but shut off the sound; that soprano nearly deafened me."

Ricky obliged, three times. Grit and Grace let their steaks grow cold.

"I've never seen that woman before." Ricky said. "If she's a choir member, she's new to me."

"Me too," Grit said.

"And the robe is different," Grace said. "The rest of the robes have dolman sleeves. Hers are kimono."

Ricky and Grit looked at Grace blankly.

"A dolman sleeve has a seam—"

Ricky interrupted, "I don't want to know," he said.

"We don't speak fashion," Grit added.

"We get it," Ricky said. "She's not a real choir member."

"Do we know she is a she?" Grace asked. "It's really hard to tell under that robe, and that hair looks fake."

"Run it again," Grit said.

On the forth go-round, Grace asked Ricky to pause at the shot of the Bible on the empty pulpit.

"Look," she said, "Lawson's glass is missing."

"Right," Ricky said. "He knocked it to the floor when he fell. Do you want to see that?" Ricky pointed the remote.

"Run it to the end again first." Grit said. "I'd like to think I can tell the difference between a man and a woman."

He couldn't. None of them could, although all agreed the hair was fake, and Grace caught a glimpse of decidedly masculine, brown footwear.

"Well, so much for that," Ricky said. "I'll back it up to where Lawson drops the glass."

The death scene from Kale's camera angle was up-close and personal. Lawson, red faced and sweating, lurched toward the camera, swiping the pulpit and slinging the water glass to the very spot where Madam X later knelt. The dying Pastor looked rapturously heavenward, clutched his chest, and in gaping profile, fell mercifully out of camera range.

The trio of would-be detectives sat waiting for closure or inspiration or both.

"Whew!" Grit said. "I don't ever want to see that again."

Ricky and Grace agreed.

"What time is it?" she asked. "I promised mother I would be home before eight."

"You can't go before you finish your steak," Grit said, "and I want to know what you think this mystery choir member has to do with Lawson's death."

"It's seven thirty," Ricky said, checking his phone. "You've got time."

"Not for both," Grace said. She pushed her plate to Grit's side of the table. "Eat this tomorrow. There's lots for me to eat at Mother's."

"So, what do you think?" Grit asked.

"I really don't know. He or she was not supposed to be there. But was it murder . . . ?"

"Yes," Ricky said. "Pastor Lawson was poisoned. Why else would someone want that glass?"

"I don't know," Grace said, "I'll have to think about it."

"Nobody does that better," Grit said.

Grace left the table and picked up her purse. "You are going to take the video to the police."

Grit nodded and moved to the door, blocking her exit.

"Close your eyes, Ricky," he said, pulling Grace close.

Ricky laughed, but turned his head as the two kissed goodnight.

# 22

# Reliable Sources

MONDAY MORNING, EARLIER THAN he would have liked, Grit arrived at the Sentinel newsroom to present his case to editor, Malcolm Combs, a balding, red-faced, pending heart attack, right out of a 1930's movie. Combs listened with one ear and some portion of his brain as he answered phones, edited copy and chomped on an unlit cigar.

Grit attempted communication. "I'm ready to do something other than obituaries," he said, hoping Combs heard.

Combs, grunted—at whom or what Grit wasn't sure.

"I want to investigate the explosion at Deep Water." Grit watched and listened closely for another acknowledgement. When Combs made passing eye contact, Grit put into evidence the "Prophet" letter and the insurance and police reports.

Combs said, "Hold on," to someone, maybe Grit, pulled the cigar out of his mouth and pressed the receiver to his chest.

"I've got someone else assigned to that story, kid, and they have all that."

Grit waved the letter. "Do they have this?"

Combs shoved a mock up of Tuesday morning's front page across the desk. "It's all in there," he said, reinserting the cigar and going back to his phone call.

The story Grit should have written was above the fold, headlined, "Bar, 'Dive', Bombed" and bylined, "Chilly Rivers," the Sentinel's part-time crime reporter and full time hack. Grit scanned the article and gritted his teeth. Rivers had garbled the information and misspelled Grit's name. He waited to point this out to Combs, but gave up after ten minutes of watching him multi-tasking himself to an early grave. Grit headed for the door.

"Hold on," Combs said.

Grit kept walking.

"Griffin!"

Grit turned; Combs put down the phone.

"I've got something for you," he said. "That was a doctor friend of mine. Off the record, Reverend Bishop is leaving the planet tonight. I want you on his obituary and a biographical piece to run on the religion page."

This was not what Grit had wanted; it was better.

"You can start with his personal secretary. Here's her name and phone number."

He handed Grit a yellow sticky note and Bishop's Vitae.

"Go ahead and write the obituary from this and whatever you get from the secretary. Keep it fluffy. Save the low-down for the bio. Find out everything—the good, the bad, and the illegal. Rumor has it the good Reverend is being investigated for tax fraud."

Grit's insides turned a back flip.

Combs wasn't finished. "About this explosion thing, I know you are personally involved, so I have an angle you can work."

Grit was speechless. Combs pulled out a folder containing news clips.

"About once a year, someone tries to figure out who that geezer on the corner of Thirteenth and College is," he said. "So far, no one has." He handed Grit the folder. "Take a look at these and see what you think. If you can tie our Moses to that letter of yours, the old buzzard might still sell papers."

Grit examined the stack of tattered newsprint. The short feature articles bore dates beginning when the self-appointed prophet showed up six years ago. Headlines included: "Who is He?" "Where Did He Come From?" "What Does He Want?" None of the writers had an actual interview. Everything was speculation.

"There aren't any quotes in these articles," Grit remarked.

Combs was back on the phone, but covered the mouth piece and answered softly, "No one has ever gotten a word out of the guy. If you do, you'll have a scoop."

Combs left his number on someone's answering machine and put down the phone.

"The Bishop story is part of your job," he said, "but you're freelance on the Moses thing. We'll pay you forty dollars per published column inch."

"Thanks," Grit said. "How soon do you need it?"

"I need the bio yesterday, and the obit most likely tomorrow." Combs answered. "But I'll give you two weeks and ten dollars a day for expenses on the Moses angle."

Grit walked out to his car marveling at God's mysterious ways.

\* \* \* \* \*

All of the Divers, even Kale, took their murder detecting assignments seriously. As soon as Kale left the meeting Sunday night, he arranged to meet Julie Washington and Tonya Hancock for lunch on Tuesday.

Monday morning, Grace spoke to several people at the funeral home about her dad's Bible before someone put Mr. Hearshell on the line.

"I sent your father's things home with Dr. and Mrs. Albrighton," Hearshell said. "Didn't they return them?"

"Yes, but not the Bible."

"That's strange. I'm sorry. I can't imagine what may have happened." A long pause. "I don't know what to say. Perhaps it was simply misplaced. I assume it had your father's name in it."

"Yes," Grace said, "The first page has a message to him from my mother with his name and her signature."

Mr. Hearshell promised to continue his search.

Grace hung up the phone, made a note to call Tabitha Albrighton and placed another call, this one to the One True Church's property insurers who agreed, after some persuasion, to look at the baptistery water heater one more time.

"But I won't be able to get an inspector out there until late this evening," the agent said.

Grace was surprised it would be that soon. Maybe her mention of a possible murder had sped up the process.

"Do I need to meet you at the church?" she asked.

"No, we obtained a key to the property when the claim was filed."

Grace thanked the agent, said goodbye and crossed one more thing off of her list.

Troy stayed up past his usual bedtime Monday researching explosive devices on the Internet. The forensic report he had from Grit showed no evidence of a timer; the killer had personally triggered the bomb during the worship service. Troy slapped his desk, "Smite them O, Lord!" he shouted, only half facetiously.

Amber hurried from the bedroom to investigate the outburst. Troy, to her relief, was fine but fixed to his computer.

"That's enough for tonight," she said.

Troy mumbled.

She ran a finger down his arm. The lace of her negligee trailed softly after. "Are you ready for bed, Honey?"

He whiffed perfume and shut off the computer.

\* \* \* \* \*

"Good morning, Ms. Summers, This is Grit Griffin from the Bennettville Sentinel calling." Grit was in his kitchen wearing the sweat pants he had slept in and eating a bagel. "I'm sorry to call you at home," he said, "but no one answered at the Tabernacle."

"You're right about that, baby," Zephonia replied. "When I found out I wasn't getting paid, I quit." She too was wearing nightclothes: a black satin gown and a velvet robe trimmed in faux leopard. But she was crouched uncomfortably beside her bed, holding a cordless phone and searching for one furry, hot-pink, bedroom slipper. "Are you calling about Reverend Bishop Reverend Bishop?" she groaned.

"Yes, Ma'am."

Zephonia spotted the slipper under the far side of the bed. "The Barkley and Jordan Funeral Home just called me about arrangements." She groaned again as she stood. "They said he died just after midnight this morning."

"I'm sorry," Grit said, mistaking her groans for profound sorrow. "So they have the body?"

"Yes, they wanted to know if the church was going to be in charge of the service and who would be paying. I just gave them a list of deacons; I don't have to deal with any of that any more!" Zephonia found the broom and sighed, "Thank you, Jesus; I have laid my burden down."

Grit applied more empathy. "I certainly understand how being personal secretary to such a busy man might be difficult."

Zephonia stooped and shoved the broom under the bed. "Nobody knows the trouble I've seen," she moaned.

"I'm sure they don't." Grit said, foregoing any further condolences. "Would you mind giving me some information for Reverend Bishop Bishop's obituary?"

"What did you say your name was?" Zephonia fetched the slipper with a mighty tug.

"Grit Griffin. I'm with the paper."

Whump! She landed on her Rubenesque derriere and dropped the phone. It slid under the bed and skidded to the far wall. Grit was treated to a cacophony of thumps, static and whistles.

Zephonia thrust the broom again and retrieved the phone on the first try. "Are you still there, baby? I'm sorry about all that. What were you saying?"

"Grit. Grit Griffin, with the Sentinel."

"Why, I saw your name in the paper this morning! That was you hurt in that explosion!"

"Yes, Ma'am, that was me. I mean I was him. I mean . . ." Grit's pronouns were a little shaky.

"But I thought the paper said 'Grin', 'Grin Griffin.'"

*Curse Chilly Rivers*, Grit thought.

"Does somebody have to pay?" Zephonia asked.

"Excuse me?"

"The obituary. When Aunty Solemnity died, the funeral home charged us one hundred and fifty dollars to put her obituary in the paper. And then the paper charged one hundred dollars per column inch to publish Aunty Euphoria's commemorative poem. It was three pages, type-written."

"No there won't be any charge. Reverend Bishop Bishop was a public figure. His obituary will be news."

"Aunt Solemnity's obituary was news to me," Zephonia declared. "That woman buried three husbands and had children by all of them. The list of survivors looked like a page from a phone book."

"About Reverend Bishop Bishop," Grit tried again. "I have the basic information, but I want to show a side of him that others may not know—any acts of kindness or benevolence done out of the spotlight."

"That man did love the spotlight. Unh huh! And he had plenty of secrets. You could say he was benevolent—benevolent to himself." Zephonia laughed.

Grit put his phone on speaker and picked up his notebook and pencil.

"Is that something you would like to talk about?"

"Baby, I've been talking to the IRS and the police, but I'm not supposed to tell you that much."

"What can you tell me?"

"I can tell you I gave information to the police that I did not give to the IRS ."

"What sort of information?"

"The sort that is going to put several people in jail. That's all I can tell you, but, if you have connections with the police, you can get the rest yourself."

Grit put down his notebook, said a quick goodbye and was ready to cut off the call and phone Hunter.

"Wait!" Zephonia commanded. "I just remembered something good The Reverend Bishop did in secret."

Grit picked up his notes, and Zephonia kept talking.

"Once a month a group of ladies met with him here at the building. I . . . uh, happened to find (Zephonia saw no need for details) the journal he kept of the meetings. Every one of those ladies was a preacher's wife, and every one was having husband troubles, and I'll tell you, from what I read, it's a good thing two of those husbands are dead; if that journal had got out, it would've killed them!"

Grit wasn't sure if she meant the ladies or the husbands, but he knew one thing, he wanted that journal, for a lot of reasons.

"Do you still have it?" he asked.

Zephonia considered saying no. It would give her two options: she could either sell the book and its damning secrets or she could destroy it.

Grit waited.

Zephonia decided that blackmail was not one of her vices, but gossip was. She would neither sell nor burn the book.

"If I let you see it," she asked, "what do you plan to do with it?"

Grit was as direct as possible, "I believe whoever tried to kill me killed Bishop and two other preachers. That journal could lead me to the killer."

For once Zephonia had nothing to say.

"Could I meet you somewhere and look it over?" Grit asked.

"I don't know." Zephonia sounded frightened. "Could you keep me out of it? I mean, I don't want to get caught up in any murders. Theft and tax evasion is as far as I want to go."

Grit saw a chance. "That journal will have to go to the police. If you give it to me, I don't have to tell them where it came from."

"Really?"

"Really," Grit assured.

"Okay," Zephonia said. "I'll meet you at the Tabernacle in half an hour. I'll be at the back door."

Grit said goodbye again, finished the bagel and called Hunter. He and the detective agreed to meet in a couple of hours, giving Grit ample time to read and make a copy of the journal before turning it over. He would stop at the paper and spit out a "just the facts, Ma'am" obituary before going on to the police station. He wondered what sort of incriminating evidence Zephonia had shared with Hunter and if the detective would be willing to share with him.

In any case, Grit would have an astounding amount of information to reveal at the Deep Water meeting that evening.

\* \* \* \* \*

Grace was still in bed. She had spent the last seven days walking on eggshells because of her mother's condition, and the effort was exhausting. Her father's death and the possibility that he had been murdered shook and depressed her. She resented spending all of her vacation and sick days confined to the preacher's house, and she was beating herself up for it. She felt shallow and selfish; everything was wrong. She needed a haircut, most of her clothes were in her apartment, and she missed her coworkers.

She got out of bed and looked in the antique mirror over her dresser. Her hair was hopeless, and her features were drawn. *You don't have a choice*, she told herself, *it's time to count your blessings.* She thought of Grit. *He's recovering well, and whether he knows it or not, he loves me!* She thought of her mom and her friends. *Mamma seems to be doing better. Maybe I can go back to work soon.* Then she remembered, *The Divers are meeting here tonight! Yeh!*

She did not have much information to reveal at tonight's meeting. Tabitha Albrighton had declared she never had Thomas' Bible and that it was not on view during the funeral. "I wondered why it wasn't there," she said, "but I assumed Dinah took it home with her."

Grace wondered if anyone would ever see the book again, but she still rejected Grit's theory that the killer took it as a souvenir. Killers only do that in fiction. As to Grit's Bible, she was certain it was under the pile of speakers at Deep Water. She would call Joe to see when the police would let someone look, but first she dressed and combed her hair.

In the kitchen, Dinah's breakfast things soaked in the sink. Grace checked outside where her mother fervently wielded a hoe. Grace fixed herself a bowl of cereal and called Joe. He had good news and bad news; the cleanup was complete, and most of the Divers' instruments, computers, speakers, and monitors were salvaged. But no one had found Grit's Bible, and all of the stuff they had left needed to be hauled out by Friday.

"I'll pass that along to everyone tonight," Grace said. "We'll take care of it." She did not want to hear the answer to her next question. "How much did the cleaning cost you?"

"Don't worry about it," Joe said. "Y'all took several hundred square feet of unusable space and made it useable. I'm coming out of all this pretty good."

"Are you sure?" Grace asked.

"Sure." Joe said. "Tell everyone, thank you."

"I will," Grace said. "Thank you, too." Grace counted another blessing and dialed Grit to tell him the good news. Someone beeped in. Grace pushed "call" and answered the beep, "Hello."

"Hello, this is James Hartford of Hartford and Hampshire. Are you the party who called about the insurance claim at Bennettville One True Church?"

"Yes. I'm Grace Willis, Thomas' daughter."

"Ms. Willis. We are preparing an official report to the police, but I'm sure you would also like to know what we found in our investigation last night."

Grace held her breath as Hartford continued.

"The heater wires were most certainly chewed through by rodents," he said.

Grace said a silent, Hallelujah.

"But," he continued, "I'm afraid the inspector found traces of peanut butter."

"Peanut butter?" Grace felt as if she had stepped through the looking glass.

"Yes, someone spread peanut butter on the heater wires and probably furnished the rats as well. I'm very sorry, Ms Willis; your father was murdered."

Grace gasped and began to cry. She ended the call as quickly as possible, picked up her cell and hit speed dial for Grit.

\* \* \* \* \*

Cupcake, the quirky café where Kale waited for Grace's friends, was one of several small shops, collectively called "Mack's Alley," located in the back of a nineteenth century warehouse three blocks north of Holy City. It served specialty sandwiches and extravagant desserts and was a favorite hangout for a group of students at New Jerusalem College who were neither socially nor spiritually chosen: those few who fell into the gap between the materialists and the zealots. The café's jazzy, avant-garde, atmosphere encouraged open-minded thinking and spiritual exploration. As a result, New Jerusalem's board of directors did all they could to discourage patronage of said establishment.

Kale took a seat near the front and watched the contrapuntal dance of hurried and leisurely shoppers moving rhythmically along the sidewalks. He spotted Julie and Tanya half way down the block obviously scanning signs and addresses. Julie, a young, single mom who worked with Grace at the car dealership, swayed seductively through the foot traffic wearing high-heeled sandals, a crocheted halter-top, and a pair of skintight capris as shiny as her tower of black hair.

Tanya wore dress slacks, comfortable shoes, and a short-sleeved blouse, her typical outfit for work at the downtown library. Her shoulder length hair fit close to her head in narrow, even cornrows that fell into soft braids. Kale remembered her saying she and Grace had been friends since high school.

If Kale had been attracted to a particular "type" of woman, at least one of these two ladies would not have fit the mold, but Kale liked women, period. He was not good looking or svelte, but the universal admiration and acceptance he bestowed on all shapes, sizes, colors, and temperaments won him plenty of female admirers—the most fervent of whom, though neither she nor Kale realized, was Maggie.

Kale greeted the two women at the door, showed them to his table and handed them menus along with recommendations. By the time the waitress noticed their arrival they were ready to order.

While they waited, Kale learned that the two had met at Deep Water—at Grace's invitation. Kale felt compelled to explore each of their spiritual situations before asking about less important things like murder. When the high-stacked sandwiches arrived, he and the ladies talked around awkward, sloppy bites.

"Grace's different," Julie said, "not judgey. She don't like what I do, but that's because she cares about me . . . and my babies."

"She has this way of letting you know she has your best interest at heart," Tanya added. "She really listens. She has . . . well," She smiled wryly, "Grace."

"I wanted to see her church." Julie said. "See what was goin' on."

"I've been to her dad's church a few times, but Deep Water is different," Tanya said. "I certainly hope y'all can get it back together." She motioned to the waitress and asked for a to-go box.

Kale wiped his chin and swallowed, "We do too," he said. "But we have to find a new place; The Dive can't insure us."

"What?" Julie asked.

"Liability insurance was too expensive even before the explosion," Kale said, "and now . . ."

"They say that in the paper!" Julie exclaimed. "'Explosion'. But I jus' hear 'pop', 'pop.' An' the lights go out an' I feel my way to that hall an' see the candles an' zip!" she motioned.

"Did you see anything or anyone on your way out?" Kale asked.

"No." She fishtailed her arm in an approximation of her path, "through the crowd, out the door, down the hall an' up the stairs; jus' gone!"

Kale and Tanya laughed.

"I'm sorry, I have to get back to work," Tanya said, standing. "But I want to tell you what I told the police. They didn't put it in the paper." She picked up her unfinished drink, her to-go box, and her purse. She pulled out a ten-dollar bill.

Kale shook his head and grabbed the ticket. "Next time," he said, then, "What did you see?"

"It could be nothing, but there was a box about the size of a cigarette lighter taped to the underside of our table. You remember where we were sitting?"

Kale nodded.

"Anyway, when I set down my purse I saw it."

"What did it look like?" Kale asked.

"It could have been a timer or a camera, even a bomb, I guess. I didn't think much about it at the time, but now I'm thinking, thank God it didn't explode!"

# 23

# Books of Revelation

"FIRST SAMUEL FIVE, VERSE THREE." Grit said. "I looked it up." He thrust his open Bible under Hunter's nose and read, "'His name was Nabal and his wife's name was Abigail. She was an intelligent and beautiful woman, but her husband was surly and mean in his dealings.'"

Detective Hunter had been sitting somewhat peacefully behind his desk when Grit charged in waving two books and a videodisk. Startled, Hunter nearly went for his gun. His heart was still pounding, and Grit wasn't finished.

"Each of the women who met with Bishop at the Abigail meetings was married to a 'surly, mean' man. All of those men were preachers, and two of them, along with Bishop, ended up dead."

Hunter made his assailant back up, literally, and explain himself. Grit showed him Bishop's journal and connected the dots.

"And those two dead preachers are Willis and Lawson," Hunter deduced, but he remained puzzled. "I can see how that might make the deaths more coincidental, but it doesn't point to murder."

"I read the whole journal. The problems those ladies were having with their husbands were the same as their sermon topics for Commandment Sunday. See . . ."

Grit handed Hunter the list of sermons from the paper with Lawson's "Thou Shalt Not Commit Adultery" and Willis's "Thou Shalt Not Bear False Witness" highlighted.

"Bishop recorded that Martha Lawson said Newell had extramarital affairs for years, and Dinah Willis called Thomas a liar."

"Not as unusual as you might think." Hunter countered.

"But my talk that night was about "honoring your father and mother, and I have struggled with that forever."

"And someone definitely tried to harm you."

"Yes."

**"She's a PK, man. You're an also ran.**

**Don't you get too close, cause the Holy Ghost,"**

Grit fumbled in his pocket,

**"gonna' take you down, better turn around,**

**get your go on dude—"**

"I'm sorry," he said. "That's Grace. She wouldn't call unless it was urgent." He opened his phone. "Grace?"

"Grit, oh Grit! I . . ." She was crying. "I know you're in the middle of something, but . . ." She hesitated then blurted, "It was murder. Someone murdered Daddy!"

"Where are you?"

"At Mother's. I haven't told her. I can't, but . . . how soon can you be here? I really need you."

"It could be another . . ." Grit looked to Hunter for confirmation, "hour?"

Hunter nodded.

"Will you be OK?"

Grace sniffed. "Yeah, I guess so. I'm just confused." She paused, "and angry."

Grit's end of the conversation made Hunter uneasy; he mouthed, "What happened?"

"Just a second, Gracey." Grit lowered the phone and spoke to the detective. "Her father's death was murder."

Hunter scowled. "Not according to the insurers and my investigators."

Grace overheard. "Grit, Grit!"

He put the phone to his ear. "Yeah?"

"Tell Hunter that the insurance company found new evidence. They are sending him a report."

"I'll let you tell him." Grit handed the phone to Hunter.

Grace related all that Hartford had told her and gave the detective the insurer's number.

Grit regained the phone, assured Grace he would be there as soon as possible and ran out of words. He was, conversationally speaking, at the place where someone needed to say "I love you."

"I . . . I'm really sorry," he said, then added, "Bye, Gracey."

He was getting closer.

Hunter ignored Grit's discomfort and went back to business. "If Willis's death was murder," he said, "that certainly complicates matters."

"And it fits in with my theory that all these incidents were related," Grit replied. "This whole mess is going to get worse before it gets better."

Hunter scanned Bishop's journal.

"If this information got out, it could ruin some powerful people. I wonder . . ." Hunter nodded thoughtfully. "You and your friends have blown a couple of big holes right through this case." He looked directly into Grit's face. "And I appreciate it."

"I've got more," Grit pulled out the DVD of Lawson's death. "You have to see this."

Hunter went to a file cabinet and pulled out an old-fashioned ledger. "I have a feeling I'm going to be needing any information you come up with, so I will let you in on something you might be able to use in your investigation."

Grit immediately recognized The Reverend Bishop Bishop's handwriting. Lists of numbers and names of various auto shops filled pages dating back at least ten years.

"What is it?" Grit asked.

"VIN numbers. Every number on these pages is a car reported stolen in Bennettville or surrounding areas. Bishop was running an auto theft ring."

"Why, in . . ." Grit barely stifled an oath. "Why would he keep a record? This could have sent him to prison!"

"It mostly kept him out. Anyone involved didn't dare turn him in; with this, he could take them down too."

"So more than one person might want to see Bishop dead?"

"Yes," Hunter said. When we found the register, we came to the same conclusion and ordered an autopsy on Bishop." Hunter said. "The results should be in any day."

Finally, Grit thought.

Hunter pointed to the register. "We're looking in here for suspects."

Grit scanned the incriminating pages and saw dozens of names, among them three area auto dealers, two pawnshops, and, to his dismay, Crutcher's Tow and Stow.

"Oh Hell!" he said, and he meant it.

\* \* \* \* \*

A team of four Internal Revenue Agents set up shop in Reverend Bishop Reverend Bishop's office in the Greater Bennettville First Methodist/Episcopal/Baptist/Holiness Alpha and Omega International Tabernacle and spent three days examining the good Reverend Bishop's papers, computer files, and financial records. They checked his phone bills, froze his bank accounts, put liens on his real estate holdings and scoured his hard drive; every name, date, or location; every deal, trade, or contract. One of the first things the investigation determined was that Reverend Bishop Reverend Bishop had created Dr. David J. Morgan in the same way Dr. Frankenstein had created his monster, by combining pieces of the dead: photo from one, social-security number from another, credentials from several. Together Bishop and his monster perpetrated financial mayhem.

The agent in charge of the investigation estimated that, after paying overdue taxes and penalties and settling lawsuits by auto insurers, Tabernacle members would be lucky to retain the building and some of the pews; everything else would have to be sold.

Before leaving with twelve boxes of evidence, the revenuers interviewed every deacon, elder, and member on the Tabernacle's roll; each answered truthfully that he or she knew nothing about the financial dealings of the congregation.

\* \* \* \* \*

Grace called her mother in from the garden. Dinah left her hoe in the garage, stopped at the kitchen stoop and stomped her feet. Rich black soil made soft, dusky footprints. She sat and pulled off her boots.

"You haven't eaten," Grace reminded her through the screen door, "and Grit will be over in about an hour. I thought you might want to clean up and eat a little before he gets here."

After half a day working in the heat, Dinah agreed she needed to eat and shower, probably in that order.

"That way, I'll be upstairs when Grit gets here," she said. "You can make my excuses to him and to your friends tonight."

"Are you sure?"

"Yes, I've got more of Thomas's things to go through and a few more letters to write."

Dinah's non-reaction to having the Divers over surprised Grace. Dr. Marvel's prescriptions were obviously dampening Dinah's fire. Grace wasn't sure that was a good thing, but she hoped it would make telling her mother about Thomas's murder less traumatic, and perhaps loosen Dinah's tongue.

While Dinah went upstairs to wash her face and hands, Grace reviewed the questions she intended to ask her mother over helpings of thawed-out casserole: *First, who was Abigail? Second, what was Dinah doing with Reverend Bishop Bishop every month? And last, why did she want Thomas buried in Texas?*

*Maybe I'd better ask the third one first*, she thought. *Asking the others will make Mother wonder where I got my information. Then the Bishop question*, Grace reasoned. *I got that one from her date book.*

She would hold off asking about the photo. *The Abigail in the picture could be a neighbor or a distant relative—not that important.* She waited until her mother was seated opposite her at the table and blessed their mystery meal before asking her first carefully worded question.

"Mom, You didn't tell me why you want Daddy buried in Texas."

Dinah did not look up from her plate, but Grace saw the color drain from her face.

"No, I guess I didn't."

Dinah was being careful also, but Grace was not giving up.

"I don't know of any family there."

Dinah looked up; her fork hovered, shaking.

"No, you wouldn't" Dinah gave Grace a hard look.

Grace grew frightened and even more frustrated. She tried a direct question.

"Then why do you want to bury Daddy there?"

Dinah strangled her fork in whitened fingers and lowered it slowly to her plate. Heavy tears made craters in her overcooked food. Grace ran around the table, threw her arms around her mom and led her to the living room couch where they sat, hugging and crying for several minutes.

"I'm sorry, Momma; I'm sorry. I didn't mean to hurt you."

"I am fine," Dinah said, blowing her nose. "I've been wanting to tell you everything for a long time."

Something about her mother's tone reminded Grace that many long-kept secrets are better left alone. She tried to take her questions back.

"It's Okay, Momma. We can bury him in Texas. I don't need to know why."

But Dinah had begun, and Grace could not hold back the tide.

"You were just a few weeks old when your sister, Abigail, died of acute leukemia," Dinah began. When she finished, Grace knew that keeping Abigail and her death a secret had been her father's idea. Somehow, to Thomas, keeping Grace ignorant made it all go away: He and Dinah had one daughter. Abigail never lived. Abigail never suffered, and Abigail did not die. The few family members who knew of the secret were warned not to speak of it. Thomas had denied his own grief so completely that he could not comfort his wife in any way.

"I found Bishop's self-help group three months ago." Dinah said. "The name seemed like a sign from God. I don't know what I am going to do now that Reverend is gone. He and the Abigails were the only people I could talk to."

"You can talk to me, Momma. I want to know everything." Grace remembered Dr. Marvel's questions about previous trauma. "And you need to tell Dr. Marvel."

"You're right. He needs to know."

The doorbell rang.

"That's got to be, Grit, Momma. I'll let you get upstairs before I let him in." Grace caught her mother's arm. "I need to share this with him," she said.

"That's fine, Gracey. No more secrets."

Grace felt a sudden surge of guilt; she had not told her mother about Thomas's murder.

The bell rang again.

"Hold on, I'm coming!"

Grace let Grit in as her mother hurried upstairs. She reached for Grit's hand, but it was full of papers. She gave him a questioning look.

"Copies of evidence," he said. "I'll show you later."

She took him to the kitchen, poured two cups of coffee, then showed him the picture of her sister.

"It isn't real to me yet," she said. "I had a sister." She sighed. "Actually, I have a sister—in heaven." Grace had a sudden thought, "Oh Grit! She's up there with my dad!" She smiled a wide, wet smile.

Grit kissed her softly by way of saying, "Yes," grabbed a napkin and dried her tears.

He pulled two stacks of stapled pages across the table, "I want to show you something. It's a record Bishop kept of his auto thefts."

"His what?"

"He was running an auto theft ring." Grit opened to a page and pointed. "'Crutcher's Tow and Stow'," He said. "Buddy and his dad will probably be arrested for auto theft and selling stolen auto parts."

Grace thought she might start crying again.

"I intend to do all I can to help Buddy beat this," Grit said. "But I'm not going to say anything until I know he's in trouble."

Grace said she would do the same, and Grit pulled out Bishop's Abigail meeting notes, explaining what they contained.

"You mean Bishop recorded everything that was said?" Grace asked.

"No, just the juicy stuff." Grit waved the stapled pages. "He had enough dicey information in here to blackmail ten or eleven very influential men."

Grit pointed to an angry, bitter quote from Dinah. Grace cringed.

"I think mother would rather die than have this get out," Grace said. "Promise me you won't show them to anyone."

"I gave the police the original; it's evidence in two murders."

"How?"

"Remember Ricky's theory that whoever did the killing was punishing hypocrites?"

"Yes."

"Well, this journal proves that Lawson was an adulterer and your father was a liar. It may even prove that Bishop was a blackmailer and a thief. The killer knew all that, saw the sermon titles when they were published at the first of the year and decided to rid the world of a few hypocrites."

Grace sat very still and looked at Grit appraisingly. Clearly he wasn't thinking about how his words sounded to the daughter of one of those "hypocrites." The accusation, especially because it was true, disconcerted and pained her. She rose to clear away the dishes and change the subject.

"Do you think I should get out the desserts for the meeting? I've had them in the freezer for almost a week."

The promise of food could take Grit's mind off anything.

"Sure," he said, "If the rest turn them down, Kale and I aren't picky."

Someone opened the front door and shouted, "Knock, knock."

"Look who's here," Grit said.

Kale and Maggie let themselves in.

# 24

# If at First You Don't Succeed

AT THE PREVIOUS DIVERS MEETING in the Willis' living room, Grace had elected to sit on the floor rather than squeeze onto the couch or perch on the arm of a chair. Tonight everyone had a conventional seat because Buddy was twenty minutes late. No one had heard from him. After Grit texted him several times with no reply, Ricky volunteered to check on him after the meeting.

Grit led an opening prayer with a special plea for Buddy, but he rushed it a bit; he wanted as much time as possible after the meeting and before his late shift at the bar to be alone with Grace. But Grace was in no mood for romance. Grit's casual reference to her father's hypocrisy was not sitting well on her stomach, and a few other organs weren't happy either.

Grit proceeded unaware of the chill.

He noticed Amber taking notes. *Speech teachers can get through a meeting faster than anyone*, he thought. He handed her a rolled up magazine. "Your gavel, Madame President."

Amber took it with a puzzled look, but thought of the possibilities—the most enjoyable of which was getting Kale's goat. She stood behind her chair and hammered for silence.

"The meeting will come to order," she said. "We have a lot to cover tonight, and Grit and Grace want us out of here as soon as possible." She gave a sidelong look at the couple. Kale whistled and hooted, and Grace flushed.

"So," Amber continued, "we're going to follow Robert's Rules of Order."

Kale groaned and gulped down a laugh.

"Cut it out," Grit told him.

Amber proceeded, "The first order of business is the minutes from the last meeting." She addressed empty space. "Madam Secretary, would you please read the minutes from our last meeting?" She picked up a notepad, assumed the role of secretary and leafed through the blank pages, "I'm sorry, Madam President," she said to herself, "we have no minutes from the last meeting."

Kale covered his mouth and turned red trying not to laugh. Grit shot him a look.

Amber resumed the role of president. "Thank you, Madam Secretary; we will now proceed to any unfinished business."

Kale fled through the front door to laugh or die, and Amber died laughing.

When she came up for air and Kale reentered, she handed him her pad and pen, "Would you please take the minutes? We need a secretary."

Rather than admit incompetence, Kale proceeded to take the following notes:

2nd Order of Business, Member Reports

Grit's Report

1. Lawson's death was murder – confirmed by insurers to Grace.
2. Bishop has been blackmailing people and running an auto theft ring.
3. Grit is writing a bio of Bishop for the paper.
4. He is writing a feature story about "Moses" with a tie-in to the "Prophet" letter and needs volunteers to watch him – Moses.

Moses Watchers, Wednesday, 6 A.M. – Friday, 12 P.M.

The following persons will park in the men's dorm parking lot, watch Moses and follow if he leaves; the object being to find out who Moses is and if he had anything to do with the murders and/or the letter:

Grit – 6 a.m. to noon

Troy & Amber – noon to 6 p.m.

Kale & Maggie – 6 p.m. to midnight

Ricky (& Buddy?) –midnight to 6 a.m.

Grace's report

1. Her father's Bible has disappeared – last seen at the viewing.
2. Grit's Bible was not found after the cleanup at Deep Water.
3. We need to get our stuff out of there - Deep Water—by Friday.
4. Joe thanks us for fixing up his basement, and we do not have to pay for the damages!!!

Troy Reports

1. The murderer could have been almost anywhere at the time of the explosion and probably used a cell phone to set off a simple stage "pot"— see handout.
2. Four such pots could have knocked down the speakers and dislodged the monitors.

Maggie Reports

1. Bishop's Bible is not at his church; was last seen at the hospital on the night he died.
2. That makes four missing Bibles, probably stolen by the murderer.
3. The murderer may have mounted a camera near the stage to determine when to set off the explosive.

~~K~~Kale Reports

~~Tonya~~ Tanya, one of our visitors, saw something that ~~was~~ could have been a miniature camera ~~fastened~~ taped to the bottom of her table. ~~K~~Kale asked the police to look for ~~goo~~ tape residue.

Ricky Reports

1. Someone took the glass and the Bible from Pastor Lawson's pulpit, and Ricky has the DVD to prove it.
2. Grit thinks it was a woman.
3. Grace thinks it was a man.

Madam President asked for further business. There were no takers. It was moved and seconded that the meeting be adjourned. The vote was Aye.

Kale closed the notebook and handed it back to Amber.

It was nearly nine, and Grit would need to leave for The Dive in forty minutes. He hinted broadly for everyone to go, and when subtlety failed, said, "Time to go. Grace and Dinah need their house back."

"I forgot," Amber said. "We haven't set a time or place to meet."

"And we need to talk about a permanent meeting place," Grace added. "And we haven't really discussed our investigation."

"Can everyone meet," Grit thought fast, "Sunday night at Deep Water to clean out our stuff? I'll find a possible meeting place between now and then, and we can check it out after." Grit waited for reactions.

Ricky frowned, "What time?"

"Seven?"

No objections. Grit remembered their lost lamb.

"Ricky, call me when you find Buddy."

"Will do."

Kale raised his hand. "I make a motion . . ."

Grit grabbed him by the back of his collar and shoved him toward the door.

"Out," he said. "Everybody!"

The laughing friends escorted Kale out the door leaving Grit and Grace to deal with unfinished business.

\* \* \* \* \*

Maggie marveled at how much easier getting her mom into bed was with Kale's help. Afterwards, they sat on the front step and talked of a time when Maggie and Loretta could be freed from alcohol.

"Has your mom ever been in rehab?" Kale asked.

"Right after Daddy died," Maggie said, "his coworkers looked in on us. When Mom started drinking the first time I was about seven. Some of them saw to it that she got help, but I don't remember exactly what. When she started up again, I was twelve, and we were alone."

Maggie and Kale talked into the morning. He learned of Maggie's dream to be a news anchor, and she discovered that he had three younger sisters; he didn't run when girls cried, and he could do some crying himself.

Just before dawn, they talked to God.

\* \* \* \* \*

Grit settled into the couch and draped his good arm across the back ready for Grace to slide on in, but she sat primly across the room in a straight-backed chair. Her contemplative stare reminded him of his Aunt Pythia's purebred Siamese.

"What's wrong?" he asked, thinking, *Might as well get it over with.*

"Nothing's wrong," she said. Her eyes were damp.

Grit knew he was in trouble.

"I just need to let you know how I feel about this . . ." she searched for words, "this murder thing with my dad."

Grit wondered why she couldn't tell him up close and personal. He wanted to hold and comfort her.

She regained her tongue, "You don't seem to understand what you imply when you start speculating." She could be very articulate when she was angry. Clarity and precise vocabulary were her shield and at times her weapon.

Grit was stunned and hurt. "Well then, why don't you tell me? What are we talking about?"

"For one thing, that Abigail journal." She pursed her lips then took a deep breath. "The secret about my sister worried my mother and ultimately hurt me, but that doesn't make Daddy a hypocrite!"

Grit opened his mouth to protest that it was the killer who made that accusation, but Grace wasn't finished.

"Only mother knew about my sister. If you think that was a motive for murder, then you are accusing her of killing all those men!"

"Whoa, whoa, whoa," Grit said. He stood and took Grace's hand. "Slow down, Gracey. Come here."

He led her to the couch, but then wisely kept his hands and arms to himself. She was crying.

"Let's both look at this again," he said. "I'm sorry if you think that I thought that; I did think it, but thinking it doesn't mean I think it's true." Grit did not become articulate when he was upset. "There have to be plenty of others who might get the wrong idea about your dad," he said. "What about the other women at those Abigail meetings?"

Grace froze. "You're right!" she said. "Anyone at that Abigail meeting could think Daddy was lying—Martha Lawson for one, and she had reason to kill Newell. Mother didn't."

Grit felt relieved, but he was still on shaky ground. He worded his next question as carefully as possible.

"Didn't your dad have some run-ins with other churches and other preachers through the years?"

Grace had to admit he did, but this was a good thing; the more suspects, the less suspicion on Dinah. "Yes," she said. "He accused any number of people of heresy. I'm sure they thought he was 'bearing false witness.'"

"And this murderer is not normal, I mean even less normal than most. He could have decided your dad was an alien from Mars!"

"But I thought you said he was reacting to the sermon titles?"

"Yes, but I just wanted you to see we aren't dealing with a rational person."

"So," she pulled away. "We're talking about someone with emotional problems."

"Yes," Grit didn't see it coming.

"Like Mother."

"Yes, I mean, no; I mean . . ."

Grace stood, "Don't you need to be at work?"

"For goodness sakes, Gracey. Don't get angry." A phrase guaranteed to make anyone angry. Grit kept his foot in his mouth. "The police even think I might have something to do with all this, and I didn't have any reason to kill any of those men."

"And mother did?"

"She had as much reason as I did, or more. You told me yourself she wasn't happy and that Thomas wasn't the greatest husband in the world."

"I think you'd better go."

"Yeah," Grit said reluctantly. "I'm working until two in the morning. I'll call you when I get to work."

"No, Mother is asleep."

"Well, I'll see you tomorrow."

"No, I don't want to see you again until this murder is resolved. I can't deal with it."

"What are you saying?"

"I'm saying I don't want to see you until you can tell me my mother had nothing to do with these murders. Can you say that now?"

Grit knew what was hanging on his answer, but he told the truth. "No."

Grace showed him out.

\* \* \* \* \*

Buddy still didn't answer his phone, and Ricky couldn't find him in any of the usual places. He called the radio station, checked the coffee shop and The Cupcake—though the latter typically closed at nine. He cruised a few parking lots and alleys, but did not find Buddy or the Crutcher tow truck. About midnight, he gave up and went home. Just outside his door, his cell signaled an unknown caller.

"Hello?"

"Ricky?" Buddy's tentative voice sounded frightened.

"Buddy! Where are you, man?"

"I, uh . . .my dad and I . . .." It took several tries for Buddy to get to the point.

"In jail!" Ricky woke his neighbors.

"Yeah, they picked us up this afternoon; put the truck in impound."

Ricky went inside. His apartment was about the size of a jail cell and just as cozy. "What's the charge?" Ricky paced between his couch and the TV.

"Auto theft and accepting stolen goods," Buddy said.

"Holy Christmas! You can't be serious."

"Ricky, I'm sorry," Buddy's voice was dead serious. "We're guilty."

\* \* \* \* \*

Usually when Grit pulled a late shift on a weeknight, he could count on business being slow—Tuesdays in particular. But he always had plenty to do. Between customers, he and Joe were up to their elbows in wood polish, floor polish, glass polish, and brass polish. As long as Joe was owner and bartender, The Dive would never become A dive.

Joe plopped down at a table to take a break, and Grit took a final swipe at the mirror behind the bar.

"The Divers decided to meet Sunday night and clear our equipment out." Grit said. "Is that OK?"

"That's fine. I'll leave the basement door open so you don't have to drag all that stuff up the stair."

"I've still got my key."

"About that," Joe said, "I had to change the lock; whoever rigged the explosion and cleaned up the evidence either got in with a key, or snuck down there from the bar. I had a new one made for you, but that's it. No more keys to anyone."

"I understand."

"How's the investigation coming?"

"Amazing! I can't believe I'm being paid to investigate a murder."

"You haven't taken up work as a PI, have you?"

"No, just on assignment for the Sentinel. I'm doing a story on Moses, that character on Thirteenth Street. The editor wants me to tie that old goat to the explosion."

"You're kidding! How could he think Moses had anything to do with it?"

"I got a threatening letter from someone claiming to be a prophet. Since our Moses dresses like a prophet, Combs thinks he could be the crazy who sent the letter."

Joe slammed his bar rag into the trash. "Ridiculous!" He nearly shouted. "You won't get a story out of that."

Grit wondered why Joe seemed to take this Moses business personally. "I might." Grit said, "The real story is Moses' identity, and I'm not going to stop until I get it."

Joe put away his cleaning things and grabbed his keys. "It's about ten minutes to two," he said. "I've got to be somewhere. You know how to close." He opened the cash drawer and grabbed the day's take. "I don't think anyone will be coming in this late," he said. "Go ahead and close us down." He wrapped the cash and credit slips in a rubber band, stuck the bundle into the safe and closed the door. "I'll count that in the morning," he said. "Is your car in the back?"

"Yeah."

Joe handed Grit the new key. "After you get the front locked up," he said, "just go through the basement and out." Joe held the front door open with one foot while he grabbed the menu placard and shoved it inside. "Good night," he said, and left.

Grit locked the doors, made sure all faucets, toilets, taps, and stoves were off then turned out lights, except those behind the bar. He put the numerous polishes back in the cleaning closet and headed downstairs, flipping switches as he went. In the basement, scarred speakers and monitors stood stacked against a wall with folded tables and chairs. Posters and decorations were down and boxed.

The remains of Deep Water neatly sorted and packed for transport saddened Grit more than the jumbled heap left by the explosion. Maybe it was the fight with Grace. Maybe it was the fear that nothing in his life would ever again be settled and safe.

He took one last look. At the far end of the room, to the left of the now missing stage, he saw his jungle drums and felt an urge to stay and pound out his frustrations, but he needed some sleep before the first Moses watch. He set his treasured instruments outside, turned out the light and secured the door. He picked up his drums and squinted into the darkness. Distant street lamps silhouetted Bennettville's eclectic skyline in a dim haze that made The Dive's isolated parking lot even darker. Somewhere close and to Grit's left an engine revved.

He crunched across the parking lot juggling car keys and drums. The nearby engine whined, and wheels skidded in gravel. Three yards ahead he saw his car. Immediately to his right was the metal wall of a dumpster.

Tires screamed. Custom halogen headlamps bloomed and wiped Grit's vision. He needed to move—fast, and he had a drum under each arm. *If I drop the drums and run, I can make it to safety.*

"Not my drums!" Grit screamed.

He threw the drums into the dumpster, grabbed the rim, vaulted over and landed in four days' worth of garbage.

Kerwham! The car hit; the dumpster crumpled, and the open lid clang-clang-clanged against the side. Grit screamed in anger. The murderous vehicle backed up and screeched into the night. Grit lay still, assessing his injuries while the dampness and goo under his back brought back memories of Grace and his kitchen floor. The only part of him that hurt was his heart.

He reached into his back pocket, pulled out his greasy phone and called the police. Caution told him, stay in the dumpster till the police arrive. Pride told him, staying will make you look like a chicken. He reached into his front pocket for his car keys and discovered a good reason to remain amidst the rubbish. He dropped to his knees and gingerly took a Braille survey of only God knew what; visibility inside the dumpster was three inches.

Two police officers arrived five minutes later; Grit was still searching through the slop. They pointed their powerful flashlights over the side, and the metal keys flashed helpfully. Grit handed his dripping drums to an officer and clambered out. He reported what little he had seen and heard, but the unfamiliar officers remained skeptical. Grit could not blame them: a man covered in garbage calls from a dumpster outside a bar at two in the morning? They administered a field sobriety test.

Before Grit was judged sane and sober, he had mentioned every Bennettville VIP he knew, including Detective Hunter. Only then did the police examine the evidence—tire tracks scorched across the parking lot and fresh streaks of deep-blue paint gouged into the dumpster.

Grit was still on the killer's hit list.

# 25

# Minor Prophets

GRACE DRANK SOME DECAF, took a hot bath and went to bed trying not to think about Grit or his suspicions, but ugly, damning evidence whirled and flapped inside her head like flying monkeys.

*The Prophet killed because he or she suspected that Lawson was an adulterer, that Willis was a liar, that Bishop was a thief and that Grit did not respect his parents.*

*Mother knows that Lawson was an adulterer that Daddy was deceitful, and she knows about Grit's troubles with his parents. It's even possible she knows about Bishop.*

*No! Mother had nothing to do with this. She was at church when Lawson died. She was in the hospital when someone tried to kill Grit.*

Grace remembered hearing her mother in the kitchen late the night before her father was murdered. *Mother wouldn't have stayed up cooking Sunday dinner if she planned to kill Daddy and Grit that morning!*

She looked across the room to her dresser. Her tear-stained reflection looked back at her with large, sad eyes. *I will not feel sorry for myself! Grit is wrong. Mother is innocent. I'll prove it! All of the Abigails knew about Lawson's adultery and Daddy's faults, and they could have learned of Bishop's illegal activities just as easily as Mother. Any of them, especially Martha Lawson, could be The Prophet.*

Her list of suspects grew. *Bishop had dangerous political and gaming friends, and a few jealous husbands wanted Lawson dead.*

She thought of Provost Chessman and others who profited from Lawson's death and of their hatred for Deep Water. *What about Bart Crutcher? Bishop would qualify as a thief in Bart's book. Bart hated Lawson for threatening to expel Buddy, and he hated Grit for dragging Buddy into Deep Water.*

Grace had no idea what Bart might have against her father. And she discounted the investigation into Bennettville's Moses as too far-fetched.

*But the mysterious choir member? Why would a choir member take Lawson's water glass and Bible unless he or she wanted to cover up a crime?*

She laid her head on her pillow, went over the list again and fell asleep counting some very black sheep.

* * * * *

Grit showered and settled in for a whole two hours of sleep before his Moses watch at six. His cell rattled with Ricky's ring-tone, and he fumbled in the dark for a second before putting it to his ear.

"I found Buddy," Ricky said.

"Thank God." Grit sat up and flipped on his lamp.

"Not really. He and his dad have been arrested."

Grit groaned.

"They've been charged with—"

"Auto theft and selling stolen goods," Grit completed. "I was afraid this would happen; I just didn't know when."

"But, how . . . ?" Ricky asked.

"I'll tell you tomorrow," Grit said. He did not want to go back over a day that had ended in a dumpster. "I've got to be on Moses watch in three hours, and I need sleep."

"Let me do it."

"But—"

"But nothing," Ricky countered. "You get some sleep and go to Buddy's arraignment. It's at one."

"I would like to be there," Grit said, "but you haven't slept either. That isn't fair."

"You can take my shift at midnight."

Ricky didn't need to twist his arm; nearly being murdered made Grit tired. It only happened once a week or so, and he wasn't quite used to it.

Grit agreed and said thanks. He put his phone on the charger and fell wearily between the sheets. He was cold and sore and, when he stopped to think about it, frightened. He thanked God for saving his life, handed Him his aches, pains, and trepidation and slept.

* * * * *

At noon, when Troy and Amber reported to the dorm for Moses surveillance, only six cars, Ricky's included, were parked in the lot. Ricky loved his slick, chrome-yellow Miata. It was the only material thing, other than unfashionable clothes, a few eating utensils, and books, that he owned.

Ricky slumped in the driver's seat, dreaming. Head back and eyes closed, he dazzled beautiful maidens and unhorsed medieval knights.

Troy jumped out of his van intending to rock the car, pound on the hood and wake Ricky in the most embarrassing manner possible.

Catching on, Amber protested, "Would you want someone to do that to you?" She indicated Moses on the opposite corner. "And we don't need to be making a lot of noise."

"This is a men's dorm. We would draw attention if we didn't make noise. Besides," he said, waving his arm, "do you seriously think Moses has not seen this car?"

Amber had to admit that was not likely, and Troy launched his attack.

Ricky's steed reared and lunged; cannon fire roared. The next shot came straight for his head, and he woke with a shout.

Moses looked over. He and Ricky locked eyes, and Moses waved his sign, "Thou shalt love the Lord thy God and Him only shalt thou worship."

Ricky waved, and Moses looked away.

"So much for stealth," Amber said. "Now what?"

"Now we eat lunch," Troy said.

He and Amber offered to share.

"No, thanks." Ricky said dejectedly. "I need to report to Grit that I have nothing to report."

"Wasn't he supposed to take this shift?" Amber asked.

Now Ricky was embarrassed.

"I took it because I thought he was too tired," he said, rolling his eyes. "Can you believe it?"

"Don't worry, you did the best you could. Go get some sleep." Troy said. "I'll call Grit. Anything in particular he needs to know?"

"Just tell him I'm sorry. If Moses went somewhere to pee or anything else, I didn't see it. So far as I can tell, he was there all night."

"Will, do," Troy said.

Ricky started his engine.

"I'll see you Thursday," he said and rumbled toward home.

Troy and Amber took their lunch and a couple of cushions across the street to a neighborhood park, sat in the shade of a Magnolia and took turns keeping watch.

\* \* \* \* \*

It was a good thing Grit had remembered to set his alarm when he went to bed, otherwise he would have slept right through to Thursday. Instead he was up at 11 A.M.

"Poor Ricky," he thought, "awake in his car for another hour. I couldn't do it."

Grit showered and dressed quickly; he wanted to get to court in time to talk to Buddy and maybe the public defender. He would not be able to do much; he couldn't bail Buddy out or hire him a lawyer, but he could show up.

He dressed less casually for court than he did for church—not having anything in particular to prove to the legal system. He chose dark chinos, a sports shirt, and socks with his sandals. He shaved his head and beard and cleaned under his fingernails. He looked like a perp freshly made over for a court appearance.

Before leaving, Grit sent another text to Grace and pretended she would read it. He was angry—not with her but with himself. He had let himself feel something he had vowed never to feel again—love. He could curse or drink or worse to make it go away, but what he felt for Grace smothered harmful intentions. Grit felt whipped. He loved Grace, but now that he knew it, she was gone.

He drove to the courthouse listening to the loudest CD in his collection, but the heavy beat did nothing to lift his spirits. It slapped against his heart, found every tender spot and left bruises.

Ancient maples, oaks, and magnolias twisted by age and disease towered over the Bennettville courthouse. Under the oldest and most misshapen, two stone tablets embodied truths beyond time or the laws of man. Grit stopped. Three of the Commandments had been defaced: "Thou shalt not bear false witness"; "Thou shalt not commit adultery"; "Thou shalt not steal." Each looked as if it had been attacked with a jackhammer. Bits of marble littered the ground. Beside a fourth Commandment, "Thou shalt honor thy father and mother" someone had written "NEXT" in permanent marker.

Grit called Hunter's cell.

"You need to get over here and see this," he said, as soon as Hunter answered.

"I've seen it," he said.

Grit wondered how Hunter knew what "it" was.

"Across the street," Hunter said, waving. "I'm coming your way. I'm testifying at the Crutchers' hearing."

Grit spotted him, waved, and shut his phone. When Hunter reached the courthouse steps, Grit quizzed him about the defaced tablets.

"Vandalism isn't my department," Hunter said. "By the time someone made the connection between the damage and the deaths, it looked like this. As I understand it, the first two were defaced a few days after Lawson and Willis died. The last one, the day Bishop finally went. 'NEXT' has been there for a week."

"It's obvious the murderer did this," Grit said.

"Or someone who reads the paper," Hunter said, "but if the killer makes good on his threat to kill you, we'll keep an eye on the tablets."

"That will do me a lot of good!"

Buddy's arraignment would start in ten minutes. Grit and Hunter climbed the impressive stone steps to the wide, columned porch and continued through sculpted metal doors to an imposing marble foyer and a row of metal detectors. Another grand, polished stair led to the second floor courtrooms.

They passed through the detectors and continued to the second floor, where they pushed through another set of sculpted doors into a dark-paneled courtroom. They found a seat on an unpadded bench near the judge. There was no time to talk with Buddy or the defender, but Hunter promised to fill Grit in on the state's case later.

Two corrections officers and a bailiff led the first four defendants into the dock. The four, handcuffed and dressed in orange jump suits, included Buddy and his dad. They sat and scanned the pews. Buddy spotted Grit and quickly dropped his head. Grit closed his eyes and wished he were anywhere else. He was not there to witness Buddy's humiliation, but he had no choice. He would explain to Buddy later.

* * * * *

Maggie thought about her and Kale's assignment as she walked from her house to the parking lot.

"Maybe," she said when she saw Kale, "Moses wears diapers."

Kale laughed then apologized, "I'm sorry; I took that out of context. I'm picturing Moses with God on Mount Sinai in a diaper."

Maggie made a face, and Kale elaborated.

"Well, Moses was up there for a long time. I don't know about him, but I wouldn't want to say, 'excuse me, God, I need to see a man about a dog.'"

Maggie would never fully appreciate Kale's sense of humor.

They crossed College and walked over to the park to relieve Troy and Amber. Kale carried a warm bag of Krystals and a couple of Cokes. Maggie had homemade cookies.

"About four thirty," Amber reported, "Moses put down his sign and walked down the street. Troy circled around behind through the alley and saw him go in the men's room at the BP station."

"The restrooms are at the side of the building," Troy said. "He has a key. He was only in there a minute or so, and he came right back to his spot."

"So we know he's human," Kale said.

"Yeah, but that's about it."

"So why don't we just stop him and ask him who he is?" Maggie asked.

"It's been tried," Troy said, "Grit showed me the newspaper clippings. No one has ever gotten him to talk."

"Why doesn't somebody just pull on that beard or tackle him?" Kale asked.

"As a matter of fact, about three years ago someone did, but an anonymous caller got him arrested for assault."

"So what can we do that hasn't been done?" Maggie asked.

"He's got to live somewhere," Troy said. "Moses could have gone home for an hour or two early this morning while Ricky was asleep, but he hasn't left since Amber and I have been on watch, so either you or Grit are going to see him leave at some point tonight. When you do, follow him."

* * * * *

After the Crutchers' hearing, Grit went back to the police station with Detective Hunter to discuss the three ongoing investigations: the auto theft ring, the preacher murders, and Grit's two near-death experiences.

"I was afraid Buddy would be arrested when I saw Crutcher Tow and Stow on that ledger from Bishop's office," Grit said. "How is he implicated?"

"I sent some officers out to local repair shops with copies of the VIN numbers from the ledger. They found stolen car parts in three shops, and the owners all rolled over on the Crutchers."

"So Bart and Buddy have been selling stolen car parts?"

"Yes, they have a chop shop out in the boonies and have sold all over the county for years. Bishop funded the whole thing and took most of the profits."

"I don't believe Buddy is involved in any of that."

"The people we questioned all remember Buddy being part of the operation."

"He's only twenty-one." Grit said. "Is there anything you can do for him?"

"If he hasn't been involved in the business for a couple of years, some of the charges could be dropped, and if he was a minor at the time, his defense could contend he was overly influenced by his dad."

Grit asked the hard question, "Do you think Bart or Buddy had anything to do with Bishop's murder?"

"There's no way to know," Hunter said. "As far as we know, Bishop died of a food poisoning."

"But food poison can be intentional," Grit said.

"But how would you prove it? The weapon is gone; no hope of fingerprints. Anyone could have prepared that tainted cake."

"What about Willis? That had to be murder. And someone is still trying to kill me!"

"We're looking into it, but we haven't tied either Bart or Buddy to Willis, and Buddy was in jail when someone tried to run you over."

*Thank God!* Grit thought. "And Lawson? Bart hated Lawson for threatening to expel Buddy."

"We don't know that Lawson was murdered, either," Hunter said.

Grit stood his ground. "The person who took Lawson's glass and Bible did it for a reason. I believe it was to cover up a murder."

Hunter went to his files. "The day after you brought me that video this was left at the station."

Hunter put on a latex glove and pulled out a drinking glass-- Lawson's. Grit was dumbstruck.

"It came with a note," Hunter said. "No prints on the box or the note." He handed Grit a Xerox copy.

```
This is the glass Pastor Lawson was
drinking from when he died. I strongly
advise you to test it for poison.
```

"We sent the glass to the lab," Hunter said, "and verified the note. The glass is the one Lawson was using. There are two sets of prints on the glass, Martha's and Lawson's, and some additional smudges made by someone with gloves."

"The mystery choir member," Grit said, then remembered, "I saw someone else handle that glass; someone dressed like a flower delivery person. He poured whatever was in the glass on the flowers. He could have put some sort of poison in the glass. Martha refilled it later. That's three people who could have poisoned him: the flower guy, Martha or the choir member."

"You've assumed several things that can't be proven. First the lab did not find any trace of poison in this glass. Skin cells from Lawson were on the rim and in the glass, so it had not been washed. And," Hunter continued, "the person who took the glass and the Bible was the choir member, not Martha or the delivery person."

"And whoever took the evidence sent you the glass to be tested," Grit said. "I don't get it. The murderer wouldn't have any reason to do that."

"Lawson wasn't murdered; he died of a heart attack."

Grit wasn't going down without a fight.

"So where is his Bible?"

"Whoever took the glass has it. Why, I don't know. They obviously cared about the man, or they wouldn't have bothered."

"But why the wig and the strange robe?"

"Plenty of women wear wigs, and she may have just picked up an old robe."

"And the commandments at the courthouse? Just a coincidence?"

"Just some crazy trying to say that these deaths are God's retribution. Anyone who reads the paper could have made that connection."

It occurred to Grit that proving Lawson was murdered might make Buddy a suspect. He changed the subject.

"Do you think the person who tried to kill me is the same one who killed Willis?" Grit asked.

"Anything is possible," Hunter answered, "but we don't have any evidence that connects the two. So far as M.O. is concerned, you couldn't get much further apart than peanut butter and gunpowder."

"I don't know," Grit countered. "Both incidents point to someone with a knowledge of electricity. The murderer had to know which wires to put on the rats' menu and how to rig a cell phone to set off an explosion."

"Neither of which is particularly difficult, but both are ingenious."

Grit landed one more punch. "A murderer that ingenious could have figured a way to make Bishop's and Lawson's deaths look like natural causes."

"Probably. But let's solve the murders we know happened before we look for murders we don't."

\* \* \* \* \*

Kale and Maggie were in the back seat of Kale's hoopty playing Rook by flashlight when Grit showed up for his surveillance shift. He pulled in behind them exactly at midnight and tapped on the back window.

Maggie jumped. "Yikes!"

"Right on time," Kale said looking at his watch. "The stroke of midnight." He did a passing Dracula impression, "The werrrry vitching hour." A dog howled. "Ah," Kale said, "'Childrrrren of the night.'"

"Stop that!" Maggie punched his shoulder. "You're creeping me out!"

Kale grabbed her hand and held it as she playfully tried to land another blow. "One of us had an eye on Moses the whole time," he reported. "He went nowhere and did nothing."

"He's all yours," Maggie added, putting down her cards. "I hope you brought something to read; you're in for a long six hours."

Grit held up his laptop, "I'm finishing my story on Bishop," Grit said, "and I'll be making notes for the Moses story—atmosphere stuff."

"'It was a dark and stormy night'?" Kale asked.

"More like 'Once upon a time'," Grit said ruefully. "This whole Moses angle is just a little too fantastic. There is no way this guy murdered three preachers while standing on a street corner in front of God and everybody."

"Our mystery prophet is due a bathroom break," Kale said, "but after that, I doubt if anything much happens."

"On the other hand," Maggie said, "So far as we could tell, he hasn't eaten or slept, so you may get a scoop." She pointed at the bag in Kale's hand and motioned it toward Grit.

Kale handed Grit the rest of Maggie's homemade cookies. "You have no idea how hard it is for me to give you these," he said.

Maggie smiled and remained in the back seat of the world's ugliest limousine as Kale moved to the driver's seat and chauffeured her home. Grit pulled into the spot they vacated and rolled down his windows. He moved to the passenger seat, pushed it back for some legroom, opened his laptop and started typing.

After two pages of Bishop's bio, Grit switched stories. He produced a plodding paragraph describing Moses' wardrobe, his walk and his lack of grooming before his own bladder began a serious monologue. He was about to abandon his post when Moses set down his sign and ambled toward the gas station. Grit let him get a couple of blocks ahead, followed and waited in the shadows. Moses stayed only long enough to do his business. Grit watched him back to his corner, but as soon as the prophet picked up his sign, Grit hurried back to the station and asked the attendant for a key to the men's room.

The key worked on the first try. Inside the restroom, a distinctly feminine form in jeans and a t-shirt stood at the sink with her back to Grit.

"Uurk!" Grit said. He pushed the door to and heard the lock click back into place. "Excuse me," he said. "I'm sorry."

His bladder continued to issue demands, but his brain began sounding another sort of alarm—a vague sense of recognition.

No, Grit thought. No way.

He wondered how and why a woman was in the men's room and if he should tell the attendant. After another five minutes he decided he would either have to get in, get the key to the ladies' room, or find a bush behind the building. He knocked on the door.

"Go away!"

Grit knew that voice.

"Haley?"

"Go away," she said again.

Grit couldn't wait. He chose the bush option, doing his best to stay hidden while keeping an eye on his ex's escape route. When he finished, he returned to the men's room door and used the key.

# 26

# In the Kitchen with Dinah

GRIT OPENED THE MEN'S ROOM DOOR; Haley Philben sat crumpled and crying in a smelly back corner. She refused his offered hand, but wiped her eyes and came out into the unflattering gas-station glare. She looked bad. Not as bad as a year ago when she returned to Bennettville in shreds, but bad. Grit noticed her hollow cheeks and sallow, cigarette skin.

As much as this woman had hurt him, he felt sorry for her, and more—not love exactly; compassion surely, and a certain need to salvage and protect—a longing for what should have been. He put an arm around her shoulders. She pulled away, still sobbing, full of guilt and fear; afraid this good man would learn how little she had cared for him and how truly insidious her betrayal had been.

He let her finish crying then led her through the back alley to his car. Open garbage cans scented the night. A sickly, stray cat darted from the shadows. Haley flinched and drew close, but distanced herself when they reached the lighted parking lot. Grit opened the passenger side door.

"Please, get in," he said. "We need to talk."

Haley again began to cry, but accepted his invitation. Grit settled into the driver's seat and listened while she briefly told the worst: the horrible trip to Las Vegas and nearly being sold, then explained about being rescued by Joe Uptain.

"So, Moses is a bunch of women," Grit said, laughing.

"Yes, we stay in the women's shelter, and Joe pays us to play Moses while we look for work or go to school."

"Really!" Grit was astounded. Joe had never said a word.

"He helped me through my pregnancy."

"Pregnancy?" Grit's mind jumped from astonishment to terror. He did some quick arithmetic.

"I had a boy. I named him Joseph after Mr. Uptain. He's five months old."

Grit relaxed; he couldn't be the father. He did not object to having children; he just preferred a little notice.

"What are you doing out here so late, anyway?" Haley asked.

"I'm doing a story for the Sentinel about Moses."

"What about him?"

"Someone calling himself 'The Prophet' tried to kill me."

She gasped, and Grit continued.

"I'm supposed to find out who Moses is and if he's responsible for my injuries."

"You can't!"

"I just did."

"No, you can't write that story! You would ruin everything! What would me and all the other girls do? The Moses gig and the women's shelter is all we have."

"No one would stop that just because they knew the truth."

"You don't understand. Joe's dad started all this. It's a . . . what do you call it? A . . . endowment! It's set up so it stops if the secret gets out." Haley seemed near tears. "None of us has ever told." She grasped Grit's hand. "You wouldn't. You can't!"

No, Grit thought. I can't. "Where can I take you?" he asked.

Haley directed him about a mile down College Street to a well-lit corner. He pulled over to the sidewalk.

"I can't let you take me all the way home,' She said. "Some of these women are in real danger from exes. Don't follow me, and don't write that story!"

"I won't," he promised again, but he had to write something.

He drove back toward his apartment lost in thought. Whatever he wrote would have to keep his readers' interest without revealing much of anything about his subject.

Good luck, Grit thought.

Ricky's ring-tone pulled him out of his quandary.

"What's up?" Grit asked.

"I'm in the parking lot ready to start my shift. Where are you?"

*Oh Crap!* Grit held his tongue. "Yeah," He said, "about that. I uh . . . I got all the information I needed. I'm calling off the watch. Sorry I didn't call you sooner."

"So who is this guy? Is he a crazy? Did he murder anyone?"

"To answer your questions: I don't know; maybe, and no."

"You don't know who he is?"

"It's a long story," Grit said, thinking, *It's a long story I can't tell.* But Ricky deserved a better answer. "I really need to get it all down on paper before I start talking." Grit said. "I'd like everyone to read it fresh in the paper, Thursday."

Ricky was being put off, but he didn't push.

Grit apologized again for not calling about the stakeout, and asked Ricky to notify the rest of the Divers.

"Not a problem," Ricky said, but he would wait until later; it was barely 6 a.m. "See you Sunday."

Ricky's salutation reminded Grit that he needed to find the Divers a meeting place, but that too could wait. He stopped at his mailbox before going into his apartment—a new daily habit—and was relieved to see nothing but bills. He washed down the last of Maggie's cookies with a glass of milk and hit the sack.

* * * * *

Ricky sat down on the futon that served as his bed and sofa and tried to relax. He felt anxious, a rare sensation. Sadness, loneliness or melancholy he knew, but this restless, I-need-to-do-something-now feeling was unfamiliar and exceedingly uncomfortable. In most situations, he could act on instinct and deal with the consequences, but something wasn't clicking. Mentally he rounded up the usual suspects: His family? All was well there. His love life? Non-existent, but that wasn't new. He sighed, rested his head on the back of the futon and contemplated the Almighty.

What, he asked, is sitting between me and peace?

Two problems settled slowly to the bottom of his clarifying thoughts. He reached in and pulled out the culprits: his claustrophobic apartment and Deep Water's dislocation. He clearly was supposed to do something about both, and God was going to make that something possible.

He leapt to his feet, forgetting that he and his pillowy futon disagreed on launch procedure, and fell back into the poofiness. He decided to stay another minute or so to ask God for directions. When he finally stood, he had a plan and not much time. "Okay, God," he prayed, "Let's get this done."

\* \* \* \* \*

Grace woke up Thursday with a plan of her own. All she had to do was show where her mother was when the murders took place, and Grit would have to acknowledge that Dinah should not be a suspect.

She dressed hurriedly and found her mother cleaning out the refrigerator. Several nondescript leftovers in various stages of decomposition sat on the kitchen table.

"We still have four casseroles in the freezer," Dinah said. "I'm getting rid of the rest of this."

Grace caught a whiff of over-ripe tuna. "Whew! Bless you. Do you need any help?"

"No, Sorry about the smell. I'll be finished shortly if you want breakfast. We've got eggs and sausage, or I could fix pancakes."

"Thanks," Grace said. "But I'm not that hungry right now." She gave her mother a hug. "I'll be up in Dad's office if you need me."

Dinah closed the refrigerator door. She looked uneasy. "What are you doing in his office?"

"I'm working on something—for Grit." *Well, I will show it to him eventually.*

"Be careful. It's a mess up there."

Grace picked up her mother's appointment calendar from the hall table and carried it upstairs where she gathered the newspaper clippings off of her dresser and walked across the hall to her father's office.

High shelves full of Bibles, commentaries, histories, and reference works loomed overhead. Hazardous stacks of periodicals and sermon outlines littered the floor and camouflaged the desk.

She found paper and pencils in the top drawer and office supplies in others. The bottom drawer was locked. She cleared a space on the desktop, sat down and started writing.

1. Bishop suffers food poisoning at Unity Picnic, Sat. afternoon, May 23
   Goes in hospital Mon., May 25
   Goes on life-support, Sun., May 31, 11:30 p.m.
   Declared dead, Mon., June 8, 11:30 p.m.
2. Lawson collapses at Holy City, Sun., May 31, 9:30 a.m.
   Delivery person empties glass
   Martha refills the glass
   Strange choir member seen taking glass and Bible, 9:32 a.m.
   Declared dead on arrival at hospital.
3. Dad, electrocuted at church, Sun., May 31, 10:30 a.m.

Memories of her father's death and her mother's screams brought tears she didn't bother to wipe. *I will not cry!* She shoved her chair back roughly and spoke aloud to her ugly thoughts, "Mother had nothing to do with it!" She stood, bumping the shelf behind her. A large, leather-bound Bible fell, landed heavily in the chair and opened to Deuteronomy, Chapter 28, the chapter used by the Prophet to threaten Grit!

Grace began laughing, crying, and hiccupping. *Breathe,* she told herself, Slow, deep breaths. She put the Bible back on the shelf, closed her eyes for a moment then continued her list.

4. Grit injured, Deep Water, Sun., May 31, 6:30 p.m.

Thinking of Grit dried her tears and stiffened her spine. *I will prove him wrong.*

It wasn't that easy—the Unity picnic for example. Grace checked her mother's calendar for May twenty-third. "Abigail meeting, M/B/E/H, 8 a.m." was the only entry, nothing to indicate that Dinah had or had not planned to attend the picnic. She could have taken the poisoned cake with her to the picnic or she could have simply delivered the deadly dessert to the church that morning. But so could anyone else! And Bishop was nearly well before his relapse Sunday night. Mother couldn't have had anything to do with the relapse; she was down the hall under sedation.

Grace turned her thoughts to Pastor Lawson. Nothing but poison could have killed him so quickly or mimicked a heart attack so closely. If the poison was in the drinking glass, it was put there sometime between eight-thirty, when the florist delivery person emptied the glass, and nine o'clock, when Lawson began to speak.

Now that she thought about it, Grace could not say where her mother was during that half hour. Typically Dinah arrived at ladies' class just at nine-forty-five. But, if she left the house early that morning, she could have gone by Holy City first. Grace shuddered; the only person who could know for sure is dead.

But, Grace reminded herself, *we have it on video; only four people touched that glass: the flower guy, Martha, Pastor Lawson, and the choir member.*

An inexplicable draft chilled the back of Grace's neck and lifted the scattered papers on Thomas' desk. She checked the tall, casement windows. Dust motes floated undisturbed in slanted shafts of sunlight, but Grace felt cold—and hungry; she hadn't had so much as a cup of coffee since yesterday. She put down her work and went to the kitchen. In the garden, Dinah dumped a bucket of moldy leftovers onto the compost pile and headed toward the back door.

* * * * *

Grit's biography of The Reverend Bishop Reverend Bishop ran in Friday's Sentinel, front page, above the fold, and bylined. Victoria Sellers had taken the day off from her real estate business to catch up at home. She read Grit's story with her morning coffee, turned the page and scanned the Police Report. Bart and Buddy's arrest headed the list. She spent the next four hours reorganizing closets, clearing her email, and trying to ignore the tug in her heart. Meta Crutcher had been her best friend.

When, for the third time, she found herself in the middle of a room, not knowing why, she gave up and called the city clerk. "How would I go about bailing someone out of jail?" she asked.

* * * * *

Dinah came in from work in the garden just as Grace reached the kitchen. "Can I get you something?" Dinah wore her shabby gardening clothes, but this morning she had combed her hair and put on a bra. She had been unusually cheerful the last couple of days, and Grace hoped Dr. Marvel would see the improvement.

"Thanks," Grace answered, "but don't bother. I'll throw something together."

Dinah went upstairs. Grace found some cheese spread, got the Ritz out of the cabinet and cut up some fresh vegetables. She was pouring tomato juice when the phone rang.

"Can you get that?" Dinah called.

Grace caught the phone in the front hall.

"Miz Willis?" the caller asked.

"This is Grace Willis."

"I'm Officer Davis with the Bennettville police. We have recovered two vehicles registered to a Thomas Alexander Willis."

Grace sat down on the stair, confused.

"Miz Willis?"

"I'm here." She did not feel "here" she felt far, far away.

"Are you related to Mr. Thomas Willis?"

"He's . . . I mean he was my father. He died a little over a week ago."

"I'm sorry. I should have recognized your name. This is Officer Davis. I met you during the investigation at Deep Water."

Grace reentered the present. "Yes, I remember. You were saying?"

"We just recovered two vehicles, a cream colored Oldsmobile and a red Taurus, registered to your father. You haven't reported them stolen."

"No, I thought they were still in the church parking lot. We left them there the day Daddy died."

"Could you come down to impound and pick them up?"

"Um . . . sure." Grace got directions.

"Impound closes at six," Davis said. "Your cars were hot-wired, be sure to bring the keys."

"Thank you, Officer. We'll be there."

Grace went back to the kitchen to finish her lunch and consider what to do next. It would take three people, one to drive to the impound and three to drive back. None of those people would be Dinah or Grit. She did not want to upset her mother, and she would not deal with Grit until her mother was exonerated. She called Ricky.

"I'll call Kale and we'll meet you at the preacher's house in an hour," he said.

Grace smeared cheese on one more cracker, washed it down with the last of her juice and went looking for car keys.

Thomas' set was in the box of personal effects returned from the coroner's office. It sat unopened on the third step of the staircase. Grace cut it open and scanned the contents, her father's watch, wallet, ring, and pocket change. His keys hung from a portrait chain Grace had given him at Christmas. She and her mother smiled insensibly from alternating sides of the plastic trinket. Grace shoved it in her pocket, refusing to cry.

"Mom," Grace called up the stairs. "I'm going to get your and Dad's cars. Have you seen your keys?"

No answer. Grace went up to check.

Dinah sat at Thomas' desk reading his Bible.

"Where did you find Daddy's Bible?" Grace gasped.

Dinah laid the book in the bottom desk drawer, closed and locked it. "It was there all along," she said.

"But we left it at the funeral home."

Dinah looked amazed, "Then how did it get in his desk?"

Grace was about to express more disbelief when the doorbell rang.

"If that's Ricky and Kale," she said, "they're early." She asked her mother again if she had seen her keys.

"Not lately," Dinah said. "They should be on the hall table."

Grace checked there again before opening the door to Ricky—and Grit.

"Kale is busy getting ready for a date with Maggie," Ricky said, "so I called Grit."

"Kale and Maggie are getting pretty tight," Grit said, smiling.

Grace bit her lip and turned away. "We can't go till I find Mother's keys," she said. "They could be anywhere."

After a fruitless, twenty-minute search, Grace sat down to think. "The last time Momma had her keys was at church the day . . . ." Grace recovered quickly. "She must have had them with her at the hospital. Her things were packed in her tapestry bag. It's in that closet." She pointed under the stair.

Grit pulled out the bag and handed it to Grace. She looked inside and backed away. "Whew! It smells like something died in there." She took the offending bag to the half-bath and dumped the contents on the counter. The missing keys and her mother's toiletries jangled against the tile but were quickly silenced by the damp, mildewed clothing that landed on top. She wrapped the smelly pile in a large towel, stuffed the keys in her pocket and carried the bundle past Grit and Ricky in the hall. "This will just take a minute," she said.

She walked quickly through the living room to the kitchen and down to the basement. She dumped the mess into the washer and set it on heavy-duty with plenty of hot water and detergent.

When she returned, she grabbed her purse, led Ricky and Grit out the door to her car and drove straight to the impound.

\* \* \* \* \*

If The Reverend Bishop Reverend Bishop had not died of food poisoning, the inevitable investigation into his finances and the subsequent damage to his reputation would have killed him.

Either way, Bishop was dead, and Bennettville, the Methodist/Baptist/Episcopal/Holiness Alpha and Omega International denomination, and the general public anticipated a grand funeral attended by the powerful and covered by the national media. Trouble was, there was no one to pay for the shindig. Bishop's supporters were busy distancing themselves, and The Reverend Bishop's holdings, including the Tabernacle, his cars, and his wardrobe, were being scavenged by his creditors and confiscated by the Internal Revenue Service.

Zephonia had not waited for the legal system to grind out the two-week's pay and severance she was owed. She pawned Bishop's gold fountain pen, his digital Bible, and his hand-tailored cashmere topcoat—three items she hoped no one would miss.

Ultimately, the Handmaidens of the Lord, Bishop's chosen help-meets, sold thirty silver serving dishes from the church kitchen and bought a pine coffin, a cheap plot in an out of the way cemetery, and a modest headstone with the inscription, "Dust to Dust and Ashes to Ashes."

# 27

# Lofty Goals

JUST OUTSIDE THE POLICE IMPOUND, a burly attendant signaled Grace to stop her car. "I need to see identification," he said brusquely. She, Ricky, and Grit pulled out driver's licenses. "Just pull in and park on the other side of the gate house," he said.

Grace parked quickly and gathered her purse as Ricky and Grit disembarked. Grit opened her door. She ignored the gesture and stepped out. Twelve-foot fences topped with razor wire rose on every side, and partially dismantled vehicles languished in ordered rows like cancer-ridden criminals awaiting clemency. Grace weighed the value of retrieving whatever might remain of her parents' cars against spending another minute in this purgatory and decided to get the heck out of Dodge. Before she could retreat, however, the lot attendant approached with a clipboard.

"Just follow me," he said.

She fell in beside Ricky, left Grit to himself and kept her eyes on the cars. A lucky few waited for their rightful owners relatively unscathed.

"Here it is," the attendant said.

Dinah's Olds was not one of the lucky. All that remained was the frame and the roof. Grace was speechless. Ricky too. Grit wisely bit his tongue. He made a closer inspection while Ricky and Grace stayed with the attendant.

"Are you sure this is my mother's car?" Grace asked.

"The VIN number on the frame matches your father's title." He spoke as if he were rendering a verdict. "Thieves always strip older cars like that; their parts fit other models."

Grace took one more look and turned away, chagrined. "I certainly didn't need to go looking for my mother's keys."

"Gracey."

Grace ignored Grit's summons and spoke to the attendant. "Could you take us to Daddy's car now, please."

The man looked down at his clipboard and pointed, "It's over—"

"Gracey!" Grit insisted. He rounded the car with his hands full of clothing. "I'm sorry to interrupt," he told the attendant, "but I think these items are involved in a murder." He turned to Grace. "Have you ever seen these before?"

Grace barely looked. "No!"

Ricky took a good look and exploded. "That's the outfit the guy wore the day Lawson died!"

"You were there?" Grit asked.

"Yeah. I was at the back waiting for Troy and Amber when the guy brought in the second flower arrangement." Ricky took the cap from Grit and inspected. "He was wearing this cap or one just like it."

Grace was confused. "Where did those come from?"

"They were in your mother's car," Grit answered.

Grace's mind raced to dark places. What was mother doing with these things?

The attendant looked aghast. "Are you saying that this stuff is evidence in a murder?"

One leg of the jumpsuit trailed in the dirt while the remainder of the garment picked up incriminating fibers from Grit's red shirt. Ricky fingered the cap absently. They were contaminating exhibits one and two.

Ricky poked the cap toward the attendant. "Here!"

"Hold on!" he said, raising his hands and backing away. "Stay here and don't move." He hurried back toward the gate. "I'll get a bag for those."

Grit looked over at Grace; she was pale and wobbling.

"Gracey!" He threw the jumpsuit to Ricky, caught Grace as she swayed and led her to the nearest derelict back seat. He sat down beside her, but she turned away. He touched her chin, gently. "Hey," He said. "Look at me."

She took a deep breath and looked into his empathetic eyes.

"It's going to be OK," he said. "This may not have anything to do with your mother."

"But I . . . but she . . ." Grace babbled.

"Those clothes could belong to the guy who stole her car," Grit said.

Grace buried her face in Grit's chest. Great, wracking sobs shook her body and his. He held her comfortingly. "We're in this together, Gracey. I'm not your enemy."

She relaxed in his arms.

Ricky approached and handed Grace his handkerchief. "Listen," he said, "why don't you let Grit take you home? We aren't going to need a third driver; your mom's car isn't drivable. I'll stay, turn over the evidence, and see about your dad's car."

Grit and Grace agreed readily.

* * * * *

"Buddy Crutcher?"

Buddy hollered, "Yo," and a balding, paunchy, corrections officer appeared at his cell.

"Somebody made your bail." The guard rattled a heavy set of keys and unlocked the door. "Follow me."

At the property room, Buddy signed for his wallet and keys. They took an elevator to the first floor, pushed through a turnstile and passed booking before reaching the street entrance where Victoria waited. Buddy remembered her face, but not her name.

"Hi, Buddy." She held out her hand. "I'm Victoria Sellers. Your mom was my best friend." A light flickered in Buddy's eyes—sparked by recognition, and hope.

* * * * *

On the way home Grace wasn't ready to talk, so Grit gave her some time. He made sure she and her mother were settled then went to see Joe. It was early, and the Dive was nearly empty. A young couple shared a booth in the back, and four German businessmen chattered at a table. No one sat at the bar. Joe looked up from his polishing. He didn't smile.

"You heard about last night," Grit said. It wasn't a question, and he didn't wait for an answer. "I need some advice. If I don't write something for the paper, I could lose my job. If I write the truth, I could ruin your ministry."

"And lose this job," Joe added without expression.

Grit sank down on the nearest barstool; this was not going well.

Joe poured him a beer. "I didn't mean that as a threat," he said. He reached behind the counter and pulled out a sheaf of papers. "You aren't the first reporter to figure out what's going on or the first to ask me what to write. I just tell them to make something up, the wilder the better."

Whatever Grit wrote, he wanted it to be true. "I'm not very good at that," he said.

Joe slid the papers across the bar. "I started collecting these a couple of years ago for the next Sherlock who cracked our cover. Take a look." Grit did as he was told while Joe explained.

"They're anecdotes and tall tales about Moses that I've heard from my patrons."

Grit took his time reading the narratives then looked up. "These people give Moses credit for everything from mayhem to miracles."

"Yeah, pretty unbelievable."

"Thanks," Grit said, gathering up the papers. "These will save my skin."

"Just be sure to get permission to quote these people," Joe warned. "I wouldn't want to violate bartender/client privilege." He was serious. "My regulars have a certain expectation of privacy."

* * * * *

"Now you and that other guy have both handled the evidence." The impound attendant was back with a couple of small garbage bags.

"He had to go," Ricky explained. "His girlfriend fainted."

The attendant handed him the bags, "Just put the hat in one and the jumpsuit in the other. They're already contaminated, but we'll do it by the book."

Ricky complied and handed the bags back. "I still need to see Thomas Willis' car," he said.

"Right." The attendant checked his clipboard and started off. "Over here."

Ricky followed, looking ahead for the Taurus.

"Tell me again." The attendant continued down the narrow path. He held the bags out to one side. "How are these things connected to a murder?"

"A man wearing that outfit was fooling around Pastor Lawson's pulpit the Sunday he died."

"Wait a minute!" The attendant turned and glared. "Are you saying Pastor Lawson was murdered? I was there. That was a heart attack, plain and simple."

"Well . . ." Ricky began to wonder about following this guy into a deserted junkyard, but he wasn't a communications professional for nothing. "I'm sorry," he said, extending his hand. "I'm Ricky Cruz. I didn't get your name."

"Conley, James Conley." James reluctantly shifted the bags to his left hand, took Ricky's right and apologized, "I just don't believe anyone would want to murder Pastor Lawson."

"You're probably right. The police are looking into an explosion downtown. They think the guy who wore these clothes could be connected to that."

Mr. Conley seemed satisfied, and they walked deeper into the yard—past a dark blue Lincoln with a deep gash in the driver's side door.

Ricky stopped. "Do you know anything about this car?"

"Why do you want to know?"

"My friend, the other guy who was here, filed a police report Wednesday morning. Someone tried to run him over and left a streak of deep blue paint on a dumpster. That gash looks fresh." Ricky looked closer.

James flipped through his charts. "Yeah, this came in last night. It's registered to . . . Holy—" He stopped short, sputtered incoherently and started again. "It belonged to Pastor Lawson!"

Ricky pressed his face to the Lincoln's tinted window. A choir robe, a wig, and a pair of men's dress shoes lay in the back seat. "Call the police," he said.

* * * * *

Grit left The Dive and went back to check on Grace. She looked better, but she still didn't want to talk. Grit walked her out the front door into the sunlight, and they sat on the front step. He took her hand and kissed it, "You're hands are cold." He rubbed them gently, and Grace warmed like a kitten in a window.

Finally relaxed, she poured out her heart, "I tried to prove you wrong about mother, but I couldn't. She could have taken that cake to the Unity Picnic. And she could have been at Holy City before Lawson collapsed."

Grit tried to say, *So could lots of people*, but failed to wedge it in.

"When I saw those overalls, and you said they came out of mother's car, I panicked. I thought she could have put those on over her dress, taken those flowers into Holy City and poisoned Newell Lawson. She knew from the Abigail meetings that Lawson was an adulterer."

"I don't think—" Grit began.

"She wouldn't; she just wouldn't. She wouldn't kill anyone!" Grace wound down.

Grit looked into her eyes. "You don't have to prove anything to me, Gracey. We're going to figure all of this out together."

She smiled. "Your article in the paper was great. I saw your by-line. Congratulations."

"Thanks." He felt as if she had handed him a Pulitzer.

Ricky pulled in the drive. He jumped out, handed Grace her father's keys and started talking—about the Lincoln, the blue paint, the choir robe, and the wig.

Grit had to repeat it all to get it straight. "The Lincoln is tied to Lawson because he owned it. It's tied to Martha because she drove it. Bishop made Bart steal it, and somebody else tried to kill me with it."

"Don't forget the robe and the wig in the back seat," Ricky said. "Whoever took Lawson's Bible wore that stuff."

"Did you find Pastor Lawson's Bible?" Grace asked.

"No. Just a blow torch and some empty cans of instant glass-froster in the trunk"

That last bit of information stopped the conversation.

Grace shook her head, "The pieces make less sense together than they do apart."

"Do the police know about all of this?" Grit asked.

"They came out to the impound before I left. They're probably still there."

Grit laughed. "You know what?"

"No, what?" Ricky countered.

"My brain is fried." He stood up. "I feel like I've been cramming for finals."

"Exactly!" Ricky agreed. "Let the police deal with it. That's what they get paid for. It's Friday night, I'm ready to howl."

Grace looked up playfully. "Is that what you do after finals? Howl?"

He gave her a quizzical look. "I suppose you have a better idea?"

"Shoe shopping?"

Grit laughed. "I'm with Ricky," he said. "We can pick up my drums on the way."

\* \* \* \* \*

Saturday morning Grit was still in bed when the phone rang.

"Detective Hunter wants to see you," Officer Davis said.

Grit threw on some shorts and a t-shirt and was in Hunter's office in fifteen minutes.

Hunter stood looking down at his desk and brooding.

"How's it going?" Grit asked.

Hunter scowled, "It's going nowhere." He waved Friday's paper. "But the bad news is I've got lots of help getting there."

"What do you mean?"

"Ever since your article came out, people from here to Washington are sure Bishop was murdered and think the Crutchers did it. I've told the desk to hold my calls." Hunter sat down and sighed. "If Bart or Buddy did it, and if the cake was the murder weapon, it's been eaten! There's nowhere to go with this."

"It wasn't Buddy." Grit said.

Hunter waved an arm. "Have a seat."

Grit did not want to stay, but he sat.

"It's not your fault," Hunter said, relaxing. "All of this would have come out eventually." Hunter caught sight of the DVD from the Holy City broadcast on his desk, and his blood pressure rose again. "It's not just Bishop they're talking about." He picked up the disk. "A bunch of these got out. The whole Zionist Christian denomination believes Lawson was murdered. I've got a list of suspects as long as . . ." Hunter whacked the disk down on his desk. "I've been watching this gad awful thing myself. Lawson pounds his Bible; Lawson drinks the water; Lawson collapses; the choir member picks up the glass and carries off the Bible—over and over again. I don't get it. The doctors ruled it heart attack. The lab assured me there was never any poison in that glass, and we couldn't do anything about it if there was. Lawson's been cremated."

"It had to be Bart." Grit said. "He hated Lawson; he hated Bishop and he hated me."

"I've come to the same conclusion, but I have no way to prove it unless we get a confession."

"What about the Willis murder?" Grit asked. "Can you connect that to Bart?"

"No. And I've got a murder weapon that could be linked to every soccer mom in the country. Peanut butter!" Hunter said it like an oath. "The one case I've got that doesn't read like a fairytale is yours. I have proof there was a crime, and I have hard evidence—the car and the explosion. But the car links the crime to two other deaths, and the explosion could've been rigged by any high school drama student."

Grit thanked God he was not a policeman. "What can I do to help?" he asked.

Hunter stood, leaned over his desk and looked at Grit helplessly. "I never thought I would say this to anyone," he confided. "Pray for me."

Grit did.

\* \* \* \* \*

Ricky didn't bother to call ahead; he was too excited. He simply showed up on the Michaelsons' doorstep.

"What's up?" Troy invited him in.

"Where's Amber."

"Right here." She came out of the bedroom. "I was on the computer."

"Can I take you two to lunch?"

"We just had breakfast," Troy answered.

"Good, I'll show my surprise first."

The Michaelsons looked at each other and shrugged. "Sure," Amber said. "Give me a minute." She returned with her purse, and Ricky led the couple out to a small, very used Honda.

"Is this the surprise?" Troy asked.

"Where's your Miata?" Amber wanted to know.

"That's part of the secret." They drove toward the center of town past the courthouse. Midday sun shone through the overhanging trees and painted the columned façade with a moving checkerboard.

"Have you heard any more from Chessman?" Ricky asked. "Some of our students won't graduate if he doesn't make allowances."

"Classes resume Monday," Troy said. "The board decided to extend the semester another two weeks."

"We have spies on the board." Amber explained.

"But what are they doing for communications faculty." Ricky said. "How—?"

"Chessman is going to let the communications students take incompletes and finish their classes over the summer by independent study." Troy said.

"Led by . . . ?" Ricky asked.

"Hold on to the steering wheel," Amber said, "Tom Dixon."

Ricky pulled to the curb. "I should have known," he said, furious. "But they had to make some kind of a deal with accreditation. Tom is just finishing his B.A."

"I didn't mean to upset you." Amber said. "Can't you drive?"

Ricky laughed. "Sure," he said. "But we're here." He climbed out.

Troy and Amber peered out their windows at the early twentieth-century neighborhood. It wasn't pretty, but it showed signs of renewal. Dumpsters, overflowing with ripped-out building innards, made the sidewalk nearly impassible. Across the street, a new Starbucks beckoned.

Ricky opened Amber's door and made a grand gesture toward the adjacent building. Plywood covered the large windows, and years of accumulated rubbish littered the entry.

"What do you think?" He asked.

Troy and Amber didn't say.

"You need to see the inside." Ricky unlocked the front door and flipped a switch. A couple of lights at the back revealed abandoned store fixtures and rickety folding chairs.

"It's mine," Ricky said. "I mean, it's ours."

"You and the bank?" Troy asked.

"Me and the bank and my landlord."

"Landlord?" Amber asked.

Ricky laughed. "I signed a long-term lease with God." He hurried to the back of the long room, "Let me show you the loft." The Michaelsons followed into the dark back room, past a small restroom, and up steep stairs. At the top, Ricky repeated his question, "What do you think?"

Troy looked at the dusty, cobwebbed corners, cracked windows, and scarred floors. "What do you plan to do up here?"

"It's his apartment!" Amber guessed.

"Yes!" Ricky said. "And Deep Water can meet downstairs."

"Oh," Troy finally got it.

"This is beautiful," Amber said. "I love the bare brick and the hardwood floors. And the windows!"

"I know it needs work," Ricky said, "but it's so much bigger than my old apartment, and I'll have lots of sun."

Troy was amazed. "This had to cost at least $300,000," he exclaimed. "How did you manage?"

"He sold his Miata," Amber said.

"Oh."

"She was my down payment." Ricky said.

"You shouldn't have." Troy was serious.

Amber shot him a look that meant hush! "Let's see the first floor again," she said.

On the way down, Ricky stomped a few stairs as if he were kicking tires. "It's really solid. Just needs cleaning up."

They reached the bottom. Troy took a look in the tiny restroom. "This is in decent shape," he said, "but you're going to need a full bath upstairs." He pulled the string hanging from the light. The bulb sizzled and went out. "This wiring isn't adequate for our equipment. We're going to be in the same shape we were in at The Dive, no insurance."

"Like I said," Ricky repeated. "It needs work."

"How are we going to pay for all that?"

Amber noticed the "we" and smiled. Troy was on board.

"The building brings in a little income." Ricky explained. "The ground floor is leased to the Bennettville One True Church on Sunday mornings. I plan to sell all of the old store fixtures, and as soon as I find another job, I'll be paying myself rent."

"How is the job hunt going?" Amber asked.

"I'm still in the praying and looking stage."

Troy walked to the front, opened the door and looked up and down the street. "How is it zoned?" he asked, still thinking about money.

"Commercial and residential."

Amber started dreaming. "It's large enough to open an art gallery or rent out studio space."

Ricky pointed up, "Talk to my Landlord."

# 28

# Come to Jesus

AFTER SIX SHORT MONTHS as a public defender, Rantham Fletcher's boyish face showed signs of fatigue. His current client, Bart Crutcher was giving him gray hairs to go with the wrinkles.

Bart paced and stared as he roamed from corner to corner of the narrow room reserved for prisoners and their counsel. "You're tellin' me you have Bishop's records?"

Fletcher nodded. "Every car you stole and every part you sold."

"Bishop's a damned idiot!"

"If we go to court, this case is going to go down in a hurry, and you and Buddy are going away for multiple counts of car theft."

Bart sat stunned. Nothing the state could do to him came near the agony of knowing he was sending Buddy to prison.

"If you take a plea," Fletcher said, " I think I can get you off with fifteen to twenty and Buddy with ten."

Bart began to swear in earnest. Great piles of expletives fell from his mouth and splattered like excrement. When he finished, he sat, put his head in his hands and sobbed violently. Fletcher thought briefly of putting an arm around the man's heaving shoulders, but before he could move, Bart was up and swearing again—swearing and crying and pounding the walls. A guard hurried in. Fletcher waved him off.

When Bart subsided, Fletcher threw him a rope. "I can get help for Buddy, if you can give me something to bargain with."

"Like what?" Bart asked.

"If you plead guilty and testify that you forced Buddy into the business, I might be able to get him a lesser sentence."

"What if I can do better than that?"

It was Fletcher's turn to ask, "What?"

"Reverend Bishop was murdered, and I know who did it."

\* \* \* \* \*

Two weeks after the horrific events of Commandment Sunday, the plight of the churches affected remained the same. At Holy City Zionist Christian, Provost Chessman saw to it that the show went on and that Newell Post Lawson remained, to all intents and purposes, alive and well.

Greater Bennettville First Methodist/Baptist/Episcopal/Holiness Alpha and Omega International Tabernacle remained in disarray. The building was open, but the furnishings, communion trays, and drapery were in the hands of creditors. The organist and choir director returned to the sanctuary but relapsed into shock upon seeing Bishop's empty pulpit. Deacon Jefferson opened the service with a prayer and stayed through a long and dismal hour that was more wake than worship.

Downtown, half of the Bennettville One True Church filed reluctantly into the dim interior of Ricky's boarded up store and logged an hour of worship. Afterwards, the elders stayed to discuss what should be done with their still unusable building and the soon-to-be-vacated preacher's house. They decided, since both were paid for, Miz Dinah could stay until they found another minister or the house was sold, whichever came first. Until then, she would receive a small stipend, and the three weeks of vacation pay Thomas had never taken. That the building should be sold was not questioned. What it would smell like when sold was anyone's guess.

\* \* \* \* \*

When Deep Water members showed up at The Dive that afternoon, Ricky was at the back door with a small U-Haul hitched to his Honda. Only Troy and Amber knew what was up. Grit unlocked the door to the basement, flipped the light and went in.

"Go ahead and get your stuff." Ricky said.

Maggie found her tambourine and hand bells; Kale retrieved his bird whistles. Troy and Amber loaded guitars and amps into their van. Ricky added some of his computer gear and stuck the rest in the back of his Honda. Grit's precious drums were already in his back seat. He and Grace loaded props, tools, art supplies, and other accumulated gear into her car.

Ricky opened the trailer. "Road trip!" he announced. "Put the tables and chairs in here," he motioned to the dark interior. "The stage platforms and those big speakers go too."

"Go where?" and other, similar questions flew.

"Just get everything stowed and follow us." Troy said.

"It's a surprise," Amber added.

* * * * *

Detective Hunter and District Attorney Wilkinson met with Bart and his attorney first thing Monday morning. The room was too warm and, except for four metal chairs and a purely utilitarian table, bare. Hunter and the prosecutor were drowsy, aggravated, and uncomfortable—Wilkinson especially—his long, bony limbs splayed around his inadequate chair like a fork full of spaghetti.

"First," Bart said. "You gotta promise me you won't prosecute Buddy. He's been out of the thievin' end of the business for years." He looked at Hunter and the D.A. for a response.

They continued to sip their coffee; he would have to say more before they made any promises.

"He was just a kid when I got him into this." Bart confessed. "You gotta promise you won't charge him or you ain't gittin' nothin' from me."

"That's not how it works," the D.A. said. "You tell us what you know, and we tell you if we need your information."

Bart conferred angrily with Fletcher.

"Just tell them what you told me," Fletcher said.

"Like I said," Bart felt uncooperative. "I know who killed Bishop."

"What makes you think he was murdered?" Hunter asked rhetorically. "He died of food poisoning."

"Did anybody pump his stomach?" Bart taunted.

Hunter checked his notes. "Bishop didn't get to the hospital until several days after the picnic. It was too late."

"I'm talking about the day he was put on life support."

Hunter looked startled. "We're listening," he said.

"What can you do for my boy?"

Wilkinson sat up straight; his knees hovered around his elbows. "Did your son have anything to do with the murder?"

"No!"

Hunter and the D.A. had a game plan. Wilkinson played the first card, "If you can persuade us you're telling the truth, I'll dismiss all charges against your son."

Fletcher gave Bart a nod.

"I killed Bishop," Bart said.

"How?" Hunter needed proof.

"Meta use' t'—"

Hunter interrupted. "Meta . . . your wife?"

"Yeah, Meta, my wife." Bart started over. "Anyhow, Meta'd buy one of them fancy chocolate cakes an' take it to the Unity picnic every year, n' Bishop'd git to it before anybody n' eat about half."

The room grew quiet and the coffee cooled.

"Well, this year, 'bout two days before the picnic, I bought the same cake an' got me some chicken blood . . ."

The room was getting stuffy.

Bart continued, "an' I mixed it with some cherry Jell-O and some Kool-aid t' cut down on the smell."

Hunter felt lightheaded.

"I cut off the top layer an' I poured that blood all over the bottom half." Bart demonstrated. "Then I jus' put the top half back on, smoothed out the icing and let 'er set." He was clearly pleased with himself.

This was the second time Fletcher had heard Bart's nauseating confession, but he gagged again.

Hunter showed a second card. "That cake killed an old man and nearly killed a two-year-old girl."

Bart grew solemn. "I didn't mean fer that t' happen. I was gonna take it away soon as Bishop did his worst." He looked to the trio of law officers for sympathy then continued without it. "Well, I was standin' there in my work clothes, waitin' when some fool policeman pulled me up an' asked me to tow a vehicle that was blockin' an exit. By the time I got back . . ." Bart's explanation trailed off with a shrug.

The D.A. did not respond.

"How do we know you aren't lying to protect your son?" Hunter asked. "That cake didn't kill Bishop. He was recovering. You had to do something else, in the hospital."

Bart looked at Fletcher who nodded again.

"I come in dressed like a nurse and give him a couple of capsules."

"The only thing in Bishop's blood was salmonella." Hunter said.

"It weren't in his blood," Bart countered. "It was in his gut." He stood in triumph and waited for someone to ask the obvious. When no one did, he continued smugly, "Ground glass . . . put the rot right into his belly."

Hunter masked his surprise. "Is that it?" he said.

Bart was confused. "What do ya' mean, is that it? Ya' wanted me to prove I killed 'im, and I did."

Wilkinson anteed up. "What about Lawson?"

Bart looked blank.

"The police found Lawson's Lincoln and the choir robe you wore when you stole his Bible."

"I didn't steal no Lincoln."

"The deep blue Lincoln with the gouge on the side." Hunter said. "The gouge you made when you tried to run down Grit Griffin."

Bart sat down. He had lost control of the interview. He started to sweat.

Fletcher pulled him aside for a conference, then addressed the D.A., "My client has no knowledge of a blue Lincoln or a choir robe."

"How about the white Old's eighty-eight and the Taurus he took from the One True Church parking lot?" Hunter asked.

Another conference. Bart remembered the Olds. "But I took that peach off the street. It was sittin' two blocks over from Holy City the day Lawson died."

"And the overalls?" Hunter quizzed.

Bart seemed baffled.

Hunter pressed on. "The overalls you wore when you poisoned Lawson."

The D.A. played his ace. "We know you sabotaged the baptistery at the One True Church and rigged the explosion at Deep Water."

Bart was angry. "If you know what I did, why are you askin' me about it?"

"You have to give us the whole truth if you want a deal." Wilkinson said. "Tell us how you killed Lawson and Willis and why you wanted Griffin dead."

Nearby a cell door slammed.

* * * * *

When Grit walked into the Sentinel Monday morning, Combs stepped out of his office and motioned him in. "Have you seen this?" he asked, handing him a copy of the Atlanta Journal. He pulled a chair up to the front of his desk. "Have a seat."

Grit sat and scanned the front page, lighting on a headline, "The Reverend Bishop Bishop Involved in Auto Theft." It was slugged Bennettville and by-lined Grit Griffin.

Combs sat down on a corner of his desk and grinned around his cigar. "The wire services picked it up. Your by-line was in papers all across the country last week." He opened the box on his desk and offered Grit a stogie.

Grit stuck one in his pocket. "Thanks."

"I'm dang proud of you, Griffin, and not just about that story. The piece you did on Moses sold more papers that anything we've printed since Reagan got himself shot."

Combs went back behind his desk and started typing. "Yep. Dang good story," he muttered. "Inspired—people love to see themselves quoted in the paper." He seemed to be talking to himself. Grit nearly missed the next question. "How would you like to come to work here full-time?"

"Excuse me?" Grit said.

"Work." Combs said. He peered around his monitor. "Do you want to work here, full-time?"

"I . . . uh." Grit's brain wasn't sending out any signals.

"Well," Combs said, "I'll let you think about it."

A lone synapse fired. "No," Grit said.

"No?"

"No, I mean . . . I mean. No, I don't need to think about it."

"Well?"

"Sure. How soon do I start?"

Combs came around the desk and slapped Grit on the back. "That's more like it," he said. "Get down to the jail. Hunter and the D.A. expect Crutcher to confess to all three murders and to rigging the explosion. Hunter promised me an exclusive if I gave you the story."

\* \* \* \* \*

Dinah would not see Dr. Marvel again until Tuesday, but Maggie needed to return to classes at New Jerusalem, and Dinah seemed to be doing well, so Grace went back to work at the car dealership Monday morning. She drove her father's Taurus so the mechanics could check it over.

Her coworkers were genuinely happy to see her. Several of the guys in cleanup found excuses to wander past her desk and speak, and when she logged on to her computer, a "Welcome Back, Grace" screen saver popped up—Julie's doing.

Grace settled into her chair at the reception desk. Life was getting back to normal. Tomorrow her mother would see Dr. Marvel, and Grace would move back into her apartment. She remembered her talk with Grit. Best of all, she thought, Grit has stopped running!

About t 3:30, Jimmy from the repair shop came by. "Can you get a ride home?" he asked.

Grace cocked her head and gave him an I-don't-want-to-hear-it look.

"We just got your Taurus up on the rack," he explained. "Your steering fluid is leaking, and we can't get to it 'til tomorrow."

"And we always run out of loaners on Monday."

Jimmy nodded.

"What about a repo?" she asked.

"Take my word on it, you don't want to drive one of those until they go through cleanup."

"Thanks," Grace said. "Don't worry about it." She called Grit.

∗ ∗ ∗ ∗ ∗

Grit turned up his CD player, bobbed his head and beat time on the steering wheel. He had a full-time job, and Bart had signed a full confession. Grace knew they were going out to celebrate, but he hadn't told her why.

Bart would be charged with one count of reckless homicide for the death of Trenton Townsend, Sr., three counts of first-degree murder for Lawson, Willis, and Bishop and one count each of attempted murder and arson for the explosion at Deep Water. In exchange for the confession, all charges were dropped against Buddy, and the D.A. would not ask for the death penalty.

Grit arrived at Bennettville Dodge a few minutes before Grace got off. He waved at her across the show room. To his right, a shiny, blue/black SUV beckoned. *I have a full time job.* He thought. *Why not take a look?* He ran his hand over the perfect finish and sniffed the interior.

"That's our latest model," Bobby John said. "We just got it in yesterday."

"Not bad."

"Are you thinking of making a trade?"

Grit took a look at the sticker price and whistled. Then he noticed the MPG and back pedaled. "No," Grit said. "I think I'll hang on to my APF."

The salesman swallowed. "APF," he said. That's uh . . ."

"Already Paid For," Grit said.

Bobby John laughed through a sickly little smile.

Grace finished up at the reception area, came over and gave Grit a quick kiss. "I need to go by the house to check on Mother and change these clothes."

"You look fine to me," Grit said automatically.

"My makeup is smeared; my hair is a mess, and I sat on a chair full of M & Ms."

"You look delicious in chocolate."

"Just take me to the house." Grace said, laughing. "I'm not going for delicious tonight, just neat and clean."

When they arrived at the preacher's house, Grace's car was missing.

"Mother said she might go grocery shopping. I guess she did."

Grit heard the concern in Grace's voice. "Is she OK?"

"Sure." Grace said. "It's just . . . Well, it's the first time she's driven since . . . "

"She'll be fine." Grit said, opening her door.

She smiled, and took his hand. "By your definition, if Mother comes home 'fine' she will be completely disheveled and covered in chocolate." Grace stopped at the mailbox and pulled out some junk mail. Once inside, she checked for phone messages—none—and ran up to her room. "I'll just be a minute."

A minute in Grace-speak could be awhile, and Grit's untold news was making him restless. He walked through the house and out the back door to the garden where late June did a dead-on imitation of July. Dinah's remaining vegetables simmered in the afternoon sun, heat silenced the insects and sent birds to roost in the quiet shade.

Near the garage, Grit stooped to look at small pieces of scorched paper, and saw snatches of print. He followed the tattered trail past the garage to the alleyway and Dinah's burn barrel. He bent into its charcoal depths and squinted as his eyes adjusted to the darkness. Under layers of discarded weeds, ashes, and spent vegetation he recognized the incinerated remains of two heavy books. One, a bit of spine attached to blackened pages, crumbled when Grit exhaled. The other, a lump of charred paper united by melted red vinyl, was readily identifiable as the remains of a Bible—his Bible.

Grit was waiting at the bottom of the stairs when Grace hurried down. She looked refreshed and beautiful in a dark brown dress and snappy turquoise sandals. Grit didn't notice, and for the rest of the evening had little to say. He barely mentioned his promotion or Bart's confession. When Grace asked what was wrong, he said he didn't feel well. He took her home early.

At her door, he gave her a quick kiss and asked, "What time do you and your mom see Dr. Marvel in the morning?"

"Her appointment is at ten. Why?"

"I . . . I wondered what time you need me to help you move back to your apartment."

"We should be finished at the doctor's a little after eleven. If you're feeling better, why don't you meet us for lunch?"

"Great," Grit said, forcing a smile. He kissed her impulsively. "I love you," he said. "No matter what happens, remember that." He turned and walked back to his car.

Grace watched him leave, then texted Maggie, **G finally told me he loves me. I should b D lirious. Why am I scared?**

# 29

# The Sheep and the Goats

"DR. MARVEL'S OFFICE HOURS on Tuesdays are nine a.m. to three p.m." At least Grit had not reached a recording.

"I need to talk to him before he sees Mrs. Willis," he said. "It's an emergency. I have some, uh . . ." Grit searched for a word he seldom used, "vital information."

"I will ask the doctor to give you a call," the woman said coolly.

*Stupid answering service.* "Please, it is very important."

She took his name and number, said, "I'll see what I can do," and hung up.

Grit had watched the DVD of Bart's confession six times. He turned it on again. *The D.A. may be satisfied with this, but I'm not,* he thought, *especially since I found those Bibles.*

Something wasn't right. Bart seemed confused and shaken. While his account of Bishop's murder covered everything from the threatening note he left on Bishop's office door to the color of the ground glass he put in the capsules, it completely omitted important details about his other crimes. His account of Lawson's murder meandered from one vague statement to another, concluding, after much prompting, with a needlessly complicated scenario involving the flower delivery, a cup of coffee in Lawson's office, and more ground glass. When Bart was pressed to explain his return to the scene in a choir robe, he rambled and finally said he came back to watch Lawson die. About the Bible and the drinking glass he said, "You say I took 'em, so I must 'a took 'em. Who knows why?"

"Willis died," according to Bart, "because he was a bastard." He did not elaborate. Questioned about the mechanics of the electrocution, Bart revealed an elementary knowledge of electricity and concluded, "It don't take no electrician to kill a man standing in water up to his arm pits and handling a microphone. You just gotta make sure the charge goes to ground—through him."

What Bart had to say about the explosion at Deep Water could have come straight out of the paper. He quoted from the prophecy Grit had received and said he tried to kill Grit because, "When Buddy got religion, he got uppity. It's bad enough he took that stuff serious, but that Deep Water weren't even a church."

Once Bart knew for sure that Buddy could not be linked to the second attempt on Grit's life, he denied having anything to do with it or the Lincoln. But that left the police with no explanation for how the wig and the robe got left in the car.

Grit shut off the video and began to pace around his couch, watching the clock. *I need to talk to Dr. Marvel.* At ten minutes to ten he reached for the phone. This time he spoke to Dr. Marvel's aide and insisted he speak with the doctor.

As soon as he was put through, Grit explained the significance of the Bibles and added, "Miz Willis had to have taken them, and burning them means she didn't want anyone to know. I don't want to cause her more pain or upset, (He was thinking more of Grace than Dinah.) but someone needs to get to the bottom of this."

Grit's rapid speech and passion made him sound a bit irrational.

"Thank you for your interest, Mr.— Griffin, did you say?"

"Yes."

"I'm sure you know I cannot discuss anything to do with a patient's condition or treatment, but I expect there is some reasonable explanation for what you saw."

"I pray you are right, Doctor, and I pray you find that reasonable explanation this morning."

\* \* \* \* \*

Dinah took her usual place in Dr. Marvel's large upholstered chair looking relaxed and calm in an eminently appropriate, tailored, top and slacks. After a few short questions, the doctor concluded she was well enough to be on her own. Before sending his aide to give Grace that information, he remembered to ask Dinah, just for the sake of putting the matter to rest, if she had burned two Bibles.

"No," she answered, picking up her purse. "I burned three." She pulled out her lipstick and mirror and retouched her lips. Then, with the same pleasant voice she used to describe the crucifixion to her third-graders, she added, "I planned and executed the murders of three men."

She paused. Dr. Marvel, aghast, retained the presence of mind to switch his digital voice recorder to AC, just in case the batteries were low.

"I'm God's prophet," Dinah said sweetly. "In the Bible, God's prophets rained down judgment on sinners. You know what a sinner is, don't you?" Dinah didn't wait for an answer. "Thomas and Pastor Lawson were sinners. God told me. We must always listen to God." Dinah held up a finger. "First I was to give them warning. I warned every one of them, but they didn't repent. So I killed them." She frowned. "Truman Griffin is a sinner, but I haven't managed to kill him, yet."

"Excuse me," Dr. Marvel said. "I'll just be a moment." He pushed a button on his desk to summon his aide. When she appeared, he took her into the hall, leaving the door ajar. "We have an emergency situation," he said quietly, "I need to cancel my appointments for the rest of the day. Please apologize to anyone waiting. And call detective Hunter at the police station. I want to speak to him." He returned to his patient, who calmly resumed her tale.

"I knew I could tell the future," she said, "but I didn't know how to use that gift. Like when Thomas was about to get fired or quit, I always knew. It would be right after I found a really good friend or a nice job or Grace had a teacher she loved. We would get comfortable and happy, and sure enough, Thomas would pull us up by the roots." Dinah made a yanking motion and looked at Dr. Marvel petulantly. "Yanking someone up by the roots is not a nice thing to do."

She stared into space. "When we left Texas . . ." she paused and squared her shoulders. Large tears spilled down her face. "When we left Texas, we left my five-year-old, Abigail, alone in a graveyard." She swallowed. "Thomas never mentioned her again. He wanted her forgotten." Dinah sighed and relaxed. "So I just kept asking God why I had this gift if it wasn't doing me or anyone else any good, and I waited." She paused.

"You waited." Dr. Marvel repeated, handing her a tissue.

"I waited for a sign." She wiped her face.

"A sign."

Dinah sat on the edge of her chair. "It said, 'Thou Shalt Not Bear False Witness.' I saw it on the street corner, and I saw it at the courthouse, and I knew God was telling me Thomas was a liar. When he pretended we never had a daughter, he was lying.

"Then I saw a little sign outside The Reverend Bishop Bishop's church that said, 'Abigails meet, eight a.m., Saturday', and I knew that was a sign from God, too—like God pointing a finger, 'Go to this meeting', so I went and met Martha Lawson and found out Newell was an adulterer."

Dr. Marvel halted her again. "Mrs. Willis, is Grace in the waiting area?"

"Yes."

"Would you mind if I called her in here so all of us could talk?"

Dinah thought for a moment. "I guess not. Amy Grace would like to know about this. When I told her about Abigail, it made her happy. We had a good talk," Dinah looked blankly into the distance, "and a good cry."

* * * * *

Amber sneezed, loudly. "That's it," she said, sniffing and wiping her eyes. "I'm not dusting another inch of anything until Ricky gets back with those masks."

Troy perched on top of a ladder, cleaning the tall, front window. He and Ricky had removed the plywood, and a few slivers of sunlight shouldered through the grime to wake decades old cobwebs and dust-bunnies. Amber imagined the dirt hissing and growling in resentment.

She did not want to think about how long it would take to make Deep Water's new accommodations conducive to worship. Just this morning, she and Troy had accepted teaching positions at the Bennettville branch of State University. Officially they were unemployed for the rest of the summer, but they would not be out of work. Not only would they be remodeling Deep Water, they would be getting ready to face a whole new group of students.

"You could take the other ladder and start cleaning the outside," Troy suggested, "get you out of this dust."

"Good idea." She went to the back room, filled a bucket with suds then hooked a hose to the faucet and snaked it out the front door. She returned for the ladder, set it up and again went back, this time for the bucket and the window-washing wand. She attached the wand to the hose and made one more trip to turn on the water. She was just climbing the ladder, wand dripping, when Ricky returned with dust masks, a box of industrial rags, and an unbelievable assortment of cleaning products.

He motioned Amber to follow him inside then called to Troy. "I picked up lunch," he said. "Are you hungry?"

They were.

Amber checked her phone; it was nearly one o'clock, and they had been working since eight-thirty. She pointed into a shadowed corner. "Could you two pull that table and some chairs over to the window? I'll go shut off the water and get my bucket."

After washing table, chairs, hands, and faces, the trio sat down to sub-sandwiches and soda.

"That's wonderful!" Ricky said when Troy told him about the new teaching positions. "I've got something to pray about, too," he added. "Community College is putting in a new TV studio and broadcast facility. It's going to be state-of-the-art hd. Bennettville is getting a pb s affiliate!" He was nearly drooling. "They're looking for a department head and a production teacher. I've had my resume in there for a year, but I'm going down there tomorrow to rattle some cages."

The Michaelsons could understand Ricky's excitement. The idea of working with up-to-date equipment and doing original broadcasting was every media teacher's dream.

Amber swallowed the last of her sub, "We can pray about that right now," she said. "What else?"

"Well," Ricky said, "Buddy is out on bail, and you'll never guess—" His phone rang. "Hey," Ricky answered. **** "Yeah" ****

"Okay" **** "Okay." He snapped it shut. "That was Grit. He and Grace are on their way over. Said they have something important to tell us."

"They're engaged!" Amber guessed.

"I don't think so," Ricky said "Grit sounded really stressed."

＊ ＊ ＊ ＊ ＊

Over the next few weeks, Grit and Grace could do nothing but marvel as they watched God take care of the impossible. By His grace, Dinah had been listed on The Bennettville One True Church's personal liability insurance, and by the grace of District Attorney Wilkinson, she was being treated in a secure ward of a private mental facility until her trial. Dr. Marvel's attorney and personal friend, Jason Callahan, would represent her. The churches affected by Dinah's crimes urged Callahan to keep the entire situation as private as possible. They had watched the media create chaos at Greater M/B/E/H and knew that newshounds were sniffing their direction.

Once again, Grit had the inside track on a sensational story that he hesitated to write.

"Better you tell it first," Combs said. "You know the truth. And you have a heart."

"I'll have to talk to Grace."

＊ ＊ ＊ ＊ ＊

Grit invited himself to Grace's apartment for lunch. When he arrived, two suitcases lay half-filled near the door to her bedroom.

"I'm taking Daddy's ashes to Texas for burial and visiting my sister's grave," she explained. "I'll be gone for two weeks."

"But . . ."

"Dr. Marvel convinced me to go. It will help give me some closure."

"And you were going to tell me when?"

"I'm sorry. I didn't make up my mind until just this minute. If I don't leave now, the media will make everything worse. Mother's safe. They can't get to her, but they could me."

Grit sat down on Grace's small couch, stricken; he was the media.

"I've been seeing headlines in my sleep," Grace said, 'Preacher's Wife Murders Two', or 'Preacher's Daughter Says, "Mother Meant Well."' Can you imagine?"

Grit could. "That answers my question," he said.

Grace sat down beside him. "What question?"

"I'm not going to write the story about your mother. I'm going with you to Texas."

"No way!" Grace jumped up from her seat. "I'm counting on you to write that story. This mess is going to get out—one way or another and sooner than later. Write the truth, and write it now!"

Grit stood and put his arms around her gently. "I love you," he said.

Grace was "D lirious."

# Epilogue

MONDAY MORNING HUNTER FILLED Grit in on the details of Dinah's confession—strictly off the record. He sat at his desk, holding a transcript of the trial.

"I can't let you have this," he said, indicating the transcript. "Too many legalities. But if you promise to talk to Dinah's lawyer before you publish anything, I can tell you how she did it."

"Done," Grit said. He settled back in his chair.

"First of all, that was Dinah you saw delivering flowers at Holy City. She did all that sleight of hand with the drinking glass and managed to doctor Lawson's Bible while she was at it."

"I don't understand."

"Give me a minute." Hunter admonished. "After delivering the flowers, she drove back to The One True Church for her Ladies' Bible class. She snuck out of there early, put on the choir garb, and drove her Olds back down to Holy City just in time to take the poisoned Bible and the drinking glass off the pulpit."

"Poisoned Bible?"

"Ricin," Hunter said.

Grit registered disbelief.

"Every time Lawson smacked his Bible, he ground ricin into his palm and breathed in spores, but I'll get to that later."

"Unbelievable!"

"Dinah walked out of Holy City dressed in that choir getup and carrying the Bible and the glass, got to the corner, and her car was gone." He chuckled. "Bart Crutcher had just loaded it into a panel truck and driven off. And," He started to laugh, "you won't believe this. She had to get back to The One True church before anyone missed her, so she went back to the Holy City parking lot and hot-wired Martha Lawson's car!"

Grit would have laughed, but Hunter was talking about Grace's mom and murder. He changed the subject, sort of. "And Dinah used Martha's car to try and kill me."

"Yep."

"Where did Dinah get ricin?"

"She grew it in her back yard."

"You think you know a person!"

"According to Dinah, that was one of her 'signs from God'. She said that, after God told her to kill Lawson, He showed her how to brew poison from the mole beans along her back fence. What she came up with was low-grade stuff, but combined with ecstasy she bought on the street and Lawson's bad heart, it was murder."

"Why did she take his drinking glass and mail it back to you?"

"Just to send us after a wild goose."

"That is really going to look bad if it comes out at trial," Grit said. "She knew what she did was wrong, or at least illegal."

"Right." Hunter said. "Her attorney will have a devil of a time coming up with an insanity case. He would have to prove she had some crazy motive for covering her tracks. It would be better for everyone if it never comes to that. Between us, I think the D.A. will find a way to keep all of this out of court. Dinah will probably end up staying where she is until she is deemed cured. If that ever happens, Wilkinson will have to decide whether or not to prosecute."

Grit sighed. "Well, we know how she killed Thomas—peanut butter and rats. Pretty elegant."

"But there was more to it; Dinah had to prime poor Rachel Albrighton to request baptism in order to get Thomas in the water, and she had to cut a good-sized hole in Thomas' waders so the water and electric charge could get to him."

"That is beyond premeditation," Grit said.

"Unfortunately, yes," Hunter said. "She would face first degree murder charges."

Grit and Hunter observed a very brief and unofficial moment of silence.

"What about the explosion?" Grit asked.

"You and your friends pretty much figured that one out," Hunter answered. "Dinah planted smoke charges at the base of the speakers and in the overhead monitor and wired them to a cell phone under the stage. That was a baby-cam under the table."

"But Dinah was under sedation at the hospital." Grit exclaimed. "Those baby cams only work within a small range."

"She must not have swallowed her sedative. We have video of her leaving and returning to the hospital in less than an hour. No one missed her."

"Right, Grace was eating with the Michaelsons."

"Dinah had taken Grace's keys from her purse. She drove Grace's car to The Dive parking lot, sat in the car and watched the service on the baby can. When you moved under the monitor, she hit speed dial and— Boom. The only reason you weren't killed is you stepped off the stage."

Grit contemplated his own demise for a nanosecond. "A couple of things still puzzle me," he said. "How did Dinah mess up the monument at the courthouse?"

"That's what the blow torch and empty aerosol cans in the back of the Lincoln were all about."

Grit considered the possibilities as Hunter continued. "Dinah went down there at night, heated up the granite with the torch then sprayed it with instant icer. It cracked like a dry engine block."

"The term 'evil genius' comes to mind," Grit said, shaking his head. "Something else bothers me, Martha Lawson. She never reported her car stolen. And she had Newell cremated within hours of his death."

"I wondered about that myself," Hunter said.

"Do you think she suspected he was poisoned?"

"Maybe yes, maybe no. Maybe she didn't care."

* * * * *

Grace's return from Texas corresponded with Deep Water's first official worship service in their new facility. She and Grit sat with the regulars, Maggie, Kale, Ricky, Troy, Amber, and Buddy, in two loose semi-circles of freshly washed chairs. Grace's friends, Tanya and Julie, sat down next to her. Buddy sat with his guest, Victoria Sellers. Kale and Maggie sat on either side of her mother, Loretta.

Zephonia Summer came at Grit's invitation. She entered in head-to-toe purple, followed by Whyneatta in a red ensemble, and Immaculata in green. The three sat down together, looking like a rainbow-powered, spiritual cheerleading squad.

Grit was pleased to see so many guests, and even more so when he moved to the center of the worshipers and discovered Rachel Albrighton and her parents seated at the back of the room. Before initiating the discussion of baptism and new beginnings, he welcomed the Albrightens into the circle.